THIS DARK HEART

Zeena Gosrani

To Holly,
For believing in me when I
didn't believe in myself.

First published in 2024
by Firefly Press
25 Gabalfa Road, Llandaff North, Cardiff, CF14 2JJ
www.fireflypress.co.uk

© Zeena Gosrani 2024

The author asserts her moral right to be identified as author in
accordance with the Copyright, Designs and Patent Act, 1988.

All rights reserved.
This book is sold subject to the condition that it shall not, by way of
trade or otherwise, be lent, re-sold, hired out or otherwise circulated
without the publisher's prior consent in any form, binding or cover other
than that in which it is published and without a similar condition
including this condition being imposed on the subsequent purchaser.

All characters in this publication are fictitious and any resemblance to
real persons, living or dead, is purely coincidental.

A CIP catalogue record of this book is available from
the British Library.

print ISBN 978-1-915444-72-1
ebook ISBN 978-1-915444-73-8

This book has been published with the support of
the Welsh Books Council.

Typeset by Elaine Sharples

Printed and bound by CPI Group UK

1

Princess Thiya of Agraal smiled down at Amara, a warmth building until she was sure she would burst. Thiya longed to run her fingers through Amara's brown hair but standing on the balcony looking down on the ballroom below meant Amara was just out of reach.

Lochan came up beside her. Out of the corner of her eye, Thiya saw her personal guardsman – her shara, Chirag – move to her right. She knew without looking that Lochan's shara, Yug, had taken up a position to their left.

Thiya spared Lochan one glance before returning her gaze to the ballroom. The waning sunlight shining through the floor-to-ceiling windows kissed Amara's dark-brown skin with a golden glow.

'What are you planning, little sister?' Lochan asked.

'Nothing.'

Amara greeted yet another suitor. Thiya watched as her own silver bangle – the one her father had given to her and all her siblings when they were born – glinted on Amara's left wrist, half hidden amongst the other bangles that circled her forearm. Thiya had given it to her before the ball, as a symbol of her love.

'It'd better be nothing.' Lochan rested his forearms along the balcony. His shoulder-length curly hair, much like Thiya's, fell in front of his face as he peered down at the room below. 'Amara needs this,' he added, having spotted who held Thiya's interest.

Thiya scoffed. Society forced women to be wives and mothers, to forge connections that other family members could exploit. If Amara didn't marry, her family would disinherit her. She could be cast out, destitute. That was the only reason Amara *needed* to marry.

'Don't be like Aunt Yesha,' Lochan said, his voice sharp. 'If you care about Amara, you won't ruin this for her.'

If she cared. Lochan had no idea how much she cared.

Thiya wrinkled her nose. 'Why do you always have to compare me to Aunt Yesha?' Every time she messed up, her brothers liked to compare her to their father's older sister: an aether mage who had almost destroyed the country.

'Because she liked to act without thinking.' Lochan poked Thiya's nose.

She swatted his hand away. 'Maybe I do think before I act. I just believe some acts are worth the punishment.' Especially if she was going to be punished anyway. 'But don't worry, I won't ruin this for Amara.'

Thiya leaned a little further over the balcony to get a closer look at Amara's next suitor, Lord Hiresh of Samka. The cold marble pressed into her stomach. She'd been doing this since the beginning of the ball and she was sure she had a bruise to show for it by now, but she didn't care. There were too many lords at this ball, lining up to greet Amara, judging her to see if she was really as beautiful as the rumours suggested (she was) and as kind (she definitely was). But mostly they were looking at Amara's father, General Sethu, trying to determine what benefits having the king's closest advisor and friend as a father-in-law could offer.

Because that was the reason for the ball – to find Amara, and every other woman of noble birth over the age of eighteen, a husband. The king threw this ball every year, and Amara had turned eighteen last month.

'That's going to be you next year,' Lochan said. 'You won't have time to miss Amara then.'

Thiya bit her lip. Lochan would never understand how unfair it was that she was expected to marry at a younger age than her brothers. Nor was it fair that she would be paraded in front of her suitors while her brothers would have freedom to choose, not that she knew who she *would* choose if she could, since Amara wasn't an option. And it certainly wasn't fair that she was expected to do all that with a smile on her face.

The suitors judged Amara. Thiya judged the suitors. General Sethu would only allow someone who could provide Amara with a good life to marry her – someone rich and well-positioned in society. But Thiya was more interested in whether they would treat Amara well.

Without warning, Lord Hiresh took Amara's hand and brought it to his lips. He said something, his mouth pulling into a smile. He didn't let go.

Amara's eyes flicked to their joined hands. She held

her polite expression, but Thiya knew she wanted Hiresh to release her. Why didn't her father stop him? Normally a look from General Sethu was enough to convince any man that touching his daughter would only end in disaster, but the general was too busy laughing at whatever Hiresh had said. Maybe Thiya needed to go down there and rip off Hiresh's arm.

'I'm serious,' Lochan said, his stern voice cutting through Thiya's violent thoughts. 'Don't sabotage Amara's chances of a good match because you want to keep her here a little longer.'

'I won't.' She had promised Amara she would behave, so she would. Lord Hiresh's arms were safe.

Thiya had known she and Amara wouldn't always be together, but that didn't stop the pain that laced her chest. She hadn't wanted to accept it. Sometimes she thought Amara was a little too accepting of her fate, facing it with a forced smile rather than the scowl Thiya would have preferred. Amara wanted to find a husband tonight to make her parents happy.

'What's the point of being miserable about something we have no control over?' Amara had said to her. 'I'd rather focus on what I can control. At least I have *some* choice in who I marry.'

A choice that didn't include Thiya, *couldn't* include her because they were both girls and part of high society.

A tear tickled her cheek. Thiya brushed it away with an impatient swipe of her hand, but Lochan had already seen. He hugged her. 'I'm sorry. I know how much she means to you.'

He knew Thiya and Amara had been friends since childhood. He did not know how their friendship had evolved into something more. But Thiya couldn't correct him, and it wasn't because her tongue felt too thick to form words. He could never know the truth.

She shrugged off his touch. 'I won't cause trouble. Don't worry.'

When Thiya looked over the balcony again, Amara was greeting a Rear Admiral who looked as old as General Sethu. Amara's smile was too tight for comfort, but only Thiya saw that. General Sethu and the Rear Admiral laughed with familiar ease. A Rear Admiral would be a good match for Amara – she could admit that, even though the thought left a sour taste in her mouth.

More tears pricked the back of her eyes, but she blinked them back as she stepped away from the balcony, unable to watch any more.

'Are you wearing trousers?' Lochan asked, eyes wide.

Glad of the distraction, Thiya smiled. 'Yes. It was Amara's idea. Kavita and I worked on them together.' She pulled at the edges of the skirt until the blue silk parted in the middle to reveal wide-legged trousers. 'Aren't they amazing?'

Lochan shook his head, but his lips twitched. 'Yes, you're definitely not like Aunt Yesha. You've really thought this through,' he said, sarcastically. 'Couldn't you have worn a sari, or even a lehenga?'

Thiya scowled. 'No.' A sari was too fiddly and the current slim-fitted style of skirt for the lehenga too restrictive. Kavita, the royal seamstress, had designed her outfit so it resembled the lehenga at first glance, the wide-legged trousers looking remarkably similar to a skirt. She'd even gone as far as to heavily embroider the waist-length blouse in shades of darker blue and purple with silver accents so the outfit didn't look too simple while still keeping the trousers light enough to dance in.

Lochan muttered something then, his eyes darkening. Thiya heard their mother's name mentioned among a few choice curse words.

'Don't worry,' she said with a grin, tapping Lochan's cheek. 'Mother will love this.' Or at least she wouldn't be able to find fault with the outfit. It was stylish and elegant while still being light and easy enough to move in. The perfect compromise.

The music playing from below changed, as the deeper, louder sound of the dhol took over. An earth mage pulled shutters across the windows, manipulating the wood so they fit perfectly into place, blocking out the night before it had a chance to fall and signal the start of curfew. Thiya had seen the mages do this so many times, and yet their display of magic never failed to leave her in awe.

The curfew had been in place since before Thiya was born, ever since the daayan first appeared. Daayan only attacked at night, so everyone headed indoors before nightfall and shuttered their windows and doors. It was unusual to party into the night given that people normally hurried home for curfew, but the guests were all staying in the palace tonight.

A fire mage lit the torches inside the palace walls, the flames shooting up to the ceiling. The candles in the chandeliers appeared to catch fire from those flames, but Thiya knew that was the fire mage as well. An air mage, created a breeze that blew around the ballroom, stopping it from getting too hot and stuffy. A titter of excitement filled the air.

'I think it's time we joined the others.' Lochan offered Thiya his arm, which she didn't take. 'You can't avoid this.'

'Are you sure? I could—'

'Thiya.'

Thiya slipped her hand through Lochan's arm before he could invoke Aunt Yesha as an insult again and let him lead her to the staircase at the other end of the balcony. Their shara followed a few steps behind.

The marble staircase was wide, with gold rails on either side. Lochan walked down the middle, and Thiya had to hitch up the front of her trousers with her left hand so she didn't trip over the hem, revealing silver mojari on her feet that sparkled in the light.

Lochan wandered over to speak to a friend. Thiya snatched a samosa from the tray of a passing servant while searching for Amara. She spotted her on the dance floor where she moved in a circle with the other dancers, clapping and stepping to the beat. Thiya could join them but the beat was too slow. She liked it better when she could spin around so fast she made herself dizzy.

Thiya took a bite of the triangular pastry and watched Amara for a while. The pastry made a satisfying crunch and the spices of the vegetable filling danced across her tongue. Amara laughed, enjoying herself now no suitors were bothering her. Everything was as it should be.

'Ah, Thiya,' her father called out to her from across the ballroom, and Thiya dragged her eyes away from Amara. 'There you are, beta.'

He strode towards her, pulling someone with him. The stranger had on a simple kurta in bronze and dark blue, but the material was expensive and expertly tailored, and despite his youthful appearance, he oozed power. A mage. Even without his uniform, Thiya knew what he was from the way he carried himself: back straight and eyes alert. Her father had been introducing her to mages since before she was old enough to attend the ball, when she used to sneak inside and sit under the drinks table in the corner, observing everything, especially the mages at work.

The man shifted his gaze, and Thiya found herself looking into stormy grey eyes.

'You have to meet Kayan. He's been telling me stories of his time in Tumassi.' Tumassi was a town to the far north of the country, on the border of Agraal and Kakodha. It used to be a vibrant trading town until the daayan appeared. Now it was the front line of defence.

'He killed six daayan in one night! Can you believe it?'

The king patted Kayan's shoulder, turned to him and said, 'I was impressed when I heard what you did, so I know my daughter will be too.'

'Thank you, Your Majesty.' Kayan bowed politely, but not before Thiya saw the haunted look in his eyes.

Since daayan were creatures of pure magic, it was almost impossible to kill one in their shadow form. But once the daayan possessed a person, killing the host would kill the daayan immediately. In order to kill the six daayan, Kayan would have had to kill six possessed people – probably people he knew. Just like the soldier she'd seen that night five years ago.

Poor Kayan. No wonder he looked haunted. Thiya hoped this chance to get away from the front line and have some fun would ease his conscience, like the king intended.

General Sethu called for her father and the king wandered away, leaving Thiya alone with Kayan. They stared awkwardly at each other for a few moments, Thiya unsure what to do, before she blurted out, 'Err ... thank you for your service.'

And that was why she didn't take part in politics. That was her older brother Shyam's job. But Kayan took her awkwardness in his stride, his smile putting her at ease.

'It's not like we had a choice.'

Thiya blinked at the sharp voice and it took her a moment to realise it hadn't come from Kayan. Kayan frowned at someone over her shoulder and Thiya turned to see another stranger with angular features. He would have been handsome if it weren't for the scowl he levelled at Thiya.

Thiya bit her tongue against her response and plastered a sweet smile on her face that she hoped would soothe the stranger's temper. 'Yes, I suppose that's true.'

All mages, regardless of gender or social status, were recruited into the army aged ten and brought to one of several training camps around the country, whether they liked it or not. It was harsh, but that was war. Without mages, the country would not have survived the threat from the daayan.

'Still, I thank you for all that you do.'

And her mother thought she spoke without thinking. She'd warned Thiya that one day her tongue would get her into trouble. *If only Mother could see me now.*

'If you really wanted to thank us, you would sort out your own family drama.'

'Isaac…' Kayan warned.

Chirag moved closer.

'No, we're risking our lives every day because her aunt created the daayan after she tried to kill her younger brother. Mages did everything they could to protect him. They even managed to kill his power-hungry sister despite most dying in the process. General Sethu's own brother sacrificed himself to save the now king – and the royal family won't do anything to fix it.'

'What do you want us to do? We don't have magic,' Thiya said.

Aunt Yesha was the last person in their family to have magic. An aether mage, she had been consumed by darkness. Her death had plunged Sanathri Jungle into shadow, from where the daayan had emerged. Aethanis were healers and destroyers. They could save a life as easily as they could take it, and her aunt had chosen to destroy.

Isaac snorted.

'Believe me, if I could do something, I would. We all would.'

'I don't believe you.' The cold in Isaac's voice seeped into Thiya's skin and she shivered. Chirag stepped in between them.

Thiya heard someone shout outside a moment before glass shattered nearby and Chirag pushed her out of harm's way. She lost her balance and fell to the floor. Pain shot through her right hip but, before she could catch her breath, Chirag wrenched her to her feet. He pushed her against the wall and crouched in front of her, assessing the threats in the ballroom.

The music stopped playing. In the distance, Thiya heard bells ringing out a familiar pattern that her brain couldn't quite grasp, the sound muffled by the blood rushing through her ears.

She peered over Chirag's shoulder, her eyes darting around the ballroom. The shutters had crashed through the windows, raining down little shards of glass onto the floor like diamonds. Guests scrambled away, their arms protecting their heads from falling glass and splintered wood. They pushed their way to the other side of the ballroom, initiating a stampede on the main entrance. Their screams filled the air, joining the shouts from outside. They all needed to get away from the open window, before shards of glass were the least of their worries.

Chirag tugged on her arm. 'We need to go, Princess.'

'Not without Amara.'

But where was she? The dance floor was empty. Thiya saw her on the other side of the room with the queen, a shara escorting them both out of a side door. Thiya sagged. They would be alright.

The mages around the room burst into action. Fire whipped around in an arc. The light seared Thiya's eyes, making it difficult to see what was happening. Chirag pulled her towards another side door and this time Thiya didn't resist.

Thiya saw a black shadow out the corner of her eye. Her breath caught in her throat. The shadow drifted in through the window, dancing just out of reach of a stream of water sent by a water mage. More screams punctured the air. Chirag tried to pull her onwards, but Thiya couldn't move. She'd never seen a daayan in its shadow form before.

The daayan's dark flickering silhouette sucked the light and warmth from the room. Thiya felt a chill deep within her bones, colder than the ice that lined the top of the Dhandra mountain range.

Guests stuck in the bottleneck at the door screamed and pushed those in front. Chirag tightened his grip around her arm, but Thiya shook him off. Fascination overrode reason. There was something about the daayan that called to her.

The daayan changed form, like smoke twisting and coalescing. It shifted from a tall flame, darker than the darkest night, to a human with impossibly long legs. It darted through the room, next transforming into a ribbon, then a snake, complete with forked tongue.

The snake slithered through the air towards her father and General Sethu. Thiya's chest tightened. The king's shara leapt to hustle him out of danger. Sethu raised a sword that flashed green with earth magic. Magic-infused swords were one of the few things that could weaken a daayan in its shadow form.

Fire flew between the general and the daayan. The daayan sprang back. The mage Kayan stopped beside Thiya, flames dancing on his outstretched palm.

The daayan dodged to the side as an air mage whipped up a gust of wind to blow it off course, but it sped straight towards Thiya's father. Thiya's scream lodged in her throat.

Kayan sent another ball of fire sailing after the daayan, but its smoky form pulled apart at the centre, creating a hole for the fire to sail through. Flames hit the king's shara, setting his clothing alight. The flames were extinguished a second later by a water mage.

Another shara pulled the king away, but the daayan followed. It sailed over the head of the first shara, shifting shape again until it resembled an arrow pointing straight at her father.

Thiya didn't hear herself scream, but she felt the pain of it as it ripped from her throat.

Kayan held more fire within his hands. He lined up his throw, his eyes focused on the king, and waited.

No! Kayan could not burn the king. She couldn't lose her father. But the daayan was about to possess him, and then he would be beyond saving.

An unfamiliar sensation rose up within her: light and love; darkness and desire. Threads of darkness and light pressed against her skin, demanding release. Thiya let them go, but instead of the feeling fading as she released it, it threatened to consume her, to split her apart.

In awe, Thiya watched as the threads of her own magic wrapped around the daayan just before it reached her father. They pulled together, squeezing until the daayan exploded in a shower of black confetti that rained down on the ballroom. Thiya blinked, and the daayan was gone.

The light and the dark threads within Thiya faded, the energy dissipating.

Her father stood where he had before. His eyes were the same dark brown that she knew and loved, and there were no prominent grey veins around them. He was alright. He hadn't been possessed.

Shaky laughter escaped her. She'd almost lost her father. Thiya looked down at her hands and body. What were those threads and where had they come from?

Her father's eyes grounded her. They were hard and cold as he stared at her like he'd never seen her before.

Oh Khal! What had she done now?

2

Thiya felt like an observer of her own body. Her legs trembled and she couldn't make them stop. She didn't put up a fight as her shara whisked her away from the ballroom. She couldn't. Everything that had happened kept playing in her head – the daayan, her father, the light and the dark twisting within her. None of it made sense.

She hoped Amara was alright. She knew she would be safe, that General Sethu wouldn't let anything happen to her, but Thiya's heart still screamed at her to turn around. Amara might be safe, but she would be frightened, wondering if Thiya was alright. She needed to get back to Amara, to hold her in her arms and chase away her fears.

Chirag led her deeper into the palace, through dark, dank corridors, the walls made of a grey stone rather than marble, to a hidden safe room. Daayan couldn't travel through walls and, with numerous walls between this room and the main palace, it would be the safest place to be. Maybe she could convince her father to let Amara come down here?

Torches sprang to life in front of her, the flames extinguishing when they passed, which made it hard to tell where they were going. Very few people knew the exact location of the room, so if a daayan did possess a member of staff, it would still be near impossible to find their way down here to attack the king.

And that daayan in the ballroom had been trying to attack the king; Thiya was sure of it. But why? Daayan weren't known to target specific victims.

She caught sight of a feiraani standing guard. Dressed head-to-toe in the black leather uniform of a mage, the fire mage blended into the shadows, but her gaze burned. Thiya wanted to hide behind her shara, to shield herself from the intensity.

The walls and floors were empty, with no carpets or tapestries to trap in the heat. Thiya shivered. The cold pressed against the bare skin on her arms and stomach, causing goosebumps. She hugged herself but, at that moment, she wasn't sure she would ever feel warm again.

Up ahead, she heard her father's voice. 'Is everyone alright?'

Then she was in her father's arms. His heat seeped into her as he hugged her close. He was safe. And whole.

'There you are.' He sighed and squeezed her tight.

His shara had led him from the ballroom ahead of Thiya, and she wondered if she had imagined his earlier expression. All she saw now was a mix of love and relief.

Her own body sagged. She felt more tired than she'd ever felt before.

'Are you alright? Are you hurt?' He stepped back enough to get a good look at her, searching for any sign of injury. He lifted her left hand. 'Where is your bangle?'

'A daayan infiltrated the palace and you're worried about my jewellery?' she asked, incredulously. She pulled her arm behind her back. She was not going to tell him she'd given her bangle – the symbol of their family – to Amara. There was no way he would approve, despite his friendship with General Sethu.

'No, I'm worried about you. What were you doing? You know the evacuation protocols. Why didn't you leave?'

Every time a daayan was spotted within the city of Kamanu, the capital of Agraal, alarms sounded and Thiya and her family made their way to this room. *Drop what you're doing and run.* The mantra had been drilled into her from a young age.

But this time had been different. This time a daayan had come inside the palace and targeted the king.

'That daayan was going to—' she choked. She remembered the way the daayan had slithered towards her father. That image would haunt her. 'Why did the daayan attack you?'

'The same reason a daayan attacks anyone. They need our flesh and blood to survive because—'

'Because they have none of their own. I know that, Father.' As well as needing blood for energy the same way humans needed food, daayan could also heal their host's body by feasting on the flesh of others, a disgusting thought and one Thiya didn't care to think about. 'I meant why did this daayan target you specifically?'

18

'Don't be silly, beta. The daayan went after me because I happened to be the first person it came across.'

No, that wasn't true. General Sethu and the shara had been in the way, and the daayan had gone over their heads. It hadn't wanted *any* human; it had wanted her father.

'And even if I had been possessed, so what? There was nothing you could have done about it. Never ignore the evacuation protocols again. Do you understand?'

But she had done something about it. Her father was standing in front of her because she had stopped the daayan somehow.

'But—'

'Leave the daayan to the mages.' His eyes were hard and his voice brooked no argument.

Thiya bit her lip and nodded.

The king's expression softened. 'Why don't you head inside and join your mother?'

'Can you bring Amara here?'

'No.' There was no hesitation.

'I'm sure General Sethu would be grateful knowing his daughter and wife are safe,' she cajoled.

'General Sethu is quite capable of ensuring his family's safety. This room is only safe if it remains secret from anyone who doesn't need to know.'

'Two more people—'

'Is two too many. My answer is no. Now get inside.' This time his request was an order and Thiya had no choice but to obey.

Four shara stood inside and outside the doorway. The swords at their hips looked ordinary, but Thiya knew they had been enchanted with magic so they could be used against daayan. As long as the magic hadn't faded during the attack.

Thiya tried not to think about that as she walked past the shara and into a large room, with a low ceiling and no windows. Despite this, the walls were made from a pale-yellow stone, which made the room appear light and airy. The only entrance was the one she had just walked through, but there was an archway that separated the front living area from her father's office.

Thiya could see her father's desk strewn with papers. This was the room where he kept all his important documents, protected by Kimi, the Goddess of Secrets. A tapestry depicting her image hung on the wall behind his desk, her finger pressed across her lips. Thiya also spotted the statue of Khalil, the God of Mischief, that she herself had hidden on a lower shelf several years ago.

Her mother sat on a sofa to the left of the doorway, hugging a blue pillow to her chest. Her brothers, Shyam and Vivek, sat on two armchairs, either side of a small, round table at the far end of the room; Lochan sat on a small pouffe near them, his legs stretched out in front of him; Ravi stood in the centre of the room.

'Finally,' Ravi said when he saw her. 'I was about to come and get you myself.' His hand went to the dagger at his hip.

Thiya snorted. He would not have been allowed to leave this room and they both knew it. 'Any excuse for a fight.'

Ravi's eyes narrowed and he took a step towards her. 'You're one to talk. Why did it take you so long to come down here if it wasn't to stay and fight yourself?' He rounded on the king. 'I told you allowing her to learn how to fight was dangerous. It's gone and put ideas into her head.'

Thiya bristled. 'What's wrong with those ideas?'

'It's made you think you can fight daayan.'

'Not daayan, people.' She closed her eyes and inhaled a deep breath. Ravi didn't know she'd almost been kidnapped as a child. Only her parents, General Sethu and her shara knew. They had allowed her to be trained so she could defend herself should the need arise again. 'You're the only one who wants to fight daayan, Ravi.'

Yes, she'd thought about fighting daayan when she was younger, being the one to defeat them once and for all – they all had – but that didn't mean she'd entertain the idea now she was older. Ravi would fight anything, as long as he was fighting. Now Thiya wondered if she should give fighting daayan more thought. She wasn't sure what had happened in that ballroom, but she knew she'd done *something*.

The king got between them, pushing them apart. Thiya blinked. When had Ravi got so close?

'No one here is fighting daayan.' The king glanced at

Thiya before glaring at Ravi. 'And Thiya's training is not up for discussion. Is that understood?'

Ravi pressed his lips together but managed to push out a, 'Yes, sir.'

Thiya joined her mother on the sofa. The musty smell that permeated the room was stronger here, but it didn't matter when her mother pulled Thiya into her arms. She tucked her legs beneath her and leaned into her mother, inhaling her jasmine perfume.

Queen Archana was tall like her daughter, with the same light-brown skin and grey eyes, but that was where the similarities ended. Her mother's features were softer, or they would have been if she wasn't suddenly looking at Thiya with a stern expression.

'What in Urvi's name are you wearing?' The queen clicked her tongue.

'A lehenga.' Thiya stood and spun around so her mother could get the full effect.

'That is not a lehenga.'

'I know it's not what you're used to, but Amara and Kavita helped me design it. I thought you would be pleased. It's still close enough to a lehenga to be acceptable, but it's trousers to make me comfortable.'

'There is nothing about that outfit that is acceptable. You represent not just this family but this country. What do you think the guests thought about us when they saw you in that? What do you think they're saying now?'

Thiya's smile faltered. 'I don't know, maybe: how did a

daayan get into the palace? Only you and father seem to be more worried about my clothes and jewellery than the daayan attack.'

Her mother cared too much about what others thought. Amara had encouraged her to find a way to compromise with her mother, but Thiya would never make that mistake again. She'd thought this outfit would please her mother as well as herself, but she couldn't get it right.

If only Amara was here. She would know how to make her feel better.

Thiya met Lochan's eye. He shrugged, his expression a mix of sympathy and 'I told you so'.

Urgh, this was so unfair. Thiya threw herself onto the other side of the sofa, as far away from her mother as possible. Her father moved to a pouffe in front of them where he shared a loaded stare with the queen.

The shara answered a knock at the door, swords drawn. One opened the door a crack, the other stood ready to attack.

Thiya saw their postures relax and a second later they opened the door wider and General Sethu walked into the room. She wanted to ask him if Amara was safe, but his hard expression stilled her tongue. He and the king disappeared into the adjoining room. They carried out their conversation in low voices, but Thiya heard enough to know they were talking about an air mage who had left his post. In his rush to get back and deal with the daayan, he had accidentally destroyed the shutter and window of the ballroom and allowed the daayan entry. The word 'execution' got thrown about a few times.

'They're rich,' Sethu said, along with something Thiya couldn't hear.

Families of mages who were convicted of treason had to pay a hefty fine, sometimes large enough to lead them to destitution. It dissuaded mages who didn't care about their own lives from disobeying the king because they didn't want to risk the lives and comfort of the rest of their family. The threats of fines and executions kept mages in line, though it was rarely needed. Most mages were happy to serve their country, to keep people safe – they thought it an honour – but there were always a few who disagreed.

Her brothers were also talking about the attack, about past and possible future attacks and about their desire to be out there, doing something. Ravi was the most vocal, but even Vivek agreed, and he rarely thought fighting was the answer. Shyam was quiet, not because he disagreed but because he preferred a cautious approach.

Lochan was the only one who didn't speak at all. Thiya wasn't sure he was even paying attention to their conversation.

The chance of another daayan attacking the palace tonight was slim to none, the safe room a precaution. The daayan had to travel a long distance to get this far south. Most possessed someone along the way and if they didn't, they were more likely to be destroyed by the sunrise before they reached the city. Daayan moved fast, but only a few moved fast enough.

She looked at her father. Her family was safe in this room, but what about Amara? Thiya should be up in the palace, not hiding down here.

Urgh, she sounded like Ravi.

There is nothing you could have done.

But she had done something, she just wasn't sure what. Or how. She didn't have magic. But Kayan did, and he'd been standing right next to her. Could *he* have done something? Could the light she'd seen have been due to proximity?

General Sethu left, but before the door swung shut behind him Thiya heard a scuffle on the other side. Ravi drew his sword. Lochan and Vivek sprang to their feet and Thiya straightened, her hand flying to the dagger strapped to her thigh.

Kayan stood in the doorway, his arms in the air, and a bright grin on his face. 'No need to stand on my account.' His voice was far too casual for someone who had swords pressed against his neck and stomach. What was he up to?

Thiya spotted Isaac just behind Kayan, his scowl fixed firmly in place. But at least his reaction made sense since shara levelled swords at him too.

'How did you get down here?' the king asked.

'We followed the general.' Kayan's grin still hadn't disappeared.

'Why?'

Isaac's scowl deepened. 'Are you the only ones allowed to hide away while the rest of your guests have to fend for themselves?' he asked.

The king's eyes narrowed. 'Who are you?'

'I apologise, Your Majesty,' Kayan said. 'I invited Isaac to come with me tonight, but he gets a little overexcited sometimes and forgets himself.' He shot Isaac a warning look. 'He serves with me in Tumassi.'

'In that case, I will forgive your impertinence, just this once. We are not hiding; we are planning. And my guests have not been left to fend for themselves. The rest of the palace has excellent security.'

'You mean mages?' Isaac grumbled.

Thiya wasn't sure why he didn't approve. Mages were their best defence against daayan. They also had walls and windows and shutters. The entire palace would be locked down, and as long as a wayward mage didn't break any more shutters, everyone would be safe.

'What is it you want?' the king asked, his voice deceptively calm.

Kayan pointed at the swords and the king nodded at the shara who relaxed their stance. None of them sheathed their swords, but they gave Kayan and Isaac enough space to step into the room.

Kayan bowed. Isaac stood with his back ramrod straight. Lochan and Vivek returned to their seats. Ravi's only concession was to lower his sword.

Kayan glanced at Thiya again. 'I came to ask if we can borrow the princess for Tumassi.'

Ravi's sword whipped straight back into the air.

Thiya straightened. 'Excuse me?'

She wasn't an object to be lent out upon request, and especially not to a battlefield. She wanted walls and a ceiling, not mud and a tent. Shyam and Vivek had to hold Ravi back. Lochan had sprung up and moved closer to Thiya. Even her mother shuffled along the sofa and took hold of Thiya's arm, as if afraid Kayan was going to snatch her away that very second.

'Why?' Thiya asked, at the same time her father said, 'No'. What did Kayan want her to do in Tumassi? She wasn't a mage, and she had no intention of making mages their tea.

Kayan turned to address Thiya, the excitement in his voice palpable. 'I have never seen anyone do what you did today.'

'Do not speak to my daughter.' The king strode into the centre of the room, placing himself between Thiya and Kayan. The shara waited for an order. Kayan took advantage of the delay.

'She can destroy the darkness,' Kayan said.

There was a plea in his voice that tugged at Thiya's heart.

'No, I can't,' she said, even as an image of the threads surrounding the daayan sprang to mind. 'If I could destroy the darkness and save my family and my people, then I would do it in a heartbeat, but that darkness over Sanathri Jungle was created by dark magic, and I'm not a mage. I can't destroy it.'

Before Kayan could respond, the king exploded. 'Get out!'

The shara grabbed Kayan and Isaac and pulled them towards the door. Mages waited on the other side, ready to neutralise Kayan and Isaac's magic should the need arise.

Kayan struggled to look at them over his shoulder. 'Please…'

'I'm not a mage,' Thiya said.

'None of us are,' Ravi added.

'But—' The shara opened the door. Kayan dug his heels in. 'She's an aethani.' He found her gaze. 'Help us.'

Thiya shook her head.

The shara pushed Kayan from the room, but not before Thiya saw his disappointment. Isaac didn't struggle, but Thiya recognised the disgust in his eyes before he followed Kayan out the door. She swallowed past the tightness in her throat. Even her mother's touch made her flinch.

Silence filled the room. Kayan's claim flew around and around in Thiya's head.

Aethani.

Aethani.

Aethani.

The weight of her brothers' stares pressed on Thiya and she looked down at her hands folded in her lap.

There were five types of mages, each one with the ability to control a different element. Feiraanis like Kayan could wield fire. Airus controlled air. Aquiras manipulated water. Terrais held power over the earth and everything that grew within it. And aethanis controlled aether, the space the other elements filled, giving them ability to heal and destroy.

Thiya's brothers had all compared her to Aunt Yesha at one point or another, but she couldn't be an aethani like Yesha. She might bend some rules from time to time, but she wasn't evil.

'Are we sure Thiya doesn't have magic?' Shyam asked, his expression neutral.

'I was tested, remember? On my tenth birthday, just like everyone else. And the mages found nothing.'

'The gods took away our magic to punish us for Yesha's actions. If they were going to return it, don't you think they would start with someone better than Thiya?'

She was glad someone was standing up for her and reminding her brothers of the obvious, but did it have to be Ravi? She held onto that anger and glared at him. 'Like you?'

Ravi shrugged with all the arrogance he could muster. 'You said it.'

'That was not why the gods took away our magic,' the king said.

'Oh sorry, it was so we could rule effectively,' Ravi said sarcastically, parroting the king's reasons for why their magic had disappeared. 'Except our ancestors had been ruling with magic for hundreds of years, and they never seemed to have a problem.'

Why couldn't her parents have sent him to live in the jungle when he was born?

'We weren't at war with daayan then. A good general doesn't charge into war. He stays back so he can observe and plan. The gods know this.'

Thiya wasn't sure whether the king or Ravi was right – though she really hoped it wasn't Ravi because his gloating would be insufferable – but she knew she didn't have magic; it was impossible.

'What did happen in that ballroom?' Lochan asked.

Thiya shrugged. 'I don't know.'

What had happened in the ballroom had to have come from Kayan. That was the only logical explanation.

'Did you freeze?' Ravi asked, a grin on his face that Thiya wanted to punch off. 'Is that why it took you so long to evacuate? You froze, didn't you?'

'Ravi, leave your sister alone,' the queen said. 'And you, don't retaliate.' She glared at Thiya. It wasn't fair.

The king held up a hand, demanding silence. 'My mages said the magic came from the feiraani.'

So it was Kayan.

'But the daayan was destroyed in its shadow form. The feiraani doesn't have that kind of magic,' Shyam said.

So, not Kayan?

'No one does,' Lochan added.

The king sighed. 'We're not sure the daayan was destroyed.'

Lochan looked horrified, his expression mirroring Thiya's. 'You think it possessed someone?'

'You said it exploded,' Ravi said.

'My mages think that was a diversion,' the king said.

'But what about the threads?' How would her father explain them? Thiya had never seen them before. She'd never even heard about them.

'What threads?' Lochan asked.

Thiya stared. Had nobody else seen them?

'It's been a long day, beta,' the king said. 'And you were close to the feiraani. His magic must be playing tricks on you.'

'Yes, that must be it.' But Thiya couldn't help but think how the daayan had disappeared after it exploded. And she hadn't seen it possess anyone. Daayan moved quickly, but that quickly? Could there really be a daayan in the palace right now? Was Amara safe?

Her brothers continued to discuss what had happened. General Sethu returned to hold more discussions with the king.

Thiya couldn't keep her eyes open any longer. She curled up on the sofa, her head leaning against the armrest. She drifted in and out of sleep, unaware of how much time had passed or how many people came in or out of the room. Whispered conversations became background noise, like the waves crashing outside her bedroom window.

It was hard to tell what time it was when her mother finally shook her awake. 'Come on.'

She sat up, a blanket sliding to the floor at her feet, and let out a yawn. It didn't feel like she'd slept long enough. Her brothers had already left, and her father was sat at his desk with General Sethu. The corridor was colder now than it had been before, but Thiya's mother held her tight as they made their way back through the palace, shara flanking them in front and behind.

Thiya paused when they left the underground tunnels and saw the shutters over the windows. 'What about the daayan?'

Her mother squeezed her hand. 'Don't worry. You're safe.'

But the sun wasn't even up and, 'Father said the daayan hadn't been destroyed.'

'It has now.'

Oh. 'Who…?'

'It doesn't matter.'

Was it her imagination or was her mother determined not to meet her eyes?

Her stomach clenched. She paused when they reached the second floor. 'I need to see Amara.'

Her mother gripped her shoulders and steered her down the corridor that led away from Amara. 'Not tonight. It's been a trying day,' she added, cutting short Thiya's protests.

'Is she…' Her breath hitched.

'She's fine,' her mother said softly. And yet Thiya needed to see that for herself. She needed Amara's comfort and guidance.

Aethani.

Amara would know what to do.

Her mother followed her into her bedroom, then walked over to the cupboard and pulled out a pair of pyjamas.

Thiya pulled one end of her chunari out from the waistband of her trousers and tried to unpin the other end from her blouse. She pulled the shoulder of her blouse up towards her neck and twisted it around to try and get to the pin underneath, but it slipped between her fingers and snagged on the translucent blue material. She groaned. It was too much – the pin, the daayan, the magic. What would she have to deal with next? Couldn't everything leave her alone for one night?

Her mother clicked her tongue. 'Why do you always insist on ruining your outfits?' She pushed Thiya's hands aside and unpinned the chunari. The long strip of rectangular material fluttered to the floor.

Thiya shrugged. 'Why is the chunari so difficult to remove?'

'You are the only one who has any difficulty.' She threw the pyjamas at Thiya. 'Get changed.' Her nostrils flared when she saw the dagger strapped to Thiya's thigh, but she didn't say anything.

Because she knew it would annoy her mother, Thiya

left her clothes on the floor and crawled into bed. The queen huffed, then bent to pick them up and draped them over Thiya's stool.

She sat down on the edge of the bed. The mattress dipped and Thiya rolled a little closer. Her mother pulled off her bangle and held it out to Thiya. 'Don't lose this one.'

Thiya shook her head. 'I don't want it.' She'd given her bangle to Amara. Accepting another tainted the gesture.

'This isn't a choice. You father insists all his children wear one, so anyone who sees you knows you are a child of the king.'

'Everyone in the palace already knows who I am.' And whenever she sneaked out, she didn't like people being able to identify her.

When Thiya didn't take the bangle her mother sighed. 'Will you, for once, do what you're told without arguing?'

Thiya took the bangle. She held it in her hand, but she didn't put it on. It was enough for her mother who pulled the quilt up to Thiya's chin and kissed her forehead. 'May Selina bless your dreams.'

Thiya didn't like her arms trapped underneath the quilt, but she allowed her mother to tuck her in all the same, realising her mother needed this. The moment she left, Thiya jumped out of bed and dropped the bangle on the pillow. She needed to see Amara.

3

Someone blocked the corridor leading to Amara's room. Thiya swore. The gods hated her. She was glad General Sethu had made sure Amara was safe, but she hated the inconvenience. This had to be payback for pretending to pray every time she was in the temple. She pressed her palms together and kept her mouth shut. What more did the gods want?

As she drew closer, Thiya caught sight of the dark blue kurta and trousers, and the swords and daggers strapped to a belt at his hips. A soldier. His arms were relaxed by his sides, but his eyes were on high alert.

He heard Thiya's approach before she even got close. 'Who's there?' he asked.

Chirag moved in front of her. 'I told you this was a bad idea, Princess,' he said.

Thiya hesitated for a moment in the shadows then strode forward into the light. Everyone knew she and Amara were friends. There was no reason why she shouldn't be here.

The soldier bowed when he spotted her, but he stopped her before she got to Amara's door. 'I'm sorry, Princess, you cannot pass.'

'But I want to see Amara.'

The soldier shook his head. 'The general's instructions

were clear. No one is allowed in or out of that room tonight.' His expression softened. 'She's safe. Her shutters are locked tight, and there are no gaps for a daayan to get through. I checked them myself.'

'I still want to see her. She may be upset after the attack.'

'I don't know…' But Thiya saw the soldier's rigid stance relax a little. 'The general wants to make sure Amara has her rest. He doesn't want her worrying a daayan is going to attack her in her sleep.'

'I won't disturb her,' Thiya said. She lowered her voice and leaned forward, like they were sharing a secret. 'I'll just poke my head in and see for myself. She'll never know I was here.'

The soldier hesitated but didn't step aside, and Thiya's irritation grew. The soldier had no right to deny her entry. She outranked him. She outranked the general.

She drew up to her full height. 'Step aside.'

The soldier swallowed. 'I … I'll need to check with the general…'

'You go do that.' She waved him away from the door. If he wanted to waste time chasing after the general, that was fine with her, especially since he would have to face the consequences of leaving his post. He wasn't going to go anywhere. He must have realised the same thing because he didn't stop Chirag from opening the door and checking for threats before signalling that the room was safe.

Thiya stood in the doorway for a moment, waiting for her eyes to adjust to the darkness. A diya sat on Amara's bedside table, a tall flame in the centre of the oil lamp. It cast just enough light to see Amara asleep on the bed, curled up under the covers, her back to the door. And to Thiya.

Thiya closed the door behind her, shutting out the protest the soldier was about to make. She made her way around the bed, her feet sinking into the shag carpet – fluffy and soft. It warmed her cold feet. She was almost around the other side when she stepped on something hard. Pain shot through her big toe and she cursed.

The quilt rustled. 'Thiya?' Amara's voice was rough with sleep and it turned Thiya's insides to liquid.

'Go back to sleep.' She pulled her right foot up and rubbed her big toe.

'What are you doing here?' Amara's voice was more alert now, but it still held that husky quality that did things to Thiya she both loved and feared.

'I came to check you were alright. I didn't mean to wake you. I can leave if you're tired.' Her fingers itched to touch Amara's skin, to see if she was as warm and soft as she looked.

'Stay.' The covers rustled again and Amara patted the bed beside her.

Thiya reached for the edge of the covers, slid inside and was immediately nestled in Amara's warmth. The scents of cinnamon and rose washed over her. Sweet and spicy, just like Amara.

She reached for Amara's face, her fingers tangling in the silky strands of her hair. She pushed Amara onto her back without releasing her hair and shifted so she was closer.

'How are you feeling?' she asked. Amara's neck was an inch from her lips and she leaned forward, pressing a light kiss against her smooth skin.

Amara's breath hitched. 'Hmmm…?'

Thiya chuckled and pulled away. 'How are you feeling after everything that happened tonight?'

'A little scared.' Amara pulled in a ragged breath. 'I tried to look for you in the crowd, but there were too many people and everything happened so fast. I found your mother.'

'I saw.'

'You did? I should have waited.' A tear slid down her cheek and Thiya hurried to wipe it away. Amara had done the right thing.

'Don't be ridiculous. I was on the other side of the ballroom and my shara got me out.'

Amara nodded. 'Good. That's good. I mean, I knew you would be safe, but…'

'I worried about you too.'

'You did?' A small smile flitted across Amara's face and she looked so hopeful. How did she not know how much she meant to Thiya?

'Of course I did, you silly goose.' She leaned down then to capture Amara's lips in a soft kiss, to feel her alive and whole in her arms. She deepened the kiss, but Amara pulled back.

'Should we be worried a daayan got so close?' Amara's gaze flickered to the curtains that hid the shutters from view, and Thiya knew she wanted to know if another daayan would breach the palace walls.

The last time it had happened had been five years ago. Night had just fallen and the window should have been shuttered tight, but Thiya had wanted to see stars. She'd seen a daayan-possessed soldier about to strike those around him with his sword. Thiya had watched as a fire mage killed the daayan and the soldier.

Now her nightmares would be filled with the daayan in the ballroom, changing shape, aiming for her father. Magic. Darkness and light.

Aethani.

She would tell Amara, but not tonight. Now they were together, Thiya didn't want to think about her fears.

'You're safe here.' She kissed Amara's forehead.

'Will you stay with me tonight? Father came to check on me, and mother stayed with me until she thought I fell asleep, but I don't want to be alone, even with the soldier outside my room.' She paused then asked. 'Is he…'

'I didn't stab him, if that's what you mean,' Thiya said, straining to keep her voice light with humour. A distraction. Amara needed a distraction. 'I left my dagger in my room.'

Amara's lips twitched. 'I didn't think you stabbed him. But I'm sure most soldiers have better things to do than babysit me. And as for your dagger, there is no way you would leave it behind.'

'If that soldier abandons his post, he will have me to answer to.'

Amara's smile was bright and full. 'How horrifying.'

'It should be.' She leaned forward again and sucked on the tender part of Amara's neck where it met her shoulder. Amara wriggled under her, but Thiya pulled back. 'As for my dagger, how dare you doubt my word?'

Amara's fingers wrapped around her upper arm and she tried to pull Thiya closer. 'Don't stop.' Her breathless, lust-filled voice made Thiya's insides spark with electricity, like she was standing in the middle of a thunderstorm that was getting wilder by the second.

Thiya sat up, the covers falling off her shoulder and pooling around her waist. She placed a hand over her heart in mock pain. 'You insulted my honour.'

'You have your dagger on you.' Amara huffed.

'Prove it.'

Amara's fingers found Thiya's knee then slid up her thigh. Thiya grabbed her wrists and lifted both hands above Amara's head. She stretched out next to Amara again, using the weight of her body to stop Amara breaking free from her grip.

'That's cheating,' Amara said when she stopped wriggling.

'Is it?'

'How am I meant to find your dagger if you don't let me use my hands?'

Thiya pretended to think about it for a moment. 'Get creative?'

Amara leaned forward and captured Thiya's lips in a deep kiss before Thiya even realised what was happening. All thoughts flew out of her head. She couldn't even remember what they were talking about. All she knew was she wanted more of Amara. She let go of Amara's hands so she could run her fingers along Amara's body.

Amara was doing the same. Her fingers trailed across Thiya's back, dipping lower until they slid into the waistband of Thiya's pyjamas. Thiya shifted closer. More. She wanted more. Their legs tangled together just as Amara deepened the kiss, her tongue darting into Thiya's mouth.

Amara yelped and broke the kiss. For a moment Thiya felt empty, and then her senses caught up to her.

'What happened? Are you hurt?' She ran her hands down Amara's arms, searching for any signs of injury.

'Why can't you wear slippers?' Amara said with a whine. 'Your feet are so cold.'

Thiya's laugh slipped out and Amara huffed. 'I'm sorry, I forgot.'

'You're lucky I love you.'

'I love you, too.'

Thiya trailed little kisses along Amara's jaw, along her cheeks and over her eyelids. Amara wriggled under her, a low moan building in her throat. She tilted her head to give Thiya access to her mouth, which she ignored. The moan turned to a groan and Thiya giggled against Amara's neck.

'I hate this,' Amara whispered.

Thiya froze, even though she instinctively knew Amara

wasn't talking about her or their make-out session. Or even what it was leading up to. She hated that their time together was limited. Amara might not get married this month or even the next, but she would soon. As would Thiya. And then whatever was between them would be over.

Thiya rolled over onto her back, giving her space to think. To breathe. Amara's breaths were just as ragged.

'We could run away,' Thiya said, though her voice lacked conviction. It was an old fantasy, one that was nice to think about from time to time but held no real possibility.

'Go live in a cottage in the mountains,' Amara continued.

'Spend our nights by the fire.'

'Sipping spiced wine.'

Urgh, no way was Thiya drinking wine. Wine addled her senses and made her lose control. Amara must have seen Thiya's expression twist.

'Fine. I'll drink the wine and you can stick to chai.'

'Better.'

Thiya rolled over to kiss her again, but Amara pulled away. 'I don't want this to change.'

'Everything changes.'

Even their relationship had changed, though Thiya couldn't pinpoint exactly when that had happened. One day her and Amara were simply friends and the next Thiya was feeling things she'd never felt before and it had excited and scared her in equal measure. She'd dreaded the thought of Amara finding out in case it made Amara hate her. And then, on her fourteenth birthday, they'd finally kissed.

Thiya still couldn't figure out who had made the first move. All she knew was that one moment they were staring at each other and the next they were kissing.

Her fantasies could not have prepared her for what she'd felt. She'd kissed the son of a servant a few weeks earlier, and the kiss had been wet and awkward. It had been a relief when he'd pulled away. But Amara's kiss had been different. It had been like breathing oxygen after holding her breath her entire life. When Amara had pulled back, Thiya had found herself leaning closer, not wanting to break the contact.

That kiss had changed her life. And now her life was changing again. This time she wasn't ready.

Amara must have sensed something in her mood because she reached up with tentative fingers to push a wayward curl behind her ear. 'I have no regrets,' Amara said, her voice a whisper, like it would disturb something important if she spoke any louder. 'I wouldn't change anything that's happened between us. Not for the world.'

'Neither would I. My life has been better for loving you.'

A sob caught in Amara's throat. Thiya slid her thumb down the side of Amara's face and under her eye, catching the tear before it had a chance to fall. Another tear joined the first.

'I'm not sure I can do this,' Amara said.

Thiya wanted to hold her again, but Amara was so stiff, she wasn't sure she would welcome her touch.

'You can,' Thiya said, trying to inject as much conviction into her voice as possible.

'How do I live with a husband not of my choosing?' Amara asked, her chin dropping, and Thiya wanted to lift it high. Amara was meant to look on the bright side. That was her way. 'Do I bear him children while I sneak out to see you every chance I get?'

'I like the idea of you sneaking away to see me,' Thiya said, earning a laugh in response. The laugh didn't mean much though. Amara was the type of person who would laugh even as she lay dying. Sure enough, the laughter faded as quickly as it came.

'I'm serious,' Amara said.

Except she wasn't. Not really. Once Amara made her vows in front of the gods, she would never betray them, even if she didn't want to marry in the first place. She would marry because it was expected of her, because she would never be allowed to marry a woman – and certainly not Thiya.

Thiya would have even less choice about her future husband. The union would be political, an alliance created to help her family, her country, her people. Her happiness wouldn't factor into the decision at all.

'I don't know how you'll live with your husband, but you'll find a way.' Thiya had never really thought about their future, had stopped herself from thinking about it on more than one occasion for the simple reason that they didn't have a future.

Amara curled into Thiya's side and Thiya slipped an arm around her shoulder, pulling her closer.

'Do you think I'll grow to love my husband?' Amara asked. 'My mother says I will, but I'm not so sure.'

Unlike Thiya, Amara had never been attracted to men. Though Thiya knew this, understood it even, there was a part of Thiya that worried Amara could grow to love someone other than her. She wanted to scream that no, Amara could never love anyone else, but did she really want Amara to live a life without love? Instead, she asked, 'Who would you choose to marry, if you could?'

'You.'

Thiya smiled at Amara's lack of hesitation. 'Apart from me.'

Amara shook her head. 'I don't want to think about it.'

'I don't think you have a choice anymore.'

Amara buried her head in her hands and mumbled something.

'I didn't hear that.' Thiya tugged Amara's hands down.

Amara sighed. 'Yash.'

The name sounded familiar, but Thiya couldn't place it. 'Who?'

'The Rear Admiral.'

'Really?' Her smile froze in place. She would not let Amara see how much that answer twisted her insides.

'Don't sound so surprised,' Amara said, lifting her head off Thiya's shoulder.

'He's old.'

'He's kind. He'll treat me well. I know he will.'

'You can't find someone younger who would treat you well? What about Lord Hiresh of Samka?'

Amara shuddered. 'He spent the entire time talking to my breasts. At least the Rear Admiral talked to *me*.'

'You do have nice breasts,' Thiya said.

Amara slapped her arm. 'Who would you choose?'

'I still have a year.' A year before she had to pander to potential suitors and hope to catch the interest of one who wasn't quite as bad as the others. And she wouldn't have Amara around for support because Amara would be living with her husband in his house and not the palace. Lochan would be here, but he didn't understand what it was like for a woman born into this world. It wouldn't be the same. 'I'm hoping someone interesting comes along before then.'

'Who do you think is interesting?'

'Someone with dark-brown eyes with flecks of gold.' Thiya leaned across and kissed the corner of Amara's eye.

'Do go on,' Amara said, a little breathless.

Thiya smiled. A lock of Amara's hair had fallen over her shoulder and curled against her breast; Thiya reached for it. 'Someone with hair as smooth as silk,' she said, as she kissed her way down Amara's neck, following the curl. 'Someone who is excited for me when I tell them I managed to land the flying kick I'd been practising for a week, who doesn't turn up their nose when they see me in my training uniform and who still hugs me when I'm covered in sweat.'

'I do like you sweaty,' Amara admitted. 'Though I prefer it when I'm the one making you sweat.'

Amara's lips found hers again and nothing else mattered for the moment – not the fact that Amara would be forced to marry someone else, not that the same fate awaited Thiya next year, and not that they might never see each other after they were married.

Amara tugged on the hem of Thiya's top and Thiya lifted herself off the mattress enough that Amara could slide it over her head. Amara's top followed, then her fingers found the string holding Thiya's trousers in place and she slipped them down her legs.

A commotion sounded outside, before the door opened and light flooded the room. Amara squealed, pressing herself closer to Thiya as if for protection. But Thiya couldn't protect her from this.

Amara's father stood in the doorway, frozen in disbelief.

The general recovered first. 'Stop what you are doing and get dressed,' he said, his voice shaking with rage.

'Is everything alright?' Isaac, the scowling mage from earlier, peered into the room. He looked at Amara and Thiya's naked state, and a grin spread across his face. The general pushed him out and slammed the door shut, but it was too late. Thiya had seen the look on Isaac's face, like someone who had just been granted his greatest wish.

From that moment, Thiya knew things would never be the same again.

4

Thiya's fingers shook so much, she struggled to light the torch on the wall using the diya. Amara had to do it for her.

'How are you so calm?' Thiya asked. Her body felt weak and it took all her effort not to touch Amara, to pull her close.

Amara shrugged, but her hands jerked as she took the oil lamp from Thiya and returned it to the bedside table. 'Why panic over something I can't control?' Translation: why show her emotions when her emotions made no difference?

Thiya scowled at the door as if she could see General Sethu on the other side.

'What do you think he'll do?' Thiya already had ideas – telling her parents at the top of the list, right below separating her from Amara.

Amara seemed to be thinking along the same lines. 'He'll probably try and marry me off sooner.'

Calm. She sounded far too calm. Why was she so calm?

'And you're fine with that?'

'Of course I'm not fine with that, but I have to marry either way. What difference does a few months make?'

'More time together.'

'Oh, Thiya,' Amara said, her voice filled with sadness and pity. Thiya didn't want her pity. 'A few months won't change the fact that we will be separated. Delaying it will only make it hurt more.'

Thiya's heart knocked uncomfortably against her ribcage. 'You don't know that.' And even if it were true, she'd take that hurt if it meant extra time with Amara.

Amara took Thiya's hand and kissed her fingers. 'I know my father. He won't force me to marry someone I really don't want to. I can hold him off for a while, but will it really help?' Tears rolled down Amara's cheeks and dropped onto Thiya's hand.

Thiya felt Amara's fingers tremble. She brought her free hand up to Amara's face and wiped the tears away with her thumb. 'Make sure he deserves you.'

Amara laughed. 'You don't think anyone deserves me.'

'And you'll do well to remember that.'

Amara leaned forward and kissed her. The kiss was short and sweet and tasted of salty tears. Amara pulled back far too soon and Thiya swayed forward.

Someone thumped on the door. Amara jumped and the distance between them grew.

Thiya's jaw clenched. 'We're changing,' she shouted.

'We should get dressed,' Amara said.

'I don't want to.' The moment she changed, she would be forced to leave this room and things would be different after that. Their parents would never allow them near each other again.

Everything was happening too fast. She was not ready. She didn't move.

Amara wandered around to the side of the bed where Thiya had flung her pyjama top and slipped it over her head. Then she picked up Thiya's clothes and handed them to her, but Thiya refused to take them.

Too soon.

Amara sighed then crouched down, Thiya's trousers in hand. She tapped Thiya's right foot, but Thiya refused to lift it.

'Please don't make this harder,' Amara begged.

It was the only reason Thiya obliged. Not for General Sethu, not for her parents and not for anyone who thought their relationship a sin.

Amara pulled Thiya's trousers up her legs and tapped her thigh. 'I was right. You were armed.' Thiya knew there were probably suggestive retorts she could make, but none sprang to mind. It was like she had been hollowed out.

Thiya tied the string around her waist and pulled the top over her head. She released a shaky breath and turned to face Amara. The light normally in Amara's eyes had disappeared and Thiya wanted nothing more than to get it back. She loved the way those eyes sparkled when Amara laughed and the way they brightened whenever Thiya looked at her.

'Are you ready?' Amara asked.

To face General Sethu? No. To face her parents?

Definitely not. But Amara had started walking towards the door.

Thiya caught her arm and Amara stopped. She slid her hand down Amara's arm to the bangle at her wrist – a thin silver disconnected band with the symbols of peace and prosperity etched into the middle. Thiya's bangle.

'Whatever happens next, remember, I will always be with you.'

Amara rested her hand on top of Thiya's. Her lips parted. Inviting. Passion flared behind those dark eyes, stoking the fire within Thiya.

General Sethu knocked on the door. 'Amara, if you don't come out now, I'm coming in to get you.'

Thiya glared at the door. Could they not have one last moment alone? But Amara moved and Thiya was forced to drop her hand.

Too soon. Much too soon.

General Sethu stood right outside. Thiya spotted the soldier blocking off access at the top of the corridor, along with Chirag.

General Sethu had to take a step back to allow Amara and Thiya out.

'What took you so long?' Sethu asked Amara.

But Thiya answered. 'Clothes are a lot harder to put on than take off.'

General Sethu's lips pressed together and he pulled Amara away from Thiya. Thiya wanted to reach out and snatch her back. Instead, she fisted her hands by her sides.

51

'We are trying to find you a husband. What did you think you were doing? How could you be so reckless?'

'Maybe Amara doesn't want a husband,' Thiya grumbled. Amara looked down at her hands, her fingers twisting together. 'Or maybe she wanted to have a little fun.' *Or maybe she's in love with me.* But even Thiya had enough sense not to say that out loud.

General Sethu's jaw tightened. 'I want to speak to my daughter. Alone.'

'What if I don't want to leave?'

'Thiya…' Amara warned. *Don't make this worse*, she seemed to say.

'Fine, I'll leave, but only because Amara asked me to.'

She started to walk away when the general spoke again.

'And Princess? I will be telling your father about this.'

She threw him a mock salute before storming off.

The further she walked away from Amara, the more the pain in Thiya's chest grew. It spread out from the centre, consuming every part of her until eventually all she felt was numb. She welcomed the numbness.

'Thiya!'

Thiya startled. Chirag stood in front of her, his brows furrowed. 'I asked if you were alright, Princess.'

Thiya shrugged.

'I'm sorry I didn't stop him, but he's the general and it was his daughter's room, and I knew he wouldn't harm you. I should have warned you...' Chirag ran his hand over his face. 'I should have knocked or shouted. I'm sorry.'

There was a weight to Chirag's words that made Thiya meet his eyes. She knew then that Chirag understood exactly what was going on between herself and Amara.

Cracks appeared in the numbness.

'It wasn't your fault. I should have known the general would want to check on Amara. I should have...'

I should have listened to my mother.

She cleared her throat. This was not a conversation she wanted to have, and especially not here with soldiers and mages patrolling the palace. She wanted to be back in the safety of her room.

Lost in her own thoughts, she didn't see Kayan until she bumped into him.

'Are you alright?' Kayan asked, holding onto her arms to steady her. He had changed out of his kurta and now wore the black leather trousers and jacket of a mage, the red bands around his wrists showing him to be a feiraani.

Isaac stood a little behind him. He wore the same uniform, only his had the green bands of an earth mage. The terrai in the palace helped maintain the gardens and close the wooden shutters at night, but she knew they had the ability to manipulate all organic material. Isaac could rip the wooden door off its hinges and grind it to dust within seconds if he wanted.

Isaac smirked at Thiya in a way that made her skin crawl.

She pulled away from Kayan. 'Shouldn't you be asleep?'

'After what happened in the ballroom?' Kayan shook his head. 'I couldn't sleep.'

'So, you thought you'd wander the corridors?'

'We thought we would patrol the corridors with the other mages, help out where we could, and then we saw General Sethu. I thought I could convince him to speak to the king on my behalf about getting you to Tumassi,' Kayan said.

'I'm not an object that can be loaned out at will.'

Isaac stepped forward. 'No, you're a mage who should be sent to Tumassi because those are your father's laws.'

Chirag tensed, his hand closing over the handle of his throwing knife. Kayan squeezed Isaac's shoulder.

Thiya's frustration bubbled over. 'What were you doing outside Amara's room?'

'That's where the general was,' Kayan said, frowning. 'We didn't know that was Amara's room.'

Isaac smirked again. Thiya wanted to punch him, but she knew that wouldn't help anyone.

'A soldier whispered something in the general's ear and he headed straight to his daughter's room, forgetting we were even there,' Isaac said. 'I wanted to know what was more important than daayan attacking the country. Now I know.'

Thiya's nostrils flared. 'Well, I hope you enjoyed the show.'

'Very much.'

Kayan looked between the two of them, a question in his eyes. She wasn't going to enlighten him. He stepped around Isaac, placing himself between them.

'We want to speak with you.'

No way was she staying anywhere near that smug snake Isaac more than she needed.

'I'm tired.' Thiya headed towards her room.

'Please.'

Thiya wasn't sure why she paused. Maybe it was the desperation in Kayan's voice, or the little hint of hope, both of which she could relate to. Or maybe it was because a small part of her wanted to hear what he had to say. Chirag stayed closer than he usually did, a comforting presence at her side.

'We want you to come with us to Tumassi.'

Thiya shook her head. 'You heard my father—'

'I'm not asking your father. I'm asking you. I know your reputation well enough to know you've left the palace without permission before. You can leave with us tomorrow, if you want to.'

Chirag tensed, but he didn't say a word.

'She won't leave,' Isaac said, disgusted.

Kayan glared at him.

Thiya had snuck out of the palace a few times with Amara. Once, she'd roamed outside with an emissary's daughter from Kakodha, the country on the other side of Sanathri Jungle. Her mother had told her to be nice to Shreya and to show her a good time. Apparently, that had not meant taking her out of the palace. Shreya had spent her entire stay talking down to Thiya, making snide comments about Agraal's daayan problem, because they never attacked Kakodha.

Thiya's parents had confined her to her room for two weeks after that and banned her from training for another week.

'What am I meant to do in Tumassi? Serve you chai? My chai is terrible, by the way.' She didn't know what she did wrong, but her chai always came out watery and with enough ginger to burn her throat.

Kayan bit his lip against a smile. 'Fight the daayan.' He sounded reasonable. He looked reasonable.

There was definitely something wrong with him.

'I'm not a mage.'

Although if she were… She could almost imagine what it would be like to hold fire in the palm of her hand – the warmth, maybe a slight tickle from the flickering flames. The power. She would love to see the look on Ravi's face if she were the one to defeat the daayan. His jealousy would entertain her for months.

Isaac pushed Kayan aside and stepped up to Thiya. Their faces were inches apart and Thiya saw the anger flash behind his dark brown eyes.

'Do you know what life is like in Tumassi? Constantly

fighting daayan but never having the power to kill them – unless they possess one of your friends?'

Thiya shook her head, swallowing around the dryness in her mouth.

'We risk our lives every night, knowing that every daayan we manage to keep at bay is one less life lost. But none of us can do what you did last night. You can stop the daayan once and for all. You can give us our lives back.'

Thiya wanted to help him, except… 'I don't have magic.'

'You do,' Kayan said.

No. There was no way. She tried to leave but Kayan blocked her escape.

Chirag pushed between them. 'You need to step back.'

Kayan did, holding his hands out, palms up.

'There's one way to be sure you're not a mage.' He offered Thiya his hand, a challenge in his eyes that Thiya understood all too well. The mage who'd tested her for magic at ten years old had held her hands. Something was supposed to happen, but nothing had. If she took Kayan's hand now, she could show him she wasn't a mage, and yet something made her hesitate. She wasn't a circus performer, she'd already been tested, and she didn't trust Kayan. But the one thing really holding her back was a voice in the back of her head saying, *What if he finds something?*

Aethani.

Like Aunt Yesha.

The darkness Yesha had created had cut off the

57

overground trade route between Agraal and Kakodha, increasing the cost of goods. The darkness had brought the night-time curfew. Agraal hadn't been the same since the daayan.

Kayan's fingers curled back into his palms. 'Why are you so determined to hide from the truth?'

'Because she's a coward like the rest of her family,' Isaac said, his expression hard. 'Your family brought the daayan into this world and you won't even help to clean up the mess.'

'That's not true.'

Thiya had a habit of messing up. She didn't want to think of the damage she could do if she were a mage. If she'd been a feiraani, then she would have set fire to her brother Ravi's things or soaked him if she were an aquira. If she was a terrai, then burying him in the ground amongst the jasmine bushes had a nice poetry about it since he hated the scent of jasmine. Or she could have summoned a gust of wind to blow him onto the summit of the snow-capped Dhandra Mountains in nothing but his underwear. Maybe she could bribe an airu to do that anyway.

Aethanis couldn't do any of that. They were healers and destroyers and she'd never destroy Ravi.

You destroyed the daayan.

But the mage test...

Her head pounded. She needed time to think.

Too fast. Everything was changing too fast.

Thiya stepped back. 'I'm tired.'

'So am I,' Isaac said.

Thiya knew he didn't just mean now.

'Help us,' Kayan pleaded. 'You can end this.'

She wanted to, but she couldn't.

'Aethanis are not evil,' Kayan said. 'They're healers. You don't have to be scared of your magic.'

She wasn't scared of her magic. She didn't have magic.

Pressure built behind her eyes. She shook her head and walked away.

Isaac's voice drifted after her. 'Do you love her?'

Thiya froze and turned back.

There was something calculating in Isaac's expression that she didn't trust.

'Would you kill daayan for her?'

Thiya's eyes widened.

'Would you do everything in your power to make the world safe for her?' Isaac continued. 'To ensure she would never have to be scared to sleep unless a soldier was posted outside her door?'

'Please, come with us,' Kayan said.

Thiya shook her head. 'I would do anything for Amara, but I *can't* kill daayan. I'm not a mage.'

'So, you don't love her,' Isaac said, his tone mocking. 'What is she then? A bit of fun?' He slunk closer, his lips curling into a vicious smile. 'Does she know? Should I tell her?'

Thiya wanted to press her dagger against Isaac's throat, to force him to swallow his insults. But he was a mage and he could hurt Chirag if not herself, so she used her words instead.

'I would go to the end of the world for Amara.'

She didn't wait for him to respond. This time when she walked away, Kayan and Isaac didn't try to stop her. But she heard Isaac speak before she reached the end of the corridor.

'Good to know.'

5

The room was lightening by the time Thiya made it back. Terrai pulled the shutters open the moment the sun crested the horizon – the moment any daayan without a human host would be destroyed by the sun.

The palace was still quiet, the usual sounds of servants scuttling around getting things ready for the morning were absent. Everyone in the palace slept late on the occasion they held a late-night function, but it would be worse today after the attack.

Thiya crawled into bed but sleep came in fits and bursts. Memories of last night broke through her calm – General Sethu's face when he walked into Amara's room, the daayan almost killing her father, somehow stopping the daayan.

Aethani.

You don't have to be scared of your magic.

The numbness cracked further, fear and pain making her chest tight. Her breath hitched. Even the sound of the waves crashing against the cliff outside her window couldn't calm her.

She didn't want aether magic. Being a healer would be fine, but she'd messed up enough times in the past because she acted without thinking. She was destined to destroy; she just knew it. She couldn't even get her outfit for the ball right, and that was after consulting with Amara and Kavita. That didn't leave much hope for any magic she might have.

Amara. She still had no idea what she was going to do about that mess. The general had caught them in bed together, practically naked. There was no way she could convince anyone they were just friends now.

She rolled onto her back and stared at the ceiling, watching the sunlight lengthen across the white marble and listening to the sea.

This was all Kayan's fault. He'd put the idea of her being an aethani in her head. Maybe she wouldn't have wandered the corridors trying to seek comfort in Amara's arms if it weren't for him. And now she wondered if she was doing the right thing. If she could destroy daayan, she owed it to her country to help.

After staring at the ceiling long enough for Thiya to realise sleep had well and truly eluded her, she dressed in her training uniform of grey cotton kurta that hit the top of her thighs, dark blue wide-legged trousers that gathered at the ankles, and soft leather boots. She strapped her dagger to her thigh and headed out the door.

Chirag had gone home to his family, but her other shara, Janav, stood outside her door. He fell into step behind her.

Amara's room was empty. Thiya swung by the bathroom but it was also empty, as were General Sethu's rooms and office and even the king's office. Where was Amara?

She glanced out the window and saw soldiers in the training ground, the only sign of life in the entire palace. There was no reason for Amara to be there, but she could have gone to find Thiya.

Thiya ran down to the training ground. She scanned all the faces, but Amara wasn't there, only Ravi, Vivek and Shyam. Lochan wasn't with his brothers, but that wasn't surprising. He normally trained with her. When her father had agreed that she be trained in combat alongside her four older brothers, only Lochan had approved. While there were some women in the army, most higher-born women were used to form alliances and produce heirs. Those who joined the army were poor with limited prospects. A princess would never be allowed to fight in a war.

Thiya did not wish to fight in a war, because that would mean her country was in danger, but she wanted to be ready if there was one. She trained to keep fit; she was aware of the threat of war on the horizon. With the daayan keeping the mages occupied, Agraal's defences had weakened. Their two closest neighbours – Kakodha and Jaankot were both sniffing around, testing their reactions. Luckily the darkness across Sanathri Jungle to the north and the Dhandra Mountains to the west meant they could only attack from the sea, and Agraal's navy was far superior to theirs.

Ravi and Vivek were sparring. Thiya watched Vivek punch Ravi, an uppercut to his abdomen that had him hunched over and gasping for breath. Shyam, perched on the fence, cheered Vivek's victory.

Vivek smirked. 'With skills like that, the daayan will run screaming.'

Ravi shook his head. 'I'd do a better job at fighting them than you.'

'Why don't we leave the daayan-fighting to the mages,' Shyam said. Ever the diplomat. He had a way with words, and his honeyed voice and even temper meant everyone liked him, a skill that served him well as the crown prince. Even Ravi couldn't keep up his anger with Shyam.

'Do we really think Thiya is a mage?' Vivek asked. It sounded like he was continuing a conversation they'd already had. Thiya froze.

'No,' Ravi said, his voice a low growl. Thiya knew better than to think he was defending her.

As the first and second in line to the throne, Shyam and Ravi weren't allowed to join the army and put themselves in danger. Vivek was the brother set to lead Agraal's army after General Sethu retired – the job Ravi wanted. Ravi took every opportunity to stand against Vivek and start an argument, and this time was no different.

'But what if—' Vivek started.

'No.' Ravi stalked off, almost bumping into Thiya on the way back to the palace.

He didn't even bother to apologise.

Shyam and Vivek stared at her. It was clear Vivek

thought she was a mage, but did Shyam believe the same? Or maybe they knew about her and Amara? Shyam and Vivek nodded at her before continuing their training. They didn't invite her to join them. They never did.

Amara clearly wasn't here, so she headed back inside.

The palace showed signs of life now, with guests emerging from their rooms and servants gathering supplies and packing their employers' belongings before they left. Thiya manoeuvred around them, trying to avoid eye contact as well as conversation. Did any of them suspect her of being a mage? Or had they heard other rumours? All the guests were in a different wing of the palace, but that hadn't stopped Isaac and Kayan from wandering around last night. Some of them might have done the same.

Thiya returned to her room in case Amara had tried to find her. Amara wasn't there, but Lochan and her mother were.

The queen rose from the chair where she had been sitting. Today she was dressed in a red and green kurta with yellow accents and fitted yellow trousers. Her oiled hair had been plaited in a single braid that hung halfway down her back and her lips were pressed together. Thiya was sure her mother knew about her and Amara.

Lochan, who had been pacing towards the window at the far end of the room, returned to his mother's side. His expression was grim.

'What are you doing here?' Thiya asked. If her mother

and Lochan were here to scold her, she wasn't going to make it easy on them.

'Your father and I spoke to General Sethu this morning,' Queen Archana said.

Thiya waited for her to continue, but the queen remained silent.

That wasn't good enough. If her mother had something to say, she had to say it outright. Thiya waited, too.

'What happened with General Sethu?' Lochan asked.

Thiya glanced at him. 'You don't know?'

But Lochan looked between Thiya and their mother, his brows furrowed. 'Mother asked me to come. She said you might need me.'

The queen kept her silence.

'Why might I need Lochan?' Thiya asked. To witness her humiliation? If they planned on using Lochan to ensure she stayed away from Amara, it wouldn't work. Even her favourite brother wouldn't be able to keep her away.

'General Sethu doesn't want you anywhere near Amara. Your father and I agreed.' The queen's voice was firm.

'I don't agree.'

The queen's eyes flashed.

Lochan frowned. 'They're friends. Have been for a long time. Why would you keep them apart?'

'Do you want to tell him or should I?' the queen asked.

Thiya's jaw clenched. So, Lochan was there to witness her humiliation.

'I love her.'

The queen held up her hand. 'I don't want to hear it, Thiya. Your sister has been carrying on a dalliance with Amara that will bring dishonour to both our families,' she told Lochan.

'I love her,' Thiya said, louder.

Lochan sucked in a sharp breath.

The queen scoffed. 'You're seventeen. You don't know the meaning of love.'

But she did. Amara was the first person she wanted to see in the morning, and the last person she thought about before bed. Whenever she was with Amara she thought she would burst from happiness, and whenever they were apart she counted the moments till they saw each other again. She valued Amara's opinion and always strove to be a better person for her.

She loved Amara.

And she was done with this conversation. If she was going to get into trouble, she might as well make it worthwhile. Except she hadn't been able to find Amara all morning.

'Where is she?'

The queen pressed her lips together and Thiya knew. The only way to keep her and Amara apart would be to send one of them away, and Thiya had to stay in the palace. She tried to think of what she'd seen in Amara's room that morning, but she hadn't focused on much besides Amara not being there.

Oh gods, there was no way, and yet her blood turned cold. She strode out of the room to the sound of her mother's protests.

Lochan caught up to her in the corridor. 'Thiya, wait…'

She didn't stop. She ran down the last corridor then came to a halt. Her hand trembled as she opened Amara's door.

Thiya saw what she hadn't seen before. The small signs of Amara's presence, her mojari peeking out from under the bed and her necklaces hanging from the frame of the small mirror on the wall, were gone.

Lochan laid a hand on her shoulder. 'I'm sorry.'

She shook her head. If he was sorry then this was somehow *real*.

'Where is she?' she choked.

'That's the other reason I came to speak to you…' Lochan hesitated.

'Where is she?'

'Gone. I overheard General Sethu and that mage from last night talking.'

'And?'

'He proposed to Amara and General Sethu accepted as long as he married her today. Amara wanted to wait for you, but the general insisted they leave as soon as possible. Now I know why.' He looked at her with a mix of curiosity and pity. Normally that would have bothered Thiya, but all she could think about was that Amara had left without saying goodbye. She might never see her again.

Her breath hitched. She scrambled for some logic, something that would tell her this was all a mistake. 'Amara said her father wouldn't force her to marry.' Her voice sounded like it came from afar.

'Amara agreed to the match.'

Drowning. She was drowning and she clutched for anything that would keep her afloat.

'But he's a mage.'

Mages weren't forbidden to marry, but it wasn't common. They had limited time off every year to visit their families. Amara would be alone most of the time. Unless that was the point? Mages didn't need a lot of money to live in Tumassi. Everything was provided for them – food, clothing, accommodation. Everything he earned would be sent back to wherever they decided to make their home. Amara could live a comfortable life. She could design clothes like she wanted. And she wouldn't have to deal with a husband when she was not attracted to men.

Thiya could be happy for her. She wouldn't rip Kayan's arms off and smack him over the head with them. She wouldn't chase after Amara and beg her to come home, to stay with her. She wouldn't ruin this opportunity for her, no matter how much she wanted to. Because Amara deserved better.

She sank onto the bed. The scent of cinnamon and rose wafted around her, the only part of Amara that lingered. A tear rolled down her cheek followed by another and another. Lochan pulled her into his arms. He rubbed her back as she cried.

The last time anyone had seen Thiya cry had been when she was thirteen years old and she'd started her monthly bleeds. She had known what they were, had been expecting them, but what she hadn't expected was the phantom hand that had tried to rip her womb from her body. One hug from her mother had let her know everything would be alright, that she wasn't alone and that she would survive.

Thiya was not sure she could survive this.

6

Thiya's chest heaved. Now that the dam had broken, the tears flooded out. All the emotions she'd been ignoring for so long rushed to the surface; everything she should have thought about before now. But knowing this separation was inevitable didn't make it easier. Her heart still cracked, each fissure sending sparks of pain shooting through her chest.

Lochan held her through it all. He knew about her and Amara now and he didn't care, which made her cry harder. She was lucky to have him as a brother.

The door opened and Thiya pulled back. Janav poked his head inside. 'There's someone here who wants to speak with you, Princess.'

'I don't want to speak to anyone.'

Janav nodded and retreated from the room.

'We can have this conversation through the door,' Kayan shouted, 'but I don't think you'd want that.'

'What now?' Thiya huffed.

Lochan got up and opened the door. Kayan held his hands up, palms facing out and the red band around his wrist on display. 'Sorry to interrupt.' Despite the apology, he was smiling. It was small, but it was there.

Khal's left testicle, he had taken Amara from her and now he had come back to gloat! She was going to make him regret that decision.

She lunged for him, but Lochan caught her around the waist before she could get far and pulled her back. She tried to reach for Kayan again, but Lochan held fast.

'Would you like me to remove him?' Janav asked.

'No,' Lochan said at the same time Thiya said, 'Yes.'

'You may leave,' Lochan said. Janav bowed and left, closing the door behind him.

Thiya blinked. Janav hadn't been her shara for long, but he answered to her, not Lochan. Chirag would never have made that mistake.

'I apologise, I didn't know he was going to do that.' Kayan's smile was gone.

'You didn't know my shara was going to be incompetent?' Thiya rounded on Lochan. 'You had no right to dismiss him.'

'I meant Isaac. Isn't that why you're crying? Although I thought you would be trying to stop him. I didn't take you for a crier.'

'What are you talking about?'

'Isaac's proposal to Amara,' Kayan said.

'*Isaac* proposed?'

'Yes.'

'Can I release you now or are you going to try and channel Aunt Yesha again?' Lochan asked.

Thiya gritted her teeth. 'I am nothing like Aunt Yesha.'

'You kind of are in that you are both aethanis,' Kayan said.

She glared at him. 'Go away.'

'But I came to offer my help.'

'With what?'

'Stopping Isaac.'

Thiya sank onto the bed. 'What's the point?'

She couldn't be with Amara, and whether it was Isaac or Kayan who had proposed made little difference. Amara had made her choice. She had chosen the mage.

'To save her from heartbreak. Or maybe humiliation. I doubt she feels anything for Isaac since they only met yesterday, and the only time she showed any emotion was when she defended you last night.'

Thiya's head snapped up. 'Amara defended me?'

'She told her father that you weren't the only one to blame for what happened between you two. She also vehemently denied it being a sordid affair like her father suggested and insisted it was a true love story. You would have melted.'

'I don't melt. And how do you even know that?'

Kayan shrugged. 'I may have eavesdropped.'

'Of course you did.'

Amara had stood up to her father – for her. Amara who never liked to break rules or make waves, who always valued her parents' approval, had told her father he was wrong. Her lips tugged into a watery smile.

'So, are you going to save Amara?' Kayan asked.

'What do you mean? Why do you care?'

'Can I not just be a nice person trying to help?'

Thiya snorted. 'You're Isaac's friend.'

'That doesn't make me a bad person,' Kayan said, which could be true, but she was sure he wanted something from her. 'Fine, I was hoping if I helped you save Amara, you would agree to help fight daayan in Tumassi. Maybe even stop them for good. I am tired of this fight. I want to go home to my family.'

'Amara doesn't need saving.' Thiya pulled the pillow over to her and hugged it close, inhaling the scent.

'Yes, she does. Isaac's not going to marry her. He wants you in Tumassi because he believes you can stop the daayan, and he got angry when you refused to even acknowledge that you were an aethani. He saw it as a betrayal. He started talking about kidnapping you. I refused to help him. But when he learned about Amara things changed. He's using her to lure you to Tumassi.'

Thiya was on her feet before Kayan had stopped speaking. If Isaac didn't marry Amara, the damage to Amara's reputation would be enough to destroy her. And it would be all Thiya's fault.

Kayan stepped out of Thiya's way, but Lochan pulled her back.

'What are you going to do?' Lochan asked.

'Stop Isaac.' Had he not been listening?

She hesitated outside Amara's room, unsure where to go. Her shara peeled off from the wall.

'I saw them in the stables before I came to find you,' Kayan said. 'They were leaving for Wangam, where Isaac's family was from. That's where Isaac told Amara they were going anyway.'

Khal, he worked fast. She started for the stables, then stopped again. She could go down to the stables, but then what? She needed soldiers and mages to help her. She needed someone who could get her both.

She headed in the opposite direction, towards General Sethu's office, Kayan by her side. Lochan was following on her heels.

Thiya spotted the king's shara outside the general's office when she knocked on the door. She didn't wait for a response before throwing it open and marching inside. The general stood behind his desk, his sword drawn. He lowered it when he saw Thiya and Lochan, but his jaw tightened and Thiya noticed he didn't sheathe it all the way.

The king stood beside the general. He frowned when he saw Thiya, which was a first.

'What do you want?' General Sethu grumbled.

'You need to call off the engagement between Amara and Isaac.'

'Do I now?' He flicked his gaze to the king.

'Thiya…' her father warned.

'Kayan said Isaac has no intention of marrying Amara.'

The general's eyes flickered to the feiraani before returning to Thiya. 'Then why would he propose?'

'To get me to Tumassi. Because he thinks I'm an aethani.'

The king inhaled sharply.

75

General Sethu lifted an eyebrow. 'Are you?'

'No,' Thiya said at the same time Kayan said, 'Yes.'

'If Isaac wanted you, he could have taken you,' General Sethu said, dismissively.

'No, he couldn't,' Kayan said. 'Thiya is too young to marry, and Isaac cannot take a princess against her will. She's always surrounded by her shara. By using Amara, he can lure Thiya away voluntarily.'

General Sethu shook his head. 'Amara is not without protection. Isaac is going to marry my daughter. I have no reason to believe otherwise. I will not call off the engagement because this is what *Amara* wants.'

Thiya flinched at the reminder Amara had chosen Isaac.

'Amara asked me for this and, since neither your father nor I want her around you, this benefits everyone. I had hoped to be there when Amara got married, but since Isaac is needed back on the front line and curfew makes travelling through the country harder, I agreed they could get married along the way. He will leave her with his family before he continues on to Tumassi. If you care about her, which I do believe you do, in your own way, you will let her go.'

'But—'

'Enough,' the king said. 'You will curb your jealousy and you will apologise to General Sethu.'

'I'm not—'

'Now,' the king said.

Thiya snapped her mouth shut. There was no way she was going to apologise for trying to save Amara. And if her father and the general weren't going to help her, she was going to have to stop Isaac herself.

'I'm going after her,' she told Lochan and Kayan after they left the general's office.

'You can't.' Lochan slapped his hand over his mouth when he realised he'd said that a little too loud. Shara stationed along the corridor threw them curious glances.

'I can.' She headed towards the door at the rear of the palace.

Lochan was not going to stop her.

'And then what? If the feiraani is right—'

'The feiraani has a name,' Kayan muttered.

Lochan rolled his eyes. 'If the feiraani is right, what will you do when you reach them? Will you go with Isaac to Tumassi or will you try and fight him? And will you be able to fight him? He's a mage.'

'She can stop him if she learns how to use her magic,' Kayan said, but Thiya ignored him. Or tried to. There was a small part of her mind that played that information around and around in her head. She could stop the daayan.

Or she could just as easily destroy the country.

'I'm not letting Amara's reputation be ruined. She doesn't deserve that.'

She opened the door and strode outside.

'I know she doesn't,' Lochan said, his voice soothing, 'and I'm not asking you to, but what if the general's right? What if Isaac really is going to marry Amara? What if she doesn't want to come back?'

Images assaulted Thiya: Amara cooking for Isaac, smiling at him, looking after their children. Thiya rubbed her chest.

'He won't marry her,' Kayan said. 'And Isaac doesn't have a family he can leave her with like he told General Sethu. They were killed in a daayan attack several years ago. He hasn't let anyone into his life since. It doesn't matter if Amara wants to marry him, because he will never marry her.'

'But General Sethu would have looked into that,' Thiya cried. The incident with Thiya had forced him to move faster, but there was no way he would have let his daughter marry someone he hadn't researched, was there?

Thiya was going to be sick.

This was all her fault.

'He must have an extended family,' Lochan said. 'Cousins? Aunts and uncles?'

'If he does, he's never talked about them. He's never been back to his family home in the eight years I've known him.'

Khal! Thiya quickened her pace to the stables. 'Where's his family home?'

'In the foothills of the Dhandra Mountains, but he won't go there. I'm sure of it.'

Thiya paused. 'General Sethu just said—'

'He doesn't have family, and he wants you in Tumassi. Why would he take Amara elsewhere when he knows you'll follow her?'

'She's not a mage,' Lochan said. 'She's not allowed in Tumassi.'

'That won't stop him,' Kayan said.

Civilians weren't allowed in Tumassi because it was far too dangerous. Even soldiers didn't venture inside. If no one else could stop Isaac, Thiya would.

'I'm coming with you,' Lochan said.

'I need you here to cover for me.'

'And have Mother kill me when she finds out?' Lochan shook his head. 'I don't think so. Besides, Mother will assume you're moping in your room.' When Thiya hesitated, he added, 'If you go, I go.' Thiya knew she wouldn't change his mind and, honestly, Thiya would be glad of his company. She nodded.

'I'll come with you as well,' Kayan said. 'I can teach you how to use your magic.'

'I don't have magic.' The reply was automatic now.

'You need my help,' Kayan said.

'I don't.'

'I'm the only one who can teach you how to use your magic, and you do need to learn, not just to stop the daayan but to rescue Amara as well. I assure you, Isaac's not the type to surrender because you bat your lashes and ask nicely.'

She'd never batted her lashes at anyone. Except maybe Amara. That one time. Never again.

'I worked in the archives for a time,' Kayan said. 'I'm one of few people who understand aether magic, who can teach you to use it. Of course, you can find one of the other mages to help you, but they'd likely drag you to Tumassi without giving you a chance to save Amara and force you into the training programme. And you won't be able to opt out because you're a princess. The law is very clear on that. Once you're a mage, your prior allegiances don't matter. You won't be a princess anymore. Your father introduced that law because too many mages from noble families were refusing to serve. He clearly forgot it would apply to his own family. Or maybe he didn't care? Either way, I am your best option.'

Thiya would happily spend the rest of her life battling daayan in Tumassi if it meant Amara was safe and happy and away from Isaac. But was she willing to become like Aunt Yesha in the process? Aethani were healers and destroyers. Was she willing to destroy for Amara?

Yes.

Kayan held out his hands again and raised an eyebrow in challenge. 'There is one way to prove you're a mage, unless you're afraid?'

She stopped, accidentally kicking a stone into a bed of roses. She wasn't afraid, at least not of magic in general. Maybe *her* magic. But if it helped Amara… She gritted her teeth and slipped her hands into Kayan's.

For a moment, she felt nothing. A smile curled her lips. There. She had been right – she didn't have magic, she wasn't an aethani and she wasn't evil. Then something changed. All at once, it felt like something was pressing against her skin, trying to get inside. Threads of darkness and light rose up within her in response. That sensation she'd felt at the ball, that mix of love and intoxication, travelled through her veins until it threatened to overwhelm her senses.

Thiya gasped, but she couldn't catch her breath. She needed it to stop.

Kayan cried out and released her hand. Everything quietened.

'What was that?' she asked, breathless.

'That was your magic.'

7

Thiya couldn't be a mage.

Kayan had done something to her, she was sure. Except Kayan didn't look smug or happy. He could be a good liar or he could simply be right.

At the moment, he was talking to a stable hand. Thiya and Lochan hung back near the entrance; the stables were too crowded for Thiya's liking. She wrinkled her nose against the smell of sweat and manure and horses.

'If the wind changes, your face will stay like that,' Lochan joked. Thiya didn't smile. Kayan was taking too long.

'They left on horseback an hour ago,' Kayan said when he finally returned.

'That's fine. If we leave now, we might catch up to them by the end of the day.' Thiya stumbled back as a stable hand passed by with a horse, the horse coming too close for her liking.

Kayan frowned. 'Is something the matter?'

'No,' she said at the same time Lochan said, 'Yes.' Thiya nudged her brother.

Kayan looked between the two of them. 'Am I missing something?'

'No,' Thiya said.

'Thiya's scared of horses,' Lochan said.

She glared at him. 'I'm not afraid of horses.'

'Did you not have riding lessons?' Kayan asked, surprised. 'I thought your mother was an exceptional horsewoman?'

The queen's reputation preceded her. It was precisely why Thiya didn't want to learn how to ride. Because everyone expected her to be the same.

'Of course I had lessons.'

'She never attended them,' Lochan said. 'She used to hide whenever someone came looking. There was one time she – oomph.' Lochan doubled over, clutching the stomach Thiya had just elbowed.

'Will this be a problem?' Kayan asked her.

'No.' She could do this to get to Amara. She strode up to the nearest horse and stroked his nose. 'I'm not afraid of horses.' They were big and smelled, and if one threw her off his back she would likely die, but she wasn't afraid of them.

'Good, then you should go pack and meet back here as soon as you're done.'

She spun around. 'Excuse me?'

'If we ride hard and change horses along the way, we can make it to Tumassi in ten days,' Kayan said. 'It's how Isaac and I got here. Make sure you pack accordingly.'

'I'm not going to Tumassi. I'm getting Amara then coming back home.'

Kayan's eyes flashed, but then his expression softened. 'We will get Amara first, but after that you have to come with me. You can either go voluntarily or Isaac can drag you.'

'I don't have to go anywhere with you.' She didn't need Kayan. She could get Amara back without her magic. She patted the dagger strapped to her thigh.

'You will continue to let people suffer and die at the hands of daayan, knowing you could have done something to help?'

Thiya pushed forward. 'That is not what I said.'

'It sounded like it.'

Lochan stepped between them. 'We can discuss this later. The quicker we pack, the quicker we find them.'

Janav stood outside her bedroom door. It didn't take much for Thiya to convince him that she was upset that Amara had gone and she wanted to sulk in peace.

Thiya had to be quiet as she packed. She didn't pack much, but she did change into a sturdier outfit of thick leggings and a short kurta along with boots. She threw more into her backpack along with a cloak and a few more weapons. Kayan was getting food, so she didn't have to worry about that. She strapped her dagger to her thigh over the leggings and slid another one into her boot. Then she climbed out the window, as she had so many times, shimmied down a tree and headed to the stables.

Outside, the front courtyard was a frenzy of activity. Carriages formed a queue along the path leading from the stables to the main gate where guests from the ball were still trying to leave. Both sides of the wrought-iron gates were thrown open to allow the carriages to roll through with ease. The line moved, albeit slowly, with soldiers helping shara guard the perimeter.

Thiya crossed the courtyard and entered the stables where Lochan and Kayan were already saddling horses.

'I can't believe I'm doing this.' She was going to ride with Lochan since his horse could easily carry the two of them, which was better than her trying to stay on and guide her own horse. Her mother would laugh if she found out about this – right after she was done scolding Thiya for sneaking out of the palace.

'It was your idea to follow Amara,' Lochan shot back from inside the stall. He hefted the saddle onto his horse and fastened the straps. 'His name is Dua.' Lochan scratched the horse's long nose.

'I don't need to know his name.'

Lochan covered the horse's ears. 'You'll upset him.'

'He's a horse. He can't understand me.'

'You'll be surprised what Dua can understand.' Lochan wagged a finger in Thiya's face. 'No being mean.' The horse snorted his agreement.

Lochan added Thiya's bag to Dua's saddle then led him through the stall door and out into the middle of the stable where the roof slanted upwards. 'Get on.'

The moment Thiya touched the harness, Dua shifted to the side and Thiya gasped. She took an involuntary step back. Maybe she was a little afraid.

'He won't hurt you,' Lochan whispered in her ear.

Her trembling fingers brushed against Dua's flanks. He was warm, his hair soft. Following Lochan's guidance, she placed her left foot into the stirrup and pushed herself up. The horse moved, but Lochan pushed her into the saddle. It was a long way down. Dua hadn't looked as tall from the ground.

Lochan swung himself behind her and settled against her back. 'Just relax and you'll stay on,' he said.

She nodded.

Kayan swung himself onto his saddle in a fluid motion that left Thiya jealous. Lochan clicked his tongue and Dua headed out of the stables, Kayan following.

They approached the gate, Kayan behind them. The path was not wide enough for a carriage and their horses, so Lochan guided Dua along the grass. A gardener yelled and a terrai followed them, straightening the blades they trampled. Thiya shouted an apology over her shoulder.

They drew closer to the gate, patrolled by soldiers, shara and mages. A carriage painted in deep shades of red and green with gold accents rolled through. Lochan pulled alongside the carriage. They had almost reached the gate when a woman came charging through from the other side, a shawl pulled over her head.

The shara and soldiers drew their weapons. One shara swung at her with a sword that lit up green with earth magic. The blade sliced through the woman's arm and she shrieked, but she kept on running, heading straight for Thiya and Lochan.

The daayan-possessed woman pulled on Thiya's arm with a grey-veined hand. 'Come with me.'

Thiya reared back and would have slid off the saddle if Lochan hadn't grabbed her kurta.

Her actions stirred a memory within Thiya – her shara lying on the ground in a pool of his own blood. A man trying to drag her away, his nails scratching her skin. Thiya trying to fight him off, her punches too feeble.

But she was stronger now.

She twisted her arm around and gripped the daayan's wrist so she could pull her closer. Then she kicked out with her leg, stomping on her chest. It should have knocked the wind out of the possessed woman, but it had little effect. The shard of ice sticking out of her chest did.

An aquira melted the icicle and blood streamed out of the woman's chest a moment before Kayan set her on fire. The daayan's grip on Thiya's arm slackened and the woman stumbled back. Only then did the flames engulf her hand.

Thiya's heart hammered. The last time a daayan had entered the palace had been five years ago. Now they'd had two daayan attacks in two days. What was going on?

'Are you alright?' Lochan asked her.

Thiya nodded. 'We need to go.'

Lochan set off again, but the gates had shut. Soldiers and shara shouted instructions at each other, more interested in the daayan than allowing carriages to leave.

One soldier stood in front of the gate. Lochan pulled Dua to a stop in front of him.

'Open the gates,' Lochan said in a perfect imitation of their father's voice. 'I want to leave.'

'A-are you sure that's s-safe, Your Highness?' He glanced around at his colleagues for help, but they were too busy to notice.

'We have a mage,' Lochan said in a lazy drawl.

The soldier nodded. 'Of course, sir.' He shouted orders up to the gatehouse.

The gates slid open, but before they could leave, someone shouted, 'What are you doing?'

Another soldier came running over to the gates, demanding they be shut.

'What's the plan?' Lochan murmured.

The gate was wide enough for their horses. Their way was clear except for the soldiers.

'I need you to step aside so we can get past,' Thiya said.

The first soldier hesitated, but the second shook his head. 'I can't do that.'

Well, she'd tried.

'Go!' she said, loud enough for Lochan and Kayan to hear.

They both hesitated. The gate was closing.

'Now!'

Lochan charged first, more trusting of her ridiculous ideas and Kayan followed a second later. Thiya clutched onto the saddle as Dua practically flew through the air towards the gate. The soldiers threw themselves out of the horses' path. She heard the shouts and cries of alarm behind her before they disappeared down the road.

8

Dua galloped towards the mansions on the other side of the road, but Lochan slowed him down as they plunged into the city streets. They had to travel through Kamanu city to head north. The streets were quieter here, where noble families slept late in their mansions or had gone away to enjoy the cooler weather on their country estates, but servants still wandered past.

The wind whipped dust into Thiya's face and tickled the back of her throat. She coughed. The city really needed some rain. She could see the plants that lined the houses wilting, the leaves burnt by the sun. The morning heat had beads of sweat rolling down her back.

Dua picked up a steady canter that was both too fast and too slow for Thiya's liking. Kayan's horse, Sona, followed close behind.

Thiya glanced over Lochan's shoulder. Soldiers were running after them, but they fell further behind with each second.

They skirted around the market square, the beating heart of the city. Vendors called out their prices, horses neighed and oxen bellowed. The stench of sweat and animal dung lingered in the air, barely covered by the smell of spices.

The crowd thickened. Their pace slowed to a walk.

Thiya couldn't see the soldiers anymore, but if they didn't speed up again they would fall even further behind Isaac and Amara.

A woman made crispy dosa in a stall ahead. Thiya watched as she spread batter across a tava in a thin layer, the masala beside it sizzling and spitting out oil as it cooked.

Thiya's stomach rumbled, reminding her that she hadn't eaten breakfast.

Amara first, then food. She would eat an entire barrel of mango and pistachio kulfi while Amara looked on disapprovingly because she hadn't eaten 'real food' first.

They left the market via the north exit and followed the road out of the city. The horses picked up their canter again; Kayan took the lead since he was the one who knew the route. Thiya knew if she followed the road north, she would hit Tumassi eventually, but she didn't know where to stop or how far they could travel before curfew – at least Isaac would have to stop for curfew too.

Kayan set a fast pace. Dua's gait was smoother than it had been in the city, but Thiya still feared she was going to slide off his back. Farmhouses, trees and fields blurred past her and she gripped the pommel tighter until her fingers hurt.

'Relax,' Lochan reminded her. She eventually got used to the movement, but soon muscles in her legs that she didn't know she had started to ache.

They approached a carriage and Kayan angled Sona

so she was between it and Dua as they passed. Lochan and Thiya averted their heads.

A man called to Kayan. 'Excuse me? Are you one of the mages who was at the palace during the attack?'

Kayan nodded without looking at him. Thiya could hear the man falter before he regained his courage.

'I wanted to thank you … for what you did…'

Again, Kayan nodded, a short incline of his head. A few seconds later, they left the carriage behind. She'd heard the rumours about Kayan defeating the daayan flying around the palace this morning. She wondered if people truly believed Kayan had saved them, or if her father had started those rumours to avoid her being found out as a mage.

They passed more carriages. Sona increased her pace and Dua followed. If anyone called out to them, they were too far away by the time it registered. They didn't see another horse. Disappointment and frustration built within Thiya.

The sun beat down on them, and without trees to provide shade, Thiya grew hot and uncomfortable, especially with Lochan so close. Her kurta stuck to her back but she didn't move away. A sweaty back was not going to be her downfall.

Thiya didn't know if it was the heat or because the horses were getting tired, but Kayan slowed the pace. It gave Thiya an opportunity to relax a little. Until Kayan spoke.

'Why don't you like horses?'

Thiya stared out into the distance. The farmland had turned wild, the grass overgrown, and a small woodland crept up in the distance. Shade. She bet it was cool under those trees.

'I like horses just fine.'

'Then why did you never learn how to ride?' Kayan asked.

Thiya could practically feel Lochan's gaze burning a hole in the back of her head. She'd always given him one excuse after another over the years: she hated horses, she wanted to spend time with Amara, she wanted to practise her martial arts. They were all reasonable excuses, but they were never quite the truth, and she was sure Lochan knew that. But Lochan didn't understand the pressure she faced to be the good daughter, to conform to society's expectations. 'We are not having this conversation.'

Kayan shrugged. 'We can talk about magic instead.'

Khal! She couldn't decide which subject was worse. No, she knew. The one where she might be evil was much, much worse.

'Being a mage doesn't make you evil you know,' Kayan said.

'I didn't say that.'

'You were thinking it.'

How did he know that? Gods, he was insufferable. And smug. She wanted to wipe the smirk off his face.

She sighed. 'How would you teach me about being a

mage?' Maybe for Amara, she would face the potential darkness.

Kayan's smirk turned into a genuine smile. 'I want you to feel for your magic.'

'How?'

'Remember that feeling when I tested you? That was your magic rising up to defend you. It's an instinctive response that every mage has, regardless of training, which is why it's so effective at identifying mages. The nature of your magic means you caused me pain. I set the kitchen table on fire during my test.'

'Then why didn't I feel it when I was ten?'

'I'm not sure,' Kayan said. 'Maybe the mage faked the testing? Though that's unlikely.' The test was carried out in front of an audience, with other mages around. There was no way a mage could pretend to test her, and there was no way she could hide her reaction or her family hide the results. She hadn't been a mage at ten. And yet she was one now. It didn't make sense. 'I don't think it matters. You are a mage now and you need to learn how to use your magic. Close your eyes.'

What was wrong with him? 'I'm on top of a moving horse.'

'You don't need your eyes to sit.'

She shook her head. 'No. I'll be no good to anyone if I die under Dua's hooves.'

'Dua won't kill you,' Lochan whispered in her ear. She ignored him.

'Fine. Don't close your eyes if you don't want to, but you do need to connect with your magic,' Kayan said.

She tried recalling the feeling but… 'There's nothing there.'

'Your magic is inside you, a part of you, yet different from anything you have ever felt before,' Kayan said gently. 'It's like seeing yourself in the mirror for the first time. You know it's you, but the image is off. I want you to find that which is different; the part of you, you have never noticed before.'

Thiya tried and failed. She huffed. 'There is nothing about me that's different.'

Thiya was spared Kayan's response when they had to stop to let a farmer cross the road with his cattle.

Kayan spoke with the farmer who seemed more than happy to talk while his cows blocked the road. Thiya gritted her teeth. Their conversation turned to travellers and Kayan asked the farmer if he'd seen another mage.

The farmer shrugged. 'I've been on the other side of that stream,' he said, pointing into the distance. 'I haven't seen anyone.'

Kayan thanked the farmer.

Thiya was not prepared for Dua to start moving again. She almost fell off him. Lochan pulled her back before she injured herself. She pressed her hand to her chest. Her racing heart knocked against her fingers.

'You never answered my question about horses,' Kayan said.

'Why does it matter?'

Kayan shrugged. 'I'm curious, and there's nothing else to do. It doesn't seem like you're scared exactly...'

'I'm not.'

'A little uncomfortable, maybe, but that's natural for someone who has never ridden before. So why didn't you learn? You've had the opportunity. Your mother is gifted, by all accounts.'

Thiya scowled. Even after she left the palace, her mother still haunted her every move. But Kayan was waiting for a reply, so she told him a version of the truth. 'I don't like something I can't control.'

Kayan nodded. 'I can understand that.'

They passed through several towns and villages. Some of the people they spoke to had seen a mage, though they couldn't be sure of his face. One person remembered a woman with him, but that had been earlier in the day. Thiya wanted to scream. It seemed that every time they were getting somewhere, her hopes were dashed.

The sun hung low in the sky when they reached the small village of Gunewa – if it could even be called a village. There were a few houses scattered on either side of the road, as well as a small temple a little further back. Kayan stopped at the only inn.

Thiya checked the angle of the sun. 'We can make it to the next village if they're not here.' She didn't like the idea of stopping here if Amara and Isaac had already gone on ahead. Pushing on would give them an advantage tomorrow.

Kayan shook his head. 'We'll never make it before the sun sets.'

He led them to the stables behind the inn and, to her annoyance, Lochan made them follow.

'We can make it if we push hard,' she said.

'We won't.' Kayan dismounted and handed his horse over to a stable boy. 'The horses are tired. We'll leave at first light tomorrow.'

Thiya felt Amara was slipping further and further away and she was helpless to stop it.

Another stable boy ran to help with Dua. Thiya wanted to shoo him away, tell him they didn't need his services because they weren't stopping, but Lochan slid off the horse. His movements were clumsier than Kayan's but he landed on his feet. He waited for Thiya.

'Are you going to stay up there all night?' Lochan asked with a chuckle.

'We've become friends.' She patted the horse's back. Dua snorted.

'Do you need some help?' Kayan asked. He raised his eyebrows in challenge.

'Wait! I think they're here,' Lochan exclaimed.

'Where?' Thiya looked around the stables but couldn't see Isaac or Amara anywhere.

'In the inn. Her horse is here.' He patted a light brown mare with a white stripe along her nose: Bandita.

They'd passed other inns along the way, but there had never been any sign of Amara or Isaac. Thiya had almost given up hope. But now she felt so close to holding Amara in her arms again.

She forced her thighs to relax and swung her right leg over, but Dua shifted at that moment and she fell – straight into Kayan's arms.

Heat washed over her and she almost fell again trying to scramble upright. Amara. She needed to find Amara. She grabbed her backpack and ran down a short gravel path and into the inn, Lochan and Kayan close behind. A bell rang when she opened the door, announcing their presence. Several heads turned their way, but most went back to their food and conversations a second later. Only the innkeeper kept his eye on them.

A girl, a few years younger than Thiya, was already pulling the shutters across the windows. She latched them in place, locking them inside, but it didn't matter. Amara was here.

Kayan spoke to the innkeeper and Thiya scanned the room. There, in the far corner, sat at the end of one of the long communal tables and tucked next to the wall was Amara. Thiya's heart skipped a beat and she started down the aisle towards her. Amara brought a handful of daal and rice to her lips and laughed at something Isaac said, her eyes crinkling in the corners like they always did when she was happy.

Thiya couldn't breathe. General Sethu was right.

Amara wanted to be here. She glanced at Kayan, wondering if he had Isaac's intentions wrong. Kayan frowned. Had he made a mistake or was Isaac acting?

Isaac sat to Amara's right, his back to the door, so he didn't see Thiya coming, but Amara looked up.

'Thiya!' she said, with a smile. 'What are you doing here?'

Isaac stiffened and turned around. Kayan approached and Thiya followed.

'Thank you for leaving without me,' Kayan bit out.

Isaac stood, putting himself between them and Amara. 'What are you doing here?'

Behind him, Amara stood and moved around the table. Isaac caught her elbow before she could get much further. Thiya dropped her backpack. She wanted to break Isaac's hand, but Amara smiled at him, reassuringly.

'I just want to give Thiya her bangle back.' She slipped Thiya's bangle off her wrist and held it up. Light glistened off the silver. Thiya had hoped Amara would keep her bangle, that a small part of her would be with Amara. Always. 'And I need to say goodbye. Everything happened so fast, we never got a chance.' Amara tried to move past Isaac again, but he held her back. Forget his hand, Thiya was going to rip his arms off.

'Why do you have to ruin everything?' Isaac asked Kayan.

Amara's smile faltered. 'I don't understand. I just want to tell Thiya I'm safe and happy.'

But Isaac knew it was a lie. Amara believed it to be true, but she wasn't safe. Thiya could see it in the hardness of Isaac's dark brown eyes.

'Get away from her!' Thiya yelled.

Amara stared. Isaac … smiled? Maybe Thiya could liberate more body parts.

'He's using you,' Kayan told Amara. Thiya waited for her reaction, ready to console her. She'd expected disbelief, anger, maybe even sadness. But Amara was not surprised.

'I'm well aware of that,' she said, 'but there's nothing wrong with wanting more leave and to be away from the front line for longer. It's a shame a mage has to marry to get extra time to see family but this arrangement works for both of us. We'll be married in name only to please my family, but once married we barely have to see each other.'

At least that explained Amara's reasons for agreeing to marry him so quickly.

Kayan stared at Isaac in disbelief. 'That's what you told her?'

'I didn't see you coming up with a better idea.' Isaac snatched the bangle from Amara's hand and shoved it at Thiya. Only instinct made her grab for it and slip it in her pocket.

Amara looked between Kayan and Isaac and shook her head. 'What do you mean?'

Thiya wanted to grab her and whisk her away somewhere no one could ever hurt her again. She wanted to hold her tight and protect her from all the Isaacs of the world.

'Let her go.' Thiya moved closer to Isaac. She tried to wedge herself between him and Amara, but there was no space. 'You have me now. I will go with you. You don't need her.'

'No. I have big plans for her, too.'

Thiya's blood ran cold. He had taken Amara to get to Thiya, to lure her here. Hadn't he? He'd got what he wanted. Amara was meant to be safe. She was meant to ride back home tomorrow and live her life. And now...

'What plans?'

Isaac's smile sent chills down her spine. 'Get to Tumassi in time, and you'll see.'

No, that was not happening. Amara was not going to become a snack for a daayan.

'I thought we were travelling to Wangam to be married in front of your family?' Amara said, her voice small.

'He has no family in Wangam,' Kayan said, softly. 'Not anymore.'

'Is that true?' Amara tried to pull herself away from Isaac, but he pulled her back. 'If you don't need extra leave to visit your family, why are you marrying me?'

Isaac gave her a little shake. 'Stop talking!'

'No.' Amara went to slap him with her free hand, but Isaac grabbed her wrist and twisted her hand behind her back. Amara cried out.

How dare he! Thiya drew her dagger, reversed the grip, and advanced. The hum of voices fell silent around them.

Isaac used his magic to rip the wooden leg off the long table and whip it towards Thiya, the wood reshaping into a thick arrow in mid-air. She and Lochan dived out of the way, Thiya landing heavily on her side, but the arrow went up in flames before it could reach them. Ash fell around them, the grey powder standing out in stark contrast against Kayan's black uniform. He hadn't moved an inch.

Thiya could barely hear Amara's voice through the sound of blood pounding in her ears. 'Ouch, you're hurting me. Let me go.'

In the few seconds of chaos, Isaac had managed to drag Amara to the front door. The innkeeper stood in front of it.

Isaac paused. 'I have no fight with you.'

'It doesn't look like the lady wants to leave,' the innkeeper said.

Amara stomped on Isaac's foot. 'I don't.' She snatched a hand free and slapped Isaac's cheek. Isaac hit her back, the crack echoing across the room. Someone shouted, but no one moved to help. No one wanted to go up against a mage.

Thiya leapt up, ignoring the sharp pain in her hip and shoulder, and ran towards them.

The door ripped off its hinges, knocking the innkeeper off his feet and banged against the adjacent wall before crashing to the floor.

The innkeeper's daughter screamed. 'Papa!' She scrambled towards him.

The night sky loomed at Thiya from the other side of the doorway, bright white stars scattered across an inky canvas.

A black shadow flickered in front, drawing closer.

'Thiya!' Amara reached for Thiya as the daayan hovered in front of Isaac.

Isaac didn't pause. 'She's inside.'

The daayan flew over Isaac's head. Isaac looked over his shoulder and his eyes met Thiya's. His smile sent a shiver rippling down her spine. Then he turned and walked out the door, dragging Amara along behind him.

Amara screamed Thiya's name.

Thiya moved to follow, but the daayan shot straight for her.

9

Flames erupted between Thiya and the daayan as Kayan intervened. Amara's cries faded and she was gone. The daayan twisted in mid-air, changing direction. Screams filled the room. Benches scraped across the floor. People ran for the stairs, creating a bottleneck at the bottom. Someone fell on the first step, but no one stopped to help. People scrambled over them to get to safety.

Kayan ran to Thiya's side, flames held in the palms of his hands. Lochan raced towards her: sword drawn. Thiya gripped her dagger tighter. Having something familiar in her hands offered her comfort even if it was useless against daayan.

The daayan dived for a table to the left of the entrance, towards a woman who had slid off her seat and was trying to crawl across the floor. Kayan threw fire between her and the daayan, sending the bench crashing into the wall. The bench caught fire, but the flames disappeared a second later.

Blood pumped through Thiya's veins, urging her to move. She needed to do something. Now. Before it was too late. If the daayan possessed someone, no one in the inn would be safe. Their determination to drink human blood and eat human flesh gave them near super-human strength. She had to stop that from happening.

Except she didn't know how to use magic.

She thought back to the attack at the palace – she remembered the threads of darkness and light. Yesha hadn't always been evil. She'd been a healer, tending to the sick and the poor, but her magic had corrupted her.

Thiya took a deep breath, and then fought against her instincts and closed her eyes. She recalled Kayan's words from earlier. *Find that which is different.*

There. Was that it? A little thread of light buried deep within her. She tried to reach for it, but darkness rushed up to meet her as well, like the darkness she imagined covering Sanathri Jungle.

Sweat slicked her palms.

The thread disappeared, the magic slipping through her fingers as quickly as it had appeared.

The daayan zipped around the room while Kayan hurled fire at it, forcing it to change direction. People cowered under tables. A few screamed.

If Thiya couldn't use magic, she wouldn't turn into her aunt. But if she didn't use magic right now, that daayan would eventually hurt someone.

She took a deep breath and tried again. A girl's scream cut through her concentration and she opened her eyes to see the daayan dive towards the young girl who had latched the shutters. Straight black hair covered most of her face, but Thiya could see the whites of her eyes as she stared at the daayan, unable to move.

Kayan threw fire at the daayan, but the girl's father

was faster. The innkeeper pushed his daughter out of the way. Hard. She slid across the floor towards Lochan, who pulled her behind him. Blood dripped from a gash on her forehead.

Kayan's flames hit the counter. Heat pulsed, before Thiya heard the roar of flames as the counter ignited. A woman screamed and ran out from the other side. She looked like the girl's mother.

Sweat beaded on Thiya's skin, but Kayan didn't extinguish the fire. Flames danced on Kayan's palm as he watched the innkeeper push himself to his feet.

The innkeeper's eyes had turned black, obscuring the whites. The colour continued to spread out, turning the surrounding veins a deep grey.

Thiya's mind screamed at her to run now the innkeeper had been possessed, but her legs wouldn't obey. Kayan looked grim and Thiya knew what he was about to do. She couldn't watch, but she couldn't look away either. If only she could save the innkeeper.

The girl barrelled past Thiya with a piercing yell and jumped on Kayan's back, knocking him off balance. 'No!'

'It's not your father. In a few moments he'll be fully possessed,' Kayan said, his voice strained. He tried to shake the girl off, but she clung to his arm, the flames on his palm dying.

The innkeeper reached for a knife on the counter before the daayan could take full control of him. His black eyes sought his wife's.

'I'm sorry,' he said, forcing the words through lips that did not want to obey.

The grey continued to spread across his cheeks and down his chin.

He turned the knife on himself.

The wife shouted out, but it was too late. The innkeeper stabbed himself through the heart, angling up through the ribs. Then he did what Thiya had been taught never to do – he pulled the knife out. Blood spilled from the wound, dripping onto the floor. He swayed on his feet.

The girl screamed, tears streaming down her face, and Thiya wanted to hug her, to take away her pain. The girl scrambled towards her father but Kayan pulled her back.

'The daayan's not dead yet.'

Blood was pooling on the floor at the innkeeper's feet. Too much blood. He would soon be dead – sacrificing himself before the daayan could take over his body completely.

The grey had spread down his neck now. Thiya had never seen the moment of possession before: how the daayan slowly infected the person, devouring them from the inside out.

The innkeeper's wife crawled towards him, reaching out to comfort him. Kayan yelled a warning, but it was too late. The daayan took control of the innkeeper's body and it pounced, using the innkeeper's weight to hold the woman in place. The daayan leaned forward in the innkeeper's body and bit her shoulder. Blood poured into his mouth.

The woman screamed and fought, kicking and hitting every inch of her husband's body she could reach. But it wasn't enough to deter the daayan from his snack. He caught her wrists and held them above her head and continued to feast on her blood.

Thiya moved forward with her dagger, but the innkeeper burst into flames before she reached him.

An inhuman cry ripped through the building. It hung in the air long after the daayan had been destroyed and the innkeeper burned. None of the flames touched the woman, but she screamed as if they had. Blood poured from the mangled flesh around her shoulder.

Kayan tried to comfort her, to reassure her that she was safe, but only the girl managed to stop her screaming. Between them, they calmed her down enough to cauterise her wound.

The mother and daughter held each other and cried as though their hearts would break.

10

Thiya had expected people to disintegrate in mage fire, to scatter into the wind as ash, but that wasn't what happened. The innkeeper's body was still there, charred beyond recognition. His wife and daughter pulled him close, speaking to him in whispers. Thiya turned away to give them their privacy.

Kayan had quashed the flames along the counter. The counter was burnt, but at least that could be fixed.

Thiya stared out of the open doorway where Isaac and Amara had disappeared into the night. She wondered if Amara was safe, and why the daayan had responded to Isaac's command. She wanted to run out the door and chase them down, but Kayan and Lochan now lifted the door between them and pushed it back into place.

'What does Isaac want with Amara?' Thiya asked. 'I offered myself to him but he wanted to keep her instead.'

Kayan heated the hinges until they slid back together and stuck, then heated the lock to hold it in place on the other side. 'I don't know.' He pulled on the door to test it, but it held fast. Amara was out there now with no way back.

Thiya reached for the bangle in her pocket and slid it over her wrist. She would find Amara and return the bangle to her – tomorrow.

'She's not a mage. Could he be trying to manipulate General Sethu?' Thiya asked.

Kayan considered this. 'To what end? The general is not in charge of mages.'

'But he could convince my father to make changes.'

'Maybe.' Kayan pinched the bridge of his nose. 'Let's get some sleep. We can try to figure out Isaac's plans in the morning.'

He walked around the counter and pulled the last set of keys off the hooks. On the shelf sat a statue of Sanchari, the Goddess of Unexpected Guests. Even in statue form, she looked like she was in constant motion.

'Should we be doing that?' Thiya glanced at the innkeeper's family, but they weren't paying them any attention. She didn't like the idea of staying down here all night, but helping themselves to a room still felt wrong.

'They need to grieve,' Kayan said, 'and we need to sleep if we want to catch up with Isaac again tomorrow.' He handed Thiya her backpack before grabbing his own then headed up the rickety staircase at the back of the inn. Thiya and Lochan followed. Thiya heard the sound of people shuffling behind their locked doors, but no one looked out to check what had happened.

'Did you know Isaac could control daayan?' Thiya asked.

'No.' Kayan found their room on the second floor, right at the end of the corridor, and opened the door. 'I

110

didn't even know that was possible. Do you think that's what he did?'

Kayan lit the sconce with a wave of his hand and a diffuse light filled the room. The space was small, only large enough for two single beds and a small chest of drawers with a bowl and pitcher on top. Shutters were already drawn tight against the windows.

'I don't know for sure, but that daayan listened to him. Could he be an aethani?'

Kayan shook his head. 'He's a terrai.'

Thiya thought back to how he'd manipulated the table to attack her. And how he'd pulled the door off its hinges with a single look. There was no denying Isaac was a terrai. But he'd controlled the daayan. He'd set it after her.

'Could he be both?'

Again, Kayan shook his head. 'It's never happened before.'

'I've never heard of someone gaining magic after ten,' Lochan said, 'and yet Thiya exists.' He closed the door and threw his backpack onto one of the beds.

'That is weird, I admit. But Isaac is not an aethani. We would have seen signs of it before now. It would have been useful on the front line.' Kayan's voice turned wistful, and Thiya remembered he wanted her to stop daayan in Tumassi, just like Isaac did. But she couldn't even stop one in an inn.

Lochan followed his backpack onto the bed and lay

down with his hands crossed behind his head. Thiya looked at the second bed.

'I'm not sleeping on the floor.' Thiya threw herself onto the other bed before anyone could argue. The bed was hard, and something dug into her right leg, but she didn't move.

'I'll sleep on the floor then,' Kayan said.

Thiya craned her neck up to see if this was some sort of trick, but Kayan shook out his bedroll between the two beds. He caught her looking and smiled. 'I'm used to catching sleep wherever I can. This is nicer than some of the places I've slept in.'

'Oh yeah? Like where?' Lochan asked, leaning forward to get a better look at Kayan.

At that moment, Thiya's stomach decided to announce her hunger to the world. Lochan and Kayan had eaten in the saddle, but Thiya hadn't wanted to take her hands off the pommel, and she was now reminded that it had been almost a day since she'd last had food. Kayan must have realised it too, because he jumped to his feet.

'Why don't I get us something to eat. Then we can discuss my sleeping habits.'

Lochan moved his bag, rearranged the pillows against the headboard and sat back, his arms crossed over his chest. Kayan returned not long after, carrying a tray with three steaming bowls. He handed a bowl each to Thiya and Lochan before settling himself onto the floor next to his bedroll to eat.

112

Thiya's nose wrinkled when she saw the contents of the bowl.

'I think it's good,' Kayan said when he saw her expression, his words muffled around the mouthful of food.

'It's daal and rice.'

'Simple food can still taste good, Princess,' Kayan said. 'Don't be a snob. Try it.'

She dipped the spoon into the brown liquid and gave it a little swirl.

'It is good,' Lochan said. He'd inhaled half his bowl already.

She took a bite – and burnt her tongue. She hadn't expected it to be so hot, like it had been freshly cooked.

'Sorry,' Kayan said. 'I'm not used to heating up food with my magic. I must have overdone it.'

'It's alright.' She lifted another spoonful to her mouth, but this time she blew on it before taking a tentative bite. The daal was hot and flavoured with chillies. It might have been the best daal she'd ever tasted. Kayan smiled knowingly. Thiya scowled.

After she'd eaten every last bite, Thiya crawled into bed. Her thighs ached and pressure had started to build behind her eyes. The food sat heavy in her stomach.

'I'm sorry I didn't stop the daayan. I searched for my magic. I saw something, but it disappeared before I could do anything,' she said.

'You did well,' Kayan said.

'Are you serious?'

Kayan laughed. 'Were you able to land a punch your first try?' he asked.

She had. The technique had been poor, the punch had had little impact and she'd hurt her wrist, but it had landed. She supposed she saw his point.

'We'll work on it. You'll get there.' He stood and collected all the bowls, piling them onto the tray. 'Now we should all get some sleep. We have a long day ahead of us tomorrow. Especially you, Thiya.'

Thiya had no problem with long days as long as they led her to Amara.

She pulled up the covers, expecting to lie awake most of the night. It was the first night she'd spent away from home, other than at the Winter Palace, and she was terrified for Amara, but sleep pulled her under the moment her head hit the pillow.

Thiya's dreams were filled with daayan, soaring flames and Amara's terrified eyes. Echoes of screams filled her ears, and she woke to one hanging on her lips. She pressed her mouth together, letting the sound die on her tongue.

Being awake wasn't much better. Every time she blinked, she saw something different. A charred body, grey veins, blood. She saw two people trying to hold each other together in the face of senseless loss and violence. One daayan and so many lives ruined. She hated this.

Why hadn't her magic worked last night? If she hadn't failed, the innkeeper would still be alive. His family would still be whole.

Thiya lay in bed until Lochan and Kayan woke, then they packed up their belongings and headed downstairs. Thiya's thighs protested with every step she took. She didn't think she'd ever been this sore, which was proof that humans did not belong on animals.

The common area was cold and dark. Kayan lit a small fire in the fireplace, but the heat barely permeated the air. Signs of the attack were everywhere – in the upturned tables and chairs, in the burnt pillows and in the scorch marks along the walls and counter – but there was no sign of the innkeeper's body or his family. Thiya hoped the two women were safe. She glanced at the door. It was still closed, so they must have retreated upstairs.

The staircase creaked as someone came down. A woman threw her room key on the burnt counter, next to where Kayan had placed theirs, then made her way to the kitchen in the back. She emerged a few moments later with a couple of stale rotli. She rolled one up and bit into the end. Yuck. Cold rotli wasn't great, but she could have at least put some ghee on it. The woman looked around at the destruction in the room and then to the three of them, her expression scrutinising as she sat down in the corner.

'Should we go?' Thiya asked.

'The sun hasn't risen yet.' Kayan made his way to the back of the room and sat down. Lochan took the seat opposite, and Thiya, after a moment's hesitation, sat next to him.

Curfew ended the moment the sun crested the horizon. Even that small amount of sunlight was enough to destroy any remaining daayan. But it was hard to know when that moment happened without opening the shutters and checking. She didn't want to wait till the sun climbed higher to leave, but she also didn't want to open the door and face another daayan. And Kayan sounded sure the curfew hadn't ended.

'How do you know?' she asked.

'I can feel it.'

'Is that a mage thing?'

Kayan considered this for a moment, frowning. 'In a way, I guess.' He lowered his voice and looked around. More people had entered the common area, and a few looked like they were trying to listen in on their conversation.

'Would I be able to feel when the sun rises?' she asked.

There were moments she knew it would come in handy, like if she wanted to watch the sunrise with Amara one day. Or watch the sun set over the Winter Palace in the Dhandra Mountains. If she knew the exact time they had to be inside, they could watch something truly spectacular. Would the ice sparkle under the light of the setting sun? Would Amara lean in a little closer for warmth, even with their steaming cups of chai?

Kayan spoke, breaking through her fantasy. 'I'm not sure. We all feel the sun in different ways. As a feiraani, I can feel the heat of the sun, but airus say the air moves faster when the sun is around, and terrais watch how the flowers respond to the sun. Aquiras feel the tide change as the moon descends, which can be a little trickier to determine because sometimes the moon is up at the same time as the sun. If you figure out how your magic responds to the sun, you'll have to let me know.'

They sat in silence after that, the room slowly filling up. Tension permeated the air. People glanced at Kayan, but he appeared relaxed and in no hurry to move. It must have been earlier than Thiya had originally thought.

After what felt like far too long, Kayan stood. 'Let's go.'

Everyone came alive at Kayan's signal. Benches scraped across floors. People picked up their bags and ran for the door. One man kicked the door because it wouldn't move.

'Who has the key?' he yelled into the room. People looked around and at each other, but of course the innkeeper and his family were not around. And anyway…

'The key won't work,' Kayan said. 'I had to weld the lock shut last night because of the damage.'

'Then open it,' the man demanded.

'That was the plan, but I need you to step aside.' Kayan didn't raise his voice, but a power radiated from him. Thiya heard the man gulp before he slipped away to the back of the crowd. She wanted to know how to do that. She could use it against Ravi any time he tried to annoy her.

Kayan melted the lock enough to open the door and headed outside. Lochan and Thiya followed. The sky was still dark, but Thiya could see the sun lighting up the horizon, the deep blues softening to purple – technically the end of curfew and the earliest she'd ever been outside. The air was cool and crisp, and there was a freshness about it she hadn't expected, the kind of freshness that happened after a rainstorm. She wondered what other experiences she'd missed out on because of curfew.

They followed the path to the stables. Both horses were saddled and ready to go. Kayan took the reins from a sleepy stable boy, straw still clinging to his clothes, and swung onto his horse. He led Sona outside to wait.

Dua snorted at Thiya by way of a greeting. Thiya sneered.

'You'll be fine,' Lochan told her, as he accepted Dua's reins from the same stable boy. 'It'll be easier today.'

She doubted that, but she reached for the reins all the same. Dua's lips pulled back from his teeth and he snorted again. Was he laughing at her? She grabbed the reins, stuck her foot in the stirrup and pulled herself onto the horse. Her movements, while not graceful, were at least smoother than yesterday.

Lochan swung himself behind her. He clicked his tongue and the horse set off.

Kayan set a fast pace, but not fast enough that he couldn't speak to Thiya about her magic after they'd travelled a few miles. 'You cannot use your magic if you cannot connect with it.'

'I tried.' The sun was out now, and the heat beat down on them. Thiya had grown the tiniest amount more comfortable on the horse, not enough to close her eyes, but enough that she was willing to turn her focus inwards.

'You felt the threads yesterday. Find that again.'

'The threads have disappeared.'

Kayan smiled. 'That's not how magic works.'

'Magic isn't supposed to suddenly appear at seventeen, either.'

Kayan didn't rise to the bait. 'You need to learn how to use your magic, not keep questioning it. Try again.'

Thiya tried to relax and control her breathing the way Kayan had shown her earlier, essentially meditating with her eyes open. She drifted inside herself, trying to find the part of her that was different, that held power.

Nothing.

'I don't have magic.'

'You do,' Kayan insisted.

'I don't.'

He reached over and grabbed her hand. Nothing.

Kayan scrutinised her expression then frowned. 'That's … odd.'

'Maybe her magic disappeared?' Lochan asked.

Kayan shook his head. 'Magic can't disappear. You're

either a mage or you're not, and Thiya is definitely an aethani.'

'Then why don't I have magic right now?'

'I don't know.' Kayan's frown deepened. Then he stopped dead. 'Unless… Can I see that bangle Amara gave you?'

'Why?' Lochan stopped their horse and Thiya glanced at the silver band that peeked out from under the long sleeve of her navy kurta.

'It was your bangle first, right?'

'Yes…'

'When I was working in the archives, I heard about some jewellery that had been created using all five elements. This was back when aether magic was more common. The bangles were said to block all magic. The wearer wouldn't be able to use their magic, but no mage would be able to use magic directly against the wearer, either. I wouldn't be able to burn you up from the inside out, or an airu wouldn't be able to rip the air from your lungs. Maybe that bangle has the power I read about.' Kayan nodded at Thiya's wrist.

Thiya removed the bangle and handed it to Kayan. This time when Kayan took her hand, Thiya felt the threads of magic rise within her in response to his magical attack. Light and dark, intoxication and desire. Her fingertips tingled.

Kayan hissed and released her hand.

Thiya stared at the bangle. So that's why her magic hadn't shown itself until now. She'd only given Amara the bangle a few days ago.

'Do you mind if I keep hold of this for now?' Kayan asked.

Thiya shrugged. It had always been a part of her, but she had no need for it now.

'Do you think Father knew?' She'd lost count of the number of times her father had told her not to remove the bangle. From Lochan's expression, he had realised the same thing.

'He may have just been trying to protect you,' Kayan said. 'That's what the jewellery was originally created for.'

'Protect us from what?'

'Mages that resent your father's conscription laws.'

That made sense, and it was better than believing her father had deliberately kept her magic from her, from the world. She wanted to believe her father would have done right by his people if he had known.

'Does this mean *I* could have magic?' Lochan asked.

Kayan held out his hand to Lochan. Lochan pulled off his bangle and slipped his hand into Kayan's.

'I'm sorry,' Kayan said a moment later.

'It's fine. I have other things I want to do than become a mage, anyway,' Lochan said, with a slight catch in his voice.

Lochan had the choice to join Agraal's army or navy. Or he could even become an ambassador with the potential to travel around the neighbouring countries. Except he hadn't shown much interest in anything. Being a mage would have given him a purpose.

'You should practise your magic,' he said to his sister.

'Lochan…'

'I'm fine.' Lochan set their horse moving again.

Thiya didn't believe him, but she nodded.

She reached for her magic.

There.

She followed that feeling. This time she felt a ball of power. Darkness mixed with light, the threads nestled together until she didn't know where one ended and the other began.

Healers and destroyers.

Her fate.

Yesha's fate.

The magic slipped away. Urgh!

Kayan had been watching her face. 'You had it.'

'And then it disappeared,' she snapped. 'Again.'

Kayan thought about this for a moment. 'You're scared.'

She was not. She wasn't scared of the daayan in its shadow form, blending in with the night, and she certainly wasn't scared of the grey veins of a person possessed. Creeped out, sure. But not scared.

'I ran towards the daayan.'

'Not of the daayan,' Kayan said.

'Then what?'

'You're worried that you'll turn evil, because society has led you to believe that all aethanis are evil. But Thiya, aether magic is not evil. Yesha might have used her magic for evil, but she made a choice, just like the rest of us do every day.' Kayan conjured fire in the palm of his hand, watching the flames dance in the breeze for a few moments. 'I can create light and warmth for someone with my magic, a shelter from the cold, but I can also use it to destroy.'

He frowned as he stared at the flames, and Thiya wondered if Kayan was thinking about what he had done last night, throwing fire around the room like a weapon. She shuddered as she remembered the destructive force. Kayan curled his fingers into his palms and the flames snuffed out.

'Magic is neither good nor evil,' Kayan said. 'It just is. You can choose a different path to Yesha's.'

Hope flared, but then she remembered the darkness inside her. It was already there. Would it grow bigger? How long before this dark heart of hers consumed her entirely?

'If you embrace your aether magic, you could potentially get rid of daayan once and for all,' Kayan said. 'And that might be the only way to save Amara from Isaac, if he's found a way to control them.'

She closed her eyes and reached for her magic again.

They ate lunch in the saddle because Thiya refused to stop. No one put up much of an argument, but she did start to regret it when she felt sick. She handed off some of her thepla to Lochan, unable to finish the spiced flatbread.

Despite their pace, Isaac and Amara remained ahead, which was almost as frustrating as Thiya's magic lessons. Finding her magic had become easier and faster, but she still couldn't hold onto it, let alone use it.

The sun had started to dip below the horizon when they reached the large town of Sambha. Kayan stopped when they spotted a group of boys playing with a ball. He dismounted and handed the reins to Lochan before going over to talk to them.

His face was troubled when he returned.

'What?' Thiya asked. 'Did they see Amara?'

Kayan nodded. 'A while ago. They're travelling faster than I'd expected, and Isaac's changed horses.' He looked across the horizon where less than half the sun was visible now. The sky to the west was painted in shades of pink and purple, but they darkened to blue and black further east. 'We need to find somewhere to stay.'

The first inn they tried was full, as was the second, but stable hands accepted their horses in the third. They walked around to the inn in time to see the shutters bang shut.

Kayan sprang forward and rapped on the door. 'It's still light outside.'

'Not for long,' the man on the other side of the door said in a lazy drawl.

Thiya pushed her way to the front. 'Then let us in,' she demanded.

A pause, then, 'We have no room.'

'Then why did you accept our horses?' Thiya asked through gritted teeth.

'The stables have room.'

'We're mages,' Lochan said. 'We can keep you safe from daayan.'

'You'll attract them, more like. You're not coming in here.'

Thiya heard the unmistakable sound of the bolt sliding into place. She banged on the door, but there was no response.

'Now what?' Lochan asked.

Thiya glanced at the horizon, at the thin sliver of sunlight still visible along the edge. They needed to find shelter, and soon. 'Can you burn down the door?' she asked, but Kayan was already leading them away.

'That won't help anyone,' Kayan said. 'I know somewhere else we can stay.'

'Why didn't you say so earlier?'

Kayan grunted. 'Didn't think of it.'

'What did the innkeeper mean about you attracting daayan?' Lochan asked. 'Is that something mages do?'

'Of course not.' Kayan huffed and adjusted his backpack so it sat higher on his back. 'It's a silly superstition, one that's usually restricted to small villages. We happen to be around when daayan attack because we are actively trying to stop them. Some people seem to see that as us attracting the daayan.'

'Will the people at this new place think you're attracting

daayan?' Thiya asked. Lochan smacked her arm and Thiya glared at him. 'What?'

'You have no tact, little sister. Can't you see Kayan doesn't want to talk about this?'

'But we're going to be staying there. We deserve to know.'

The sun had dipped below the horizon now, the last of the sun's rays their only protection against daayan. The shades of red and orange that painted the sky would have been beautiful if they weren't so close to curfew. They could still go back and force their way into the inn.

Kayan sighed and rubbed his nose. 'The guesthouse is run by the mother of a mage I used to work with. I haven't seen her since her daughter's funeral.'

'Oh,' Thiya said. 'I'm sorry.'

Kayan nodded.

The sky had darkened to shades of deep blue and purple by the time Kayan stopped outside a house made of light grey stone and situated on a riverbank. The shutters were drawn over the windows, but Kayan climbed the steps leading to the front door and rang the bell.

Thiya heard a muffled voice from the other side of the door. 'Who's there?'

'Kayan.'

A bolt slid back and a small window opened in the door. An eye blinked at them. 'Show me your face.'

Kayan conjured a small ball of fire and let it hang in the air above his face.

'Now your companions.'

The flames moved over to Thiya's head, hovering there for a few seconds before showing Lochan's face.

Without a word, the woman shut the window. The door opened. 'Well don't just stand there, come inside.' She ushered them through the doorway, her gaze flicking across the deserted street and the darkening sky.

The moment they were inside, the woman slammed the door shut and slid home the bolt. The light flickered in the torches along the wall.

'It's safe,' she yelled, and it was like the house breathed a sigh of relief.

They were in a long hallway, stairs leading up from one side, and several doors leading off the other. One door was ajar and Thiya heard the sound of voices within.

The woman swept past Thiya and pulled Kayan into a hug, her black hair falling over his shoulder. 'Oh, it's so good to see you.' She pulled back enough to look at his face. 'How have you been, and why are you out so late?'

'We lost track of time.'

'Then it's a good thing you came to me.' She reached for Kayan's chin and angled his face towards the light. 'Have you been sleeping?'

'Whenever I can.'

She clicked her tongue. 'They work you too hard.'

'We work as hard as we need in order to protect this country.'

'Sarika was the same, always sacrificing herself for everyone else.' The woman shook her head.

'Would you rather the daayan destroyed the country?' Thiya asked.

The woman glared at her. 'I would rather my daughter did not die for a hopeless cause. I would rather more mages not join her.'

'Maybe the cause is not quite so hopeless anymore,' Kayan said. The woman narrowed her eyes, but Kayan shook his head. 'I'm still working on it but, in the meantime, let me introduce you to Princess Thiya and Prince Lochan of Agraal. Thiya, Lochan, this is Prisha.'

Prisha scrutinised Thiya and Lochan, and Thiya had to fight the urge to fidget. Prisha was not her tutor and Thiya had done nothing wrong.

'You are full of surprises,' Prisha said with a smile. 'But you two might want to keep those titles to yourself. Not everyone around here is happy with your family. Come on, I suspect you might be hungry. Food is already on the table. You can leave your bags here and head on through.'

Thiya glanced at Lochan who shrugged and followed Kayan through the open door to a dining room.

There were five tables in the room. A group of six were squashed onto a table in the corner. Next to them, one woman sat on her own, scowling at her plate. There was a long buffet table set up against the wall with bowls of biryani, potato and chickpea curry and garlic naan. Thiya breathed in the aroma. Her mouth watered.

'Well, don't just stand there,' Prisha said. 'Grab a plate. Help yourself.'

She was supposed to serve herself? But she followed Kayan's example and filled a plate with food before bringing it over to an available table. The sound of chattering around them filled their comfortable silence, until the woman's words on the next table caught Thiya's attention.

'I wish the daayan *had* possessed the king. Then maybe the royal family would start taking our struggles seriously.' Her curls, held back by a pink scarf, bounced around her animated face.

The man sat opposite her looked aghast. 'You can't mean that.'

Lochan and Thiya locked eyes.

'I do. What have they ever done for us, other than hide in their fancy palace and pretend there's nothing wrong with the world? They go and throw their extravagant balls while we die every day.'

One ball a year, not plural. And they were for a good cause. They built alliances and created trade deals during that ball. This woman clearly didn't know a thing.

'They're tradition.'

That's right, Thiya thought, mentally applauding the man.

The woman snorted. 'Tradition just means they can do something problematic and no one argues. Tradition is something they hide behind and use to control other people. It's not something to be proud of. If it were, they wouldn't need someone like you trying to defend them

129

with *tradition*. It's because of tradition I can't officially marry my wife.'

Thiya frowned. Her and Amara couldn't share their love for one another because of tradition, but that wasn't the fault of her family. They too were caught up in the trap of tradition.

The man held up his hands. 'Alright, you might have a point about the ball, but wishing the king dead is a step too far.'

'Hey now, there'll be no talk of treason in this house,' Prisha said as she walked past, checking to see if anyone needed anything.

'It's not treason if it's true,' the woman said with a shake of her head. 'You think Prince Shyam is going to be any better than his father?'

Thiya's fingers curled into her palms. Lochan put a staying hand on her arm. Prisha noticed the exchange and frowned. 'How are you enjoying your food?' she asked.

But Thiya couldn't answer. This woman didn't know her brother. Shyam was the best of them. He *cared*. Really cared. He was constantly challenging their father about lowering taxes for the poor and giving incentives to farmers to grow more crops and hire more hands. Not that her father didn't care. He did.

'He is just like his father. He will ignore us because he doesn't want to know the world is not safe.'

'That is not true.' Thiya didn't realise she'd spoken aloud until two pairs of eyes turned to stare at her.

'Would anyone like more naan?' Prisha asked, loudly.

130

'What would you know about it?' the woman asked, and Thiya saw her lips were painted the same shade of pink as her scarf.

Plenty, but Kayan kicked her under the table before she could answer.

'I thought so,' the woman said when Thiya didn't reply. 'You know I'm right. Everyone knows I'm right, they're just too scared to admit it. Just like they're too scared to admit they wish that feiraani had let the king die. The royal family will never act against the daayan until one of them dies.'

'They are acting. There's an army of mages who protect the country,' Thiya cried.

'Yes, *our* people. The ordinary citizens of Agraal.' The woman glanced at Kayan's uniform. 'How many of the royal family have sacrificed themselves for the country?'

'The royal family don't have magic,' Thiya said before Kayan could reply. Then she thought of the bangles and her own unexpected magic. But her family loved this country. They *cared*. There was no way her father had intentionally hidden her magic.

Prisha tried to intervene, but the woman ignored her. The woman wandered over to their table. 'So they say. But don't you think it a little convenient that they went from having the strongest magic in the country to having none, right when the daayan appeared?'

Threads of magic swirled inside Thiya, almost as if they agreed with the woman's words. 'The gods—'

The woman pounded her fist on the table, rattling the

cutlery. 'I know the story. I don't believe it. The royal family are liars and cheats.'

Each accusation was a physical blow, landing at the centre of Thiya's chest. If she hadn't been sitting, it would have knocked her off her feet. The woman was still talking, still *lying*, about her family, but the words didn't register. Thiya wanted her to stop. She *needed* her to stop. The king must have been trying to protect his family. There was no evidence he knew he was hiding their magic, even Kayan said so.

The magic inside her grew stronger, the threads of darkness and light rising to the surface.

'They're not going to thank you for defending them,' the woman said. 'The king will sooner throw you onto a fire than shake your hand. You're delusional if you think he cares about you.' She nodded at Kayan. 'At least the mage knows I speak the truth.'

'Everyone's entitled to their opinions,' Kayan said, evenly.

'You agree with her?' The woman's harsh laugh rang through the air. 'You think the royal family appreciate your sacrifice?' She laughed again.

'Maybe we should change the subject,' Prisha said.

Thiya watched a thread of her magic wrap around the woman's body. 'Of course they appreciate his sacrifice.' Her own heart beat a little faster.

'Do you agree?' the woman asked Kayan.

Kayan hesitated, and the woman's smile widened like a predator about to catch an unsuspecting prey. 'I think the royal family can change,' Kayan said, his eyes on Thiya. 'If they did find a mage in the family, for example, they could prove their worth by sending her to Tumassi.'

Prisha's eyes widened.

'They would never do that,' the woman said.

'They might be reluctant at first,' Kayan conceded, 'but I have faith they would do the right thing.'

Kayan met her eyes, but Thiya wasn't sure she was doing the right thing. She was following Isaac and heading to Tumassi because of Amara. Of course she would destroy daayan if she could while there, but Amara was her priority. Maybe the woman was right about her even if she was wrong about the rest of her family. She squirmed under Kayan's gaze and the belief she found there. Belief in her.

'Ha! The last member of the royal family who had magic almost destroyed this country for her greed, or have you forgotten about Yesha?' She leaned closer to Kayan. 'Those royals only think about themselves. There is no way any of them would sacrifice themselves for the likes of us.'

Thiya's heartbeat sounded disjointed. There was a second, quieter echo a fraction behind the first.

The woman was wrong, but Thiya knew she wouldn't want to hear that. She wanted to blame someone else for her misfortunes. It didn't matter what Thiya did, she would never please this woman. She would just find someone else to blame for her troubles.

The second heartbeat grew stronger. It belonged to the woman. Thiya wasn't sure how she knew that, but she did. The same way she knew she could make it stop – make *her* stop. The threads of magic pulsed.

The woman shrieked, her hand flying to her chest. She collapsed against the table. Thiya could feel her ragged breaths. The man screamed the woman's name, but Thiya couldn't hear him over the sound of roaring in her ears. A dark, heady sensation coursed through Thiya. She wrapped more threads of magic around the woman's heart and squeezed. She could do whatever she wanted and no one could stop her. She could get Amara back. They could be together. Forever.

Heat seared her wrist, and Thiya cried out. She blinked and the room came back into focus in time for Thiya to see Kayan pull his fingers back. Thiya's skin was red and blistered where he had touched her.

'What in Khal's left butt cheek…?'

'I had to stop you making a mistake you would later regret,' Kayan murmured. He jerked his chin towards the woman who lay on the floor, panting heavily, but she'd stopped clutching her chest. Had Thiya done that?

Lochan seemed to think so. His eyes were wide and he looked at Thiya like a stranger. 'You had this really intense look on your face,' he said, his voice hollow.

Bile rose up Thiya's throat.

'What was that?' the man asked. He stood and rounded on Kayan, the only mage in the room. 'What did you do?'

Prisha moved between them. 'Your friend had a heart attack.'

The man shook his head. 'I'm a physician. I know heart attacks. That was magic.' His eyes narrowed on Kayan again.

'Feiraanis burn,' Prisha said. 'They don't cause heart attacks.'

'But—'

'Go check on your friend,' Prisha told him.

Kayan pulled Thiya to her feet. Her legs shook. 'We need to leave.' He nodded at Prisha as he led Thiya away. Thiya glanced over her shoulder to see the man crouched over his friend, but his eyes followed them out the door.

Prisha went with them. 'I hope you know what you're doing,' she said in the hallway.

'I have no idea what you're talking about,' Kayan said.

Prisha's eyes flashed. 'My father was a mage before the daayan. I know magic when I see it. *You* might not have the ability to affect that woman, but that doesn't mean someone didn't use magic on her.' Her eyes flicked to Thiya.

Shame washed over her and Thiya shrank back.

'She can stop them,' Kayan said, softly.

'But will she?'

Thiya looked away first.

Kayan slid open the bolt and pushed Thiya out into the night. 'Give her a chance,' she heard him say before he and Lochan followed.

Thiya could still feel that dark, heady sensation within her telling her to go back, to finish what she'd started, to give into the darkness.

135

11

Kayan pulled Thiya away from the house before dropping her hand.

'Are you alright?' Lochan asked. He'd picked up their packs on the way out, and he handed Thiya hers. His hand twitched in the air between them as if he'd been about to offer comfort then thought better of it. Yesterday Thiya would have been upset, but today she felt numb.

Lochan had a right to fear her. She'd almost killed someone. Like in the ballroom, she had no idea what she'd done, and yet there was no denying she *had* used magic. She'd felt the darkness coursing through her.

The numbness started to subside, replaced with disgust and self-loathing. She was evil. Maybe it was a good thing she hadn't known about her magic sooner. How many people would she have killed otherwise? She'd almost murdered that woman. Thiya didn't like her views, but that didn't mean she deserved to die.

'We need to move,' Kayan said, looking up at the night sky.

The moon was not full, but it was bright enough to cast a silvery light across the road. Stars dotted the rest of the sky, from little pinpricks of light to beams the size of Thiya's fist. The sight took her breath away. The last and only time Thiya has seen the night sky, she'd been distracted by a daayan, and she hadn't had the time to appreciate the beauty. Thiya could have stared at the sky for hours if the threat of daayan wasn't hanging over their heads.

They headed through the town and back towards the stables. Thiya's legs felt heavy and she stumbled over her feet a few times.

'We need to leave,' Kayan said. 'Prisha won't say anything, but her friend seemed to realise we were somehow responsible for what happened, even if he doesn't quite know how. It won't be long before soldiers are upon us.'

While the soldiers could be dealt with, it would delay them further and that was not something Thiya was willing to risk.

Like in the inn, Kayan melted the lock before pulling the stable door open. Liquid metal ran down the doorframe. He used his magic to light a torch on the wall and Lochan headed straight for Dua.

A stable hand lay asleep on a bale of hay just inside the doorway; her short hair fell across her face and a soft snore sounded from slightly parted lips. She didn't stir as they passed.

Lochan had opened the stall door and was crouched down so he could shake Dua awake. Dua whined.

Kayan placed a finger on his lips.

'Dua won't wake up.' Lochan's whisper carried around the stables, but the girl didn't stir.

'Then leave him.' Kayan was already saddling Sona.

She had opened her eyes the moment Kayan had approached.

Thiya crept a little closer and saw Dua asleep on the floor. Lochan stroked his nose and this time he did open his eyes – only to huff air into Lochan's face before closing his eyes again. At another moment in time, Thiya would have found it funny.

'Get another horse,' Kayan said, nodding to the horses at the far end of the stables that the inns kept for mages, royals and other important members of society to use at short notice. Sona was saddled and ready to go.

Lochan shook his head. 'I can't leave Dua.'

'No horse can handle this entire journey alone, not at the pace we're travelling and certainly not carrying two riders,' Kayan said, harsher than Thiya had heard him before.

'But Dua…'

'Will be safe where he is,' Kayan said.

Lochan crouched down to whisper something to Dua before leaving and closing the stall door. Thiya chewed on her lower lip and watched as Lochan selected a chestnut brown horse around the same size as Dua. He led that horse over to Kayan and handed over the reins before saddling a third horse.

Thiya's eyes widened. 'Why do we need three horses?'

Kayan and Lochan both turned to stare at her, then at each other.

Kayan shrugged. 'She's your sister.'

138

Lochan shook his head. 'I lay no claim over that.'

'Hey!' She was right there.

Lochan stepped forward and placed his hands on Thiya's shoulders. 'Little sister, there are three of us,' he said, like that explained everything.

'And?'

'The *three* of us need *three* horses.'

'I don't know how to ride a horse,' she hissed.

Lochan didn't look concerned. 'You've been doing fine until now. You sit on her and she'll follow the others.'

'What if she doesn't?'

'She will.'

'But what if she doesn't?'

'She will.'

'But what—'

'We'll be able to travel faster this way. We just need to be on the lookout for daayan,' Kayan interrupted. 'We'll get to Amara faster. And we need to be away from this town by morning if we don't want to be caught.'

She looked at the horse again, watched the way his nostrils flared. Could she stay on top of a horse without Lochan's support?

Kayan helped her mount. She gripped the reins tight, her body locking into place.

'Don't pull on the reins,' Lochan said. He tapped her fingers until she loosened her grip. 'You'll be fine,' he said, running a hand down the horse's neck. 'You'll see. She's a good horse. Aren't you?' The horse leaned closer to Lochan's touch.

Kayan melted what remained of the lock. 'A good shove will allow them to open it in the morning, but it'll stay closed for now.' He led the way down the road.

Lochan had told the truth. Thiya's horse followed the others without issue. Kayan set a fast-walking pace. Despite the moon's light, the buildings cast deep shadows into the street. Who knew what lurked in the dark, or if the shadows themselves were the danger. The hairs on the back of Thiya's neck stood on end.

The horses' hooves were too loud in the night. An owl hooted overhead, making Thiya jump. Wind rustled leaves in the trees. Too loud. She knew those sounds, had listened to them from her own bed. But sounds that had brought comfort before, now turned menacing.

Something moved in the shadows and Thiya's mouth went dry. 'How…' She swallowed. 'How do we know if there is a daayan nearby?'

'We don't,' Kayan said. 'Not until it attacks us.'

'Can you not…' Another movement. It was the tree leaves. It had to be the tree leaves. Kayan threw her a curious glance, encouraging her to finish her question. 'Can you not sense them?'

'No, although you might be able to.'

Because she had the same magic as Aunt Yesha – the same magic that had created daayan, had made Thiya almost kill someone.

She pressed her fingers against her burnt wrist. The throbbing pain helped ground her.

'How does it feel?' Kayan asked, dropping back to ride beside her.

Thiya shrugged. After what she'd done, she wasn't sure she had a right to complain about a little burn.

'I'm sorry,' Kayan said.

Thiya had been expecting his anger. She would have *deserved* his anger, but she couldn't detect any.

'You did that?' Lochan asked, outraged.

Kayan nodded. 'I had to get your attention somehow,' he told Thiya. 'You weren't responding to anything else.'

'It's fine.'

'It's not fine,' Lochan yelled. A bird startled and took off from a nearby tree. 'He hurt you.'

'He saved *her*,' Thiya said quietly. She could still see those fear-filled eyes, feel her own darkness, that desire to destroy. She shuddered.

'I'm still sorry for hurting you,' Kayan said.

Thiya shook her head. He had nothing to apologise for. 'Thank you.' *For pulling me out of the darkness, for saving that woman's life, for not letting me become a murderer.* She couldn't say those words out loud, but Kayan seemed to understand.

'You should be able to heal it. I can help you—'

'No!' Her magic was too dangerous to use. What if she tried to heal herself and ended up killing Lochan, Kayan or even herself? She deserved to feel the sting from the burn while it healed. She deserved so much worse.

Kayan frowned. 'I've told you; you don't have to be scared of your magic.'

'I'm not.'

'Everything in this world is balanced and that includes our magic.'

'Easy for you to say. You didn't almost kill someone,' she muttered, but of course Kayan heard.

His voice hardened. 'I've killed using my magic, more times than I care to count. Most of them my friends. Fire can bring heat on a cold day, but it can also burn.' His eyes darkened with memories, and Thiya wondered what he was seeing. The innkeeper? Friends in Tumassi? Maybe she had more in common with Kayan than she thought.

Except feiraanis weren't feared in the same way as aethanis. And for good reason. The darkness, and the power that had come with it, had been intoxicating.

Kayan blinked. 'Aethanis are healers. They can affect any part of the human body. You have the ability to make people better, but that also means you can use your magic to hurt them as well. *You* get to decide what to do with it.'

Not long after they left the town, Kayan steered the horses off the path and into the fields.

'Where are we going?' Lochan asked.

'Those trees just ahead,' Kayan said, pointing into the distance, towards shadows. 'I want to camp somewhere we can't be seen from the road, just in case someone decides to follow us.'

Without the buildings, there were fewer shadows here than there had been in town, which would make it easier to spot daayan. But there was also nowhere to hide. Thiya could see the outline of the jungle stretching up into the hills beyond, but they were too far away.

'A—are you sure this is wise?' Thiya asked when she saw where Kayan intended to stop for the night. He conjured small balls of fire, which hung low in the air above their heads like flickering stars – too low for anyone riding past to see.

'Yes. We don't have many other options.' He got out the tent.

The trees formed a warped semi-circle that hid them from view of the road and the surrounding farmhouses, so Thiya could understand the logic, but they were still far too exposed. And there was no way she was sleeping on the floor – thin material the only barrier between her and daayan. She didn't care that mages did it all the time.

'There was a barn a little further back.'

She was suggesting a barn? Khal, she must be desperate.

Kayan pulled the tent out of the bag, and oh gods, the material was even thinner than she'd realised.

'Even if there are no humans sleeping in the barn to see to the animals' needs in the middle of the night, farmers get up at first light. We would meet them on our way out and the fewer people who see us after this evening the better.'

Shame flooded Thiya and she kept her mouth shut, even when Kayan pulled thin metal poles from the bag. There was no way that was going to hold the tent up. But he and Lochan worked together to pitch the tent and, to their credit, it did stand upright. But it was still so thin.

'If you can't sense the daayan, how will we know they're coming?' asked Thiya.

'The daayan can't travel through solid objects,' Kayan reminded her.

She knew that, but the tent didn't look solid. And in the palace… 'We have to put shutters over our windows.'

'To stop them breaking, like at the ball. And to stop the light leaking out and attracting daayan to the towns,' Kayan said.

Lochan peered inside. 'It's not as bad as it looks,' he said, though his voice lacked conviction.

'Your magic protects you better than anyone in the country,' Kayan said.

Her magic was her biggest enemy.

'You need to learn how to use it. We'll practise some more now,' Kayan said, his words urgent. 'If Isaac can really control daayan, no one else will be able to stop him. No one else can save Amara.'

Thiya sucked in a ragged breath. Gritting her teeth, she followed Kayan's lights inside.

Thiya sat in the middle of the tent, as far away from the walls as possible, and eyed the flames that danced over her head, casting diffuse light across the tent but no heat. She rubbed her arms.

'Can you light a proper fire?' she asked Kayan.

Kayan considered her for a moment. 'I will create a fire, if you use your magic.'

'I've already used it,' she muttered.

'You need to learn how to use it intentionally.'

'I don't—'

Kayan glared, stilling the words on her tongue.

It wasn't that cold. With three of them in a small space, it should warm up soon enough. She rubbed her arms a little faster.

Lochan sat in the opposite corner of the tent, next to the door. He was supposed to be keeping an ear open for any noise that could suggest a daayan was outside, but he was more interested in the contents of the backpack. Kayan's enchanted sword was now on the floor by his side.

The temperature dropped. Icy air, colder than that on the Dhandra Mountains, pressed against Thiya's skin until she couldn't feel the tip of her nose. Her chattering teeth was the only sound she could hear.

Lochan didn't seem to mind the cold. His eyelids dropped the way they did when he was tired and comfortable. Kayan continued to stare at her, the corner of his lips twitching. Understanding dawned. Khal, he was lowering the temperature around her on purpose.

'Warm the tent,' she told Kayan.

'Stop running from your magic.' He didn't even deny that he was responsible for the cold.

Khal! Kayan wasn't going to back down and Thiya had now lost feeling in her fingers.

'Fine,' she said through gritted teeth.

'Fine, what?'

Khal's left butt cheek, he had to be kidding! She wriggled her toes before she lost feeling in those as well.

'If you restore the heat, I will try and connect with my magic.'

Kayan shook his head. 'You can already connect. You need to learn how to use it. And you can't pretend you tried, then claim it didn't work.'

'Fine.' She almost bit her tongue; her teeth were chattering so hard.

'Promise?'

'Kayan! I can't keep any promises if I die from the cold!'

Kayan waved away her concerns. 'It's not cold enough to kill you for at least another few minutes.'

To her relief, Kayan raised the temperature until it felt like a spring afternoon. It still took another few minutes for the feeling to return to her fingers and nose.

'Are you ready?' Kayan asked.

'Can I at least eat first?'

Lochan was already eating paratha and plantain crisps.

'After.'

'But—'

'Stop stalling. Close your eyes,' he said. When Thiya complied, he continued. 'Find your magic within.'

All Thiya saw was the back of her eyelids. She thought she saw a flicker of light, but she was sure that was from one of Kayan's flames. Just when she was about to give up, she saw her power.

Her muscles tensed.

'Do you have it?' Kayan asked.

'I think so.' There was a swirling mass of light and dark in her very centre. Flesh and bone may have held her together, but these threads of magic knit through every fibre of her being in a way that left her breathless. She wanted to shy away from it, but she held on.

Kayan wrapped his fingers around her wrist, his grip loose but firm. 'Push me off.'

Now this she could get on board with. Eyes open, she threw her hands out, shoving against Kayan's shoulders so he fell onto his back. She bit her lip to keep from laughing at his startled expression.

Kayan pushed himself upright. 'I meant with your magic,' he grumbled.

'You should have been more specific.' Thiya chuckled. Kayan's jaw clenched.

She closed her eyes. This time she didn't have to reach for her magic – it was right there, waiting.

Kayan wrapped his hand around Thiya's wrist once

more. 'Pull some of your magic up to the surface,' he said. 'Not all of it – I would like to live – but enough to throw me off.'

The tent fell silent apart from the crunching of plantain crisps as Lochan bit into them.

Thiya reached for the magic. She pulled a strand the size of a fine tapestry thread and brought it up to the surface, the darkness and light twined together.

You're just like Aunt Yesha.

She faltered, but Amara's screams when Isaac had dragged her from the inn made her hold on. She still felt that warm glow of the light and the seductive intoxication of the darkness, but it was more subdued this time. The darkness didn't overwhelm.

Now what?

She was aware of the tent around her, could still hear Lochan munching away and feel Kayan's relentless stare and the weight of his expectations. His fingers were warm against her wrist. She wrapped the thread of magic around Kayan's hand where he touched her skin, pushing it through the same way she had physically pushed against his shoulders with her hands.

His arm flew back with such force, his hand bounced of the tent wall behind him. But Kayan was smiling. 'That wasn't so hard, was it?' Kayan's expression had softened and Thiya couldn't help but smile. She'd done it. She'd used magic when she'd wanted and how she'd wanted, and she hadn't hurt anyone.

'Try again, but this time use a little less magic,' he added, wryly.

Thiya suppressed a yawn and tried again. And again. And again. But every thread of magic she pulled was too much. Kayan kept crashing to the ground. Thiya would be surprised if he didn't have bruises, but his excitement seemed to overcome any pain.

Another yawn escaped and Thiya hit her nose in her rush to cover her mouth.

'I think we should stop for the day,' Kayan said.

'No, I think I almost had it that time.' She reached for her magic again, but Kayan placed his hand over hers.

'You've used a lot of magic today. You're tired. You need to rest.'

Thiya scoffed. 'You're still using magic and you're fine.' She pointed to the flames dancing around the tent.

'I'm much stronger than you,' Kayan said.

'Show off,' Thiya muttered.

'When you're forced to practise using your magic for at least twelve hours a day for the next eight years, you can show off too.' His words weren't mean, but Thiya felt shame wash over her. She'd never thought to learn about life inside the training camps before. But mages had to survive an entire night using magic without rest.

Kayan pulled over the bag of food to see what Lochan had left them and handed Thiya a paratha, but even eating that took effort.

By the time she stretched out on her side of the tent,

she didn't care that she was essentially sleeping outside – until Kayan extinguished his flames and plunged them into total darkness.

'Can you conjure the flames again?'

'Are you afraid of the dark?' Kayan teased.

'No,' Thiya lied, 'but it's too hard to see anything. Lochan just kicked the back of my knee.'

'I did not,' Lochan said.

'I'll be keeping watch,' Kayan said. 'Get some sleep. If we're attacked by daayan, I'll protect you.'

Thiya bristled. 'I don't need protection.'

'That's the spirit. I'll wake you when it's time for your shift.'

Despite her tiredness, Thiya didn't sleep well. Lochan's shoulder dug into her arm on one side and her face pressed against the tent wall on the other. A stick or a stone pushed into her hip, but since it was underneath the tent, she could not get to it. She kept thinking about the woman at the inn who would have died if Kayan hadn't stopped Thiya, and she remembered Prisha asking if Thiya would stop the daayan. Kayan's faith in her made her squirm.

'I have faith in you, too,' Amara whispered in her dreams. She leaned over Thiya, her thick hair unbound. Thiya wanted to run her fingers through it.

'What if I hurt someone?'

The woman's screams from the guesthouse rang in her ear and she fisted her hands. She couldn't bear the thought of hurting anyone, especially Amara.

But Amara took Thiya's hand and gently released her fingers, one by one. Thiya's body loosened.

'You are nothing like Yesha.'

'But—'

'No.' Amara kissed her knuckles. 'Yesha cared about herself. You care about other people.'

'I care about you.'

She still wondered whether she could stop the daayan, whether she even wanted to. How was that better than Aunt Yesha?

'Because you're questioning it,' Amara said. 'Do you think Yesha ever questioned her actions when she killed those mages in the jungle?'

Amara's finger brushed the inside of Thiya's wrist. Pain flared and Thiya winced. Amara examined the burn. The skin was still red and angry. And hot. Very hot.

'Does it hurt?' she asked.

Her wrist throbbed, but right now, everywhere Amara touched ignited, sending sparks shooting along her skin.

'Not at the moment,' she said, her voice rough.

Amara pressed her lips to the burn. Thiya's wrist flared hotter, but the mix of pleasure and pain made her toes curl. A moan escaped her lips.

Amara smiled in satisfaction. 'Next time it hurts, that

should make it feel better. And if that doesn't work, you can try this.' Amara kissed her way up Thiya's arm, feather-light kisses that made Thiya squirm. It was not enough.

Amara fanned kisses along Thiya's collarbone and over to the sensitive spot on her neck. Thiya's back arched off the floor. Amara nipped the skin, the short spike of pain made Thiya cry out. She wanted more. She pulled Amara closer and captured her lips in a kiss.

Just like she remembered.

Exactly like she remembered. Amara smelt like cinnamon and rose petals.

But this wasn't real.

Amara pulled back; her brows furrowed. 'What's wrong?'

'Where are you?' Thiya brushed her finger over a cut on Amara's lower lip. Amara didn't seem to notice.

'Right here.' Amara pressed her hand against Thiya's pounding heart. Her lips followed the hand and Amara kissed her way down Thiya's stomach. Thiya couldn't remember when her kurta had come off, but oh she didn't care. A low growl caught in the back of her throat.

More. She needed more.

As if she heard her thoughts, Amara looked up at her from under long lashes and grinned. Mischief lit her eyes.

Desire flared, hot and heady.

Amara slid up her body and nipped Thiya's ear. Not the direction Thiya wanted Amara's mouth to go, but

Amara whispered things in her ear that had her whole body heating.

Her magic stirred.

Amara gasped. 'Thiya!'

There was no teasing to her voice now, only fear and pain. But desire gripped Thiya. Her magic held Amara's heart in its grip.

'Thiya!'

Amara hit her.

Thiya's magic squeezed.

'Thiya!' Amara clawed at Thiya's face, but the pain increased the pleasure.

'Thiya!' Amara shook her.

'Thiya.' The voice grew deeper, the shaking more insistent. 'Thiya, wake up. It's your turn to keep watch.'

Kayan crouched over her. He handed her the enchanted sword. It hummed in her hand and she almost dropped it.

Thiya was fully clothed inside the tent. Amara had disappeared, and her heart yearned for something that hadn't been real.

Kayan settled into the space on the other side of Lochan. The moment he closed his eyes, he was asleep, his breathing soft and even. How did he do that? Thiya didn't think she would ever sleep again. She could still hear Amara's screams echoing inside her head. She'd done that. The last remnants of desire fled her body. Her skin felt cold and clammy.

153

She focused on her surroundings and let the minutes turn into hours.

Shadows moved across the surface of the tent. An owl hooted. Something crunched outside. Thiya stilled. Was that a footstep?

She pushed herself to her knees. Leaves rustled overhead, but no other noises sounded.

She exhaled.

She looked to her left. At some point, Lochan had rolled towards Kayan and now he lay encircled in Kayan's arms, both sound asleep. She smiled, but her happiness for her brother was marred by the bitter pang of jealousy. How she wished she could wake up in Amara's arms.

It was almost time for Lochan's shift, but she decided against waking him. She couldn't sleep anyway. At least one of them could be happy.

12

The sun had risen over the horizon by the time they reached the next village, casting the jungle creeping up behind it in shadows. The air was more humid here and sweat rolled down Thiya's back despite the early hour, so it was a relief to step into the inn behind Kayan.

'You just missed them,' the innkeeper said when Kayan asked about Isaac and Amara.

Khal! Isaac was always one step ahead.

The innkeeper looked from Thiya to Kayan and Kayan's uniform.

'Where have you come from?' he asked, eyes narrowing. 'Is it just the two of you?'

Warning bells rang in Thiya's mind. They needed to get out of there. Kayan lied in response to his questions and thanked the innkeeper for his time before heading for the door.

'Wait—'

Nope. They both ran outside. Lochan met them with their horses.

'We need to leave,' Lochan said, throwing each of them their reins and climbing onto his horse. 'There are soldiers looking for a feiraani and his two companions after an incident last night at a nearby inn. That's us, by the way.'

'We figured,' Thiya said. 'That innkeeper suspected us.'

'At least Prisha managed to keep our identities a secret,' Kayan said, mounting his own horse.

But how long would that last? Khal! If there were soldiers after them, it wouldn't be long before the shara got involved. She couldn't let them drag her home, not without Amara.

Once they were all mounted, Kayan led the way out of town. 'We need to get off the road.'

'We need to find Amara,' Thiya said. 'If she's on the road, I'm following it.'

'You can't help her if you're caught.'

'We're already behind,' Thiya snapped.

Kayan pulled his horse to a stop just outside of town. 'If we cut through the jungle, we can stay out of sight of the soldiers and get ahead of Isaac and Amara so we can ambush them in daylight when Isaac can't call on the daayan, if he can really do that. But it will mean more camping. No beds. No wash facilities … if you think you can cope.'

Thiya's cheeks heated as she remembered the fuss she'd made that morning about having to relieve herself behind a tree.

'For how long?' she asked.

'A few days.'

She shook her head. She did not want to repeat the experiences of last night and this morning, but she could survive being dirty, sweaty and itchy for Amara.

156

'Fine.'

'Then let's go.' Kayan guided his horse off the road.

'Wait, is no one going to ask me if I'm fine with camping?' Lochan smirked.

Thiya patted Lochan's shoulder. 'No.'

Moving off the road, they followed a narrow dirt path around steep hills, following the river in the valley. But the path was not as well maintained as the roads, and they had to be careful their horses didn't get hurt. Despite the slower pace, Kayan assured them they were making good time.

Along their path sat the occasional farmhouse or cluster of houses nestled on the edge of the jungle. They set up camp along the treeline that night, which might have been a mistake since Thiya woke at the smallest of sounds – tigers prowling the undergrowth for their next meal, the screech of bats in the trees. She stifled a yawn as they entered a small village on the second day to get some food. Villagers eyed them sharply, treating them with distrust or outright contempt.

'They don't get many travellers here,' Kayan said. 'Most people who travel use the main road. There's no good reason for strangers to be here.'

A lot of people refused to talk to them, although there was one man who sold them a loaf of bread for double what it was worth. Thiya saw the boarded-up windows and the hungry children staring at them from the doorway and was glad when Kayan handed over the money without protest or complaint.

There were other houses in disrepair. Some had their windows smashed, one was missing a door and the roof had caved in on another. A lot of the houses were empty. Abandoned, Thiya realised.

'What happened here?' she asked.

'People left,' Kayan said. 'The village is too small for mages, let alone soldiers, to be posted here. When the trade routes closed and curfew was introduced, villages like this suffered. No one came here, no one helped.' He nodded to a house with broken windows. 'The nearest town with soldiers is Liggan and that's half a day's ride away. Crime went up. People moved away because they couldn't afford to stay. They abandoned their homes in search of work in larger towns.' He nodded at a house where a tree's roots had grown under the foundations and the wall was starting to warp and buckle.

Thiya's magic stirred within her, like it wanted to heal the place. 'How sad.'

'This isn't even the worst place I've seen,' Kayan said. But when Thiya asked him to elaborate, Kayan shook his head, his eyebrows drawn together.

They skirted around another village the next day. Thiya could see damaged buildings with roofs and walls crumbling in.

'How did this village sustain so much damage?' Thiya asked Kayan. Daayan could not do this, surely?

'Vishtak.'

'What?'

'It's a last resort,' Kayan said, his lips tightening. 'When there are too many daayan to deal with individually. Throw an explosive and get rid of the threat in one go.'

And kill everyone at the same time. 'That's … horrible.'

'It's necessary,' Kayan growled.

Thiya wondered how many times he'd used vishtak.

Again, her magic stirred, stronger this time, but there was nothing to heal. Nothing in the village was alive.

She would need to bring the plight of these villages to her father's attention when they got back home. There was no way he knew about this.

Thiya had continued to practise with her magic as they travelled. But though she found it easier to sense her magic, she still had trouble shaping it so it did what she wanted, and those few times she succeeded, her control was off. She used too little magic or far too much. She didn't understand the balance.

'What's that?' Lochan asked, pointing into the distance.

It was a woman in a green and gold sari.

'Do you think she's alright?' Lochan asked.

'No.' Thiya could see the woman's movements were unbalanced and heavy. There were rips in her sari and what looked like blood on her bare feet. When she drew closer, Thiya saw the grey veins and black eyes. Thiya swallowed.

159

Daayan.

The possessed woman saw them. She went still. Her muscles tensed, her body coiled, ready to pounce.

Kayan's horse jerked and snorted and Kayan jumped off before the horse could throw him. The moment the horse realised he was free, he bolted.

Thiya and Lochan both dismounted, and Lochan gripped the reins.

Kayan pushed Thiya and Lochan behind him a moment before the daayan leapt up, her head angling for his neck. A high-pitched shriek escaped her lips. Thiya saw the front of her sari catch fire. Kayan held more fire in his palms.

Thiya could stop this. It was just like she'd practised with Kayan when she pushed him over, except this time she was going to kill a daayan, the evil creatures that had been terrorising her country, her people, for years.

Her magic flared, wanting to be used. She pulled at a thread and stopped, no idea what to do with it.

'Thiya, hurry,' Kayan cried.

The magic slipped from Thiya's grasp and her eyes flew open. The woman had stumbled back, and she patted out the fire on her sari with her bare hands, oblivious to the blistering skin. She snarled like a feral animal.

Lochan struggled with the remaining horses. His movement caught the daayan's attention and she leapt from Kayan to him. The impact pushed Lochan onto his back, the daayan landing on top of him. The horses fled.

No! Not Lochan. She couldn't lose Lochan.

Thiya reached for her magic again, snatching at the threads. Her whole body shook. What if she failed and Lochan…

She was not going to fail. She wrapped a thread of magic around the woman.

Lochan fought the woman, but the pain from her blows had no impact. Lochan would lose, and when he did Thiya would lose him.

Thiya wanted to tell Kayan to kill her, but this woman deserved to live too.

She felt the darkness inside the woman, like a mirror to her own. Aether magic coming from the daayan. The woman's heartbeat was slow, sluggish, like it was struggling to beat against the darkness.

You have a choice. Kayan had told her that more times than she could count. Thiya could save her people – save this woman.

Thiya concentrated on the daayan within, just as the woman evaded Lochan's punch and bit his shoulder.

Lochan screamed.

Sweat beaded Thiya's forehead.

Thiya felt the daayan's hold on Lochan loosen as her magic squeezed. The daayan exploded, black sparks leaping from the woman's skin. The grey veins receded and the woman's eyes changed from black to a golden brown.

A wave of dizziness overcame Thiya and she reached out to Kayan for support.

'Are you alright?' he asked.

Her heart raced, but she nodded.

Lochan got to his feet; his hand pressed against his injured shoulder. 'You did it.'

The woman collapsed, her eyes rolling into the back of her head.

Thiya stumbled over to the woman, her knees barely able to support her weight. Kayan knelt beside her.

Kayan's fire had burned the woman's flesh from her neck, down the right side of her body and along her right arm. Her sari stuck to her wounds in places and her chest rattled with each laboured breath.

Her eyes flickered open. She looked around before focusing on Thiya. Her brown eyes were soft and tears collected along the lower lid.

'Thank you,' she whispered. Her eyes closed. Her heart stopped beating.

13

Thiya waited for the woman's chest to rise again, but she remained perfectly still – no flutter of lashes, no twitch of her fingers.

Kayan pressed two fingers against the left side of the woman's neck – the side that had sustained the least amount of damage. He pulled back after a while, his shoulders hunched.

No! The woman couldn't die. Thiya had saved her. She'd killed the daayan.

'How do I heal her?' Thiya drew up strands of her magic and wrapped them around the woman, ignoring the headache that had started to build.

'You can't.' Kayan sniffed. 'She's sustained too many injuries.'

She couldn't be dead. Thiya sobbed.

'Are you alright?' Lochan asked.

She shook her head. She'd failed.

What if she failed Amara too?

'It's not your fault she died,' Kayan said. 'You gave her something no one ever thought was possible. You gave her back her life, even if it was just for a moment.'

'I failed.'

'You allowed the woman to die as herself. I've watched friends die as daayan, so believe me when I say that means a lot. You *did* save this woman.'

Tears pricked the back of Thiya's eyes. She blinked and looked away.

'And think of how many more lives you could save,' Lochan said, a little wobble in his voice.

She glanced at Lochan's wound. The bleeding had stopped, but the flesh was red and mangled.

'Can you heal it?' Kayan asked her.

She wanted to, could feel her magic responding, but she wasn't sure that was a good idea. 'I have darkness inside me,' she said, her voice barely above a whisper.

Kayan shrugged. 'So do I. So does everyone. The difference is mages can see the darkness inside them. That's your magic. It's there to remind you of what you can do, what you are capable of. The good and the bad.'

'You don't understand…'

'What else do you feel inside you?'

'Excuse me?'

'Besides the darkness, what else do you feel?' Kayan asked. 'For example, mine is warm and cold, passion, seduction and destruction. It smells of cloves and cinnamon and singed hair. What does your magic feel like?'

'It's not the same,' Thiya said.

'Are you going to let your brother suffer because you're scared?'

'I'm fine,' Lochan said, but Thiya saw the way he gritted his teeth.

'You need to stop running from the darkness,' Kayan said. 'Without darkness, there can't be light. You can do a lot of good if you embrace your magic. I believe in you.'

Tears welled. Lochan pulled her into a hug, and this time Thiya sank into his embrace. 'You can be annoying, but you are not Aunt Yesha.'

And she wasn't alone. She had her brother and Kayan. And Amara was waiting for her. Her heart seemed to grow too big for her chest.

Thiya cleared her throat and stepped back. 'Let's get you healed up.' She pulled at a strand of her magic and stepped closer to Lochan.

Her world swayed. Lochan's arms wrapped around her. 'Whoa, are you alright?' He looked down at her in concern, and Thiya realised she was leaning heavily against him. When had that happened?

She nodded, or at least she thought she did. Lochan's worry deepened and he glanced at Kayan.

'She must have used too much energy,' Kayan said. 'She's tired.'

Thiya tried to protest, but she couldn't.

Kayan cleaned Lochan's wound as best he could then wrapped it in his undershirt. 'It should heal by itself, but it'll leave a scar.'

'Don't women like scars?' Lochan asked, a mischievous smile playing around his lips.

Kayan nodded. 'Men too.' Their eyes met. Neither moved for a few seconds, then Lochan cleared his throat and looked away.

165

'We should leave,' Lochan said.

'Let's give this woman a proper send-off.' Kayan straightened her body and crossed her arms over her chest. He stepped back and set fire to her, releasing her soul. Thiya sent a prayer to Gayan for the woman's next life to be better than this one.

The horses hadn't gone far. They found them taking shelter in the jungle. Once Lochan had calmed them down, they continued on. Thiya was barely able to cling to the saddle, she was so drained after using her magic.

They rejoined the main road early the next morning. Kayan checked in at the local inn and found no one had seen Isaac and Amara, so maybe they had not passed through yet. At least the three of them were ahead and able to lay their ambush.

'Continue until the trees crowd the path,' Kayan said.

'Is that wise?' Thiya asked.

Isaac was a terrai. He would be in his element. Quite literally. The vegetation surrounding the road was thick – extending up into the hills on the left where streams trickled down towards the river.

'Surprise will work in our favour. We can hide in the trees. Plus, I'll have you on my side,' he said.

Except Thiya didn't think she was going to be much

help. Isaac had spent years learning to use his magic in combat. Thiya still struggled to control hers.

'I'll also have this.' Kayan held up Thiya's bangle. 'Isaac is strong, but if I can cut off his magic, I might stand a chance of overpowering him.'

Lochan stopped where Kayan indicated. The air was thicker, the water hanging heavy in the air. Mud splashed Thiya's leggings when she climbed off her horse.

Thiya followed Kayan down a narrow, muddy path. She saw a cottage in the distance, peeking out from between trees. A part of her wondered who would live in such isolation. Another part of her thought it would be the perfect place for her and Amara. Just the two of them. No one to disturb them. No one to judge them.

'What are you smiling about, little sister?' Lochan asked.

'Nothing.'

He nudged Thiya's shoulder. 'It's interesting how nothing seems to bring out such strange reactions in you.'

Oh, if he wanted to play, she would be happy to oblige. 'What's happening between you and Kayan?'

'Nothing.' His ears reddened. His eyes flicked to Kayan who was tying up his horse a short distance away. Their eyes met and Lochan quickly looked away.

'Such strange reactions indeed.' She finished tying her own horse to a tree. When the horses were secure, they returned to the road and waited. Lochan's horse was still with him, and he held tightly to her reins.

'This will work out,' Kayan said after a while. Was he trying to convince her or himself? He listed off everything that was on their side, which mostly consisted of surprise, surprise and more surprise. But it had to work, because if it didn't, Amara…

She was not going to think about that.

Lochan caught her wrist as she paced past the tree he hid behind for the umpteenth time. 'I'll get Amara to safety.' She knew he would do everything in his power to ensure Amara was safe so she and Kayan could focus on dealing with Isaac.

The image of the daayan-possessed woman flashed into her mind. She would not let anyone else die. Not this time. She bit her lip and glanced at the sun. Where were they?

Lochan's fingers tightened around her wrist. He looked past her, onto the road. Thiya glanced back to a horse ridden by a man wearing black leather and a woman sat behind him, her long hair bouncing in a single plait against her back.

Amara.

14

The plan felt trivial now Amara was so close. Thiya was about to spring out from her hiding place, not caring about the consequences, until Kayan wrenched her back.

'Don't,' he said, his gaze on Isaac.

From the corner of her eye, Thiya saw Lochan slip away into the jungle with his horse, but Kayan didn't move.

Isaac and Amara drew closer, and still Kayan didn't move. Surely they were close enough?

Thiya pulled at a thread of magic, getting ready. She could see Amara's high-necked, long-sleeved pink kurta, more modest than anything she'd ever worn before.

Thiya searched her for signs of injury, but there were no visible cuts or bruises. There was nothing in the way Amara sat that suggested hidden injuries, but Thiya noticed there was no laughter on Amara's face. Even when Amara didn't smile, her eyes normally shone with mirth. Isaac had driven that from her.

Kayan sent flames erupting along the path in front of Isaac and Amara. Their horse startled, his front legs flailing in the air. Amara screamed, her arms tightening around Isaac's waist to keep from falling. Khal! That wasn't the plan. Thiya was meant to push Isaac off the horse, but Amara's hold on him meant she would fall as well.

Lochan rode up beside Isaac and Amara at that

moment and tried to pull Amara onto his horse, but Amara's eyes were squeezed shut. She screamed again and tightened her grip around Isaac's waist.

She was going to hurt herself. She was going to ruin her rescue!

Thiya broke cover and ran towards Amara.

'Let go,' she yelled at Amara.

'Don't,' Isaac growled.

Amara didn't move. She screamed as the horse bucked, but her scream was more pain than fear or surprise. She bit her lower lip, the screams subsiding, as she tightened her hold on Isaac.

Why was she listening to *him*?

Thiya tugged on Amara's arm. 'Let go,' she urged.

'Stop,' Amara whimpered, and Thiya heard the strain. She grabbed a thread of magic and wrapped it around Amara, wanting to know what was going on.

Thiya felt Amara's heartbeat, heard it surround her, loud and erratic. There was a darkness seeping into Amara from a new bangle around her wrist. It was the darkness of aether magic. Black threads writhed inside her, feeding on her energy. The darkness grew stronger as it leeched her strength.

'I've got you,' Thiya said, reaching for more magic. But Isaac had managed to get his horse under control, and he swung his legs over the saddle, almost kicking Thiya in the face before his feet hit the ground.

Thiya leapt out of the way and focused on Amara. If

she could destroy daayan, she could destroy whatever was inside Amara as well. She pulled another thread of magic and wrapped it around the dark aether.

Isaac pulled Amara off the horse and Amara winced. The face of the woman Thiya had almost killed flashed through her mind, and she hesitated.

Isaac's arm wrapped around Amara's waist, pressing her against his body. Amara tried to pull away, but Isaac tightened his hold.

'Leave her alone!' Thiya cried. She started for Amara, but Isaac sent a branch crashing into her back. She flew forward, throwing her hands out to break her fall. Pain burned her palms where the road scraped the skin off, blood mixing with mud and damp leaves.

Amara gasped. 'Thiya!'

Thiya pushed herself to her feet and wiped her stinging hands on her leggings. 'Let her go, coward!'

Isaac's eyes flashed. 'How dare you call me a coward when you've hidden your magic for years to avoid serving in Tumassi!'

'I didn't know I had magic,' Thiya said.

From the corner of her eye, she saw Kayan creeping around behind Isaac.

Isaac scoffed. 'I don't believe you.'

'It's the truth. I'll even come with you to Tumassi now. Just let Amara go.'

Isaac shook his head. 'She stays with me. You'll follow anyway.'

I have big plans for her. Isaac had said that earlier in the inn. But Thiya still couldn't figure out what he wanted with Amara.

'She has no magic,' Thiya begged. Sweet, sweet Amara would never hurt a fly. She did not deserve to be a part of Isaac's games. 'She cannot help you, but I can. I can stop the daayan, the fighting, the conscription of mages. We can do it together.'

'You don't know what I want.'

Kayan had got behind Isaac and he threw fire at his back. Isaac twisted at the last second and bent a tree into the road in front of him to absorb the flames. Charred leaves crackled and fluttered to the ground. Isaac's horse reared back before running off into the jungle. Thiya dived out of the way to avoid being trampled. She staggered to her feet and ran over to Amara, praying Kayan would keep Isaac's attention.

Amara wrapped her fingers around Thiya's wrists, her grip a little too tight. 'You need to leave,' she said, her voice low and urgent.

'Not without you.' She tugged on Amara's arm.

'I can't.'

'Because of this bangle?' The bangle still spilled darkness into Amara. All Thiya needed was—

Amara pushed her out of harm's way as Isaac sent a tree branch careening towards her. Thiya fell flat on her back. The branch flew over where she had been standing moments before.

Isaac advanced on Amara.

'Run!' Thiya shouted. But Amara remained rooted to the spot.

Lochan jumped off his horse and tried to usher Amara to safety. He tugged at her hand, but she fought him off, accidentally hitting his injured shoulder. He cried out and dropped her hand.

Isaac dragged Amara to Lochan's horse. Kayan threw more fire at Isaac, but Isaac made the earth rise up to intercept the fire. The soil sizzled where the fire heated the water within. Steam billowed into the air, obscuring Isaac from view.

'Let her go,' Kayan cried.

'You know this needs to happen,' Isaac said.

Kayan directed more fire towards the sound of his voice. The steam thickened. Then, spikes made of soil shot out of the steam. Kayan incinerated them before they sliced through his body. Kayan and Isaac were too evenly matched. Thiya needed Amara to leave so they could all get out of here.

She staggered to Amara. 'Go with Lochan.'

Isaac's attention was on Kayan. She had the opportunity to run, and still Amara shook her head. 'There's something you need to know. Isaac knew you were a mage before he came to the palace,' Amara murmured.

What? A chill trickled down Thiya's spine. 'That's impossible.' She hadn't even known herself.

'And yet he knew.' Amara glanced at Isaac as he

173

swung a particularly nasty-looking spiked branch at Kayan's head. 'And that's not all. I overheard him speaking to someone. They want you to free Yesha.'

'Aunt Yesha?'

'Yes,' Amara said, wide eyed.

'But Yesha's dead.'

'She's alive,' Amara insisted.

Kayan's fire flew past, too close for comfort.

'We can figure it out later. We need to leave.' She took Amara's hand, but Amara pulled away.

'If I go with you, the magic in this bangle will kill me.'

That was not happening. 'Then we find a way to take it off.' She reached for Amara's wrist again, but Amara hid it behind her back.

'Isaac will send daayan to attack everyone I care about,' she said, her voice hollow.

'I can't leave you with him.'

'You don't have a choice.'

Thiya shook her head. She didn't care about anyone else. She only cared about Amara. 'What does he want with you, anyway?'

'I don't know.'

Thiya strained to hear her around the sound of the cracks and splutters from Isaac and Kayan's fight. They needed to leave.

'Do you trust me?' Thiya asked.

Amara nodded.

Thiya held out her hand again. 'I can stop the daayan.

I can keep Isaac from hurting your family, and I can stop that bangle from hurting you. But I need you to come with me. We're stronger together. Always were, always will be.'

After a moment's hesitation, Amara took her hand.

They'd only taken a few steps when Amara screamed and thrashed, trying to get away from something invisible attacking her from all directions. The darkness wasn't just leeching energy from her, the threads were digging into her muscles and bones.

Thiya didn't have to search for her magic this time. It was already there. She wrapped a thread around Amara, commanding it to heal and destroy the darkness within.

Amara screamed louder, as her body became a battleground.

Khal! Thiya needed to remove that bangle, that's where the aether was coming from.

Amara swayed and Thiya pulled her into her chest, running her hand up and down her back. 'I've got you,' she whispered.

She pulled Amara's wrist towards her and ran her finger over the edge of the bangle. The jewellery looked like a vine wrapped several times around Amara's wrist to create a bangle an inch thick. Thiya twisted Amara's wrist, but she couldn't see where the vine started or ended. She tried to slip her finger underneath, but there was no room. It was pressed tight against Amara's skin.

The earth shook as Isaac sent a tree crashing to the

ground. When the dust settled, Kayan was standing on top of the trunk.

Lochan drew his sword and thrust at Isaac, but Isaac sent a branch to knock the sword out of Lochan's hand. Kayan threw fire at Isaac from the other side.

'You need to leave,' Amara said, her voice strained. 'Before he gets you, too.'

'Not without you.' Thiya pinched the vine bangle between her fingers, but it was stronger than it looked. No matter how much she tugged, it wouldn't move. She pulled the dagger from its sheath and pressed the tip against it. Amara made a sound of protest.

'Trust me,' she said.

She was not going to hurt Amara, but if she could cut the vine deep enough, she might be able to rip the bangle off.

Lochan shouted out.

The ground under Thiya started to shake. The soil shifted under her feet, rippling like a wave and throwing her off balance. Amara reached for Thiya. Her hand was clammy but it was perfect because it was Amara's. Thiya squeezed gently.

Amara cried out again.

'What's happening?' Thiya asked.

Isaac pulled Amara away from Thiya.

Kayan was wrapped up in branches, leaves stuffed into his mouth. Lochan lay on the ground, a gash bleeding on his forehead. And Amara…

Amara's face was pinched, her lips pressed together. The aether was attacking her body again.

'Let her go.' Thiya's voice cracked. 'Please.' It left a sour taste in her mouth, but for Amara she would beg.

Isaac shook his head and, if Thiya wasn't mistaken, he looked at her with pity. 'If you want to see Amara alive again, get to Sanathri Jungle before the new moon.'

'Why are you doing this?'

'Because it's what must be done.'

'What do you want with her?'

'Not me.'

'Who?' Thiya asked, even though Amara had already told her. Even though it was impossible.

But Isaac didn't answer. He pulled Amara towards Lochan's horse and Thiya lunged for her. Amara dug her heels in but Isaac leaned in. 'That was nothing compared to what I could do to you, the pain I could make you feel, make your family feel. Would you like to hear your girlfriend scream?'

Amara's eyes flicked to Thiya.

'Get on the saddle,' Isaac growled.

I'm sorry, Amara mouthed before reaching for the reins. A breath hissed through her teeth as she tried to pull herself onto the saddle. Isaac tried to help her and she shoved him off. 'Don't touch me.' Her jaw tightened, but she pulled herself up. Isaac climbed up after her.

Thiya would not let Isaac take Amara from her. Not again. Her dagger lay on the ground where she'd dropped it at her feet. She picked it up and marched over to Isaac. She would spill Isaac's blood to get Amara back. It was no less than he deserved.

Isaac was too high up on the horse for Thiya to do much damage, but there was a spot on the thigh that, if she hit it, would bleed freely without medical intervention. She pulled her arm back and aimed.

Isaac twisted around. His lips pulled back in a snarl. 'Don't. You'll upset your aunt if you stab me.'

15

Thiya tightened her grip on her dagger and advanced. 'My aunt is dead.'

Amara started to scream. The darkness ripping into her muscles.

'You're killing her,' Thiya cried.

'I'm not the one doing that. I warned you your aunt would be upset if you stabbed me.' Isaac's voice was cold and emotionless. 'But don't worry, Yesha doesn't want to kill her just yet. Although she will if you force her hand.'

Thiya sheathed her dagger reluctantly.

'I don't understand. How is this happening? How is Yesha still alive?' she asked.

'Your father's mages didn't do a very good job of killing her when they had the chance,' Isaac said. He stroked a finger down Amara's cheek. 'Did they?'

Amara frantically shook her head.

Isaac set off, the horse kicking dust into Thiya's face. She coughed, pressing her arm over her nose and mouth. Tears slid down her cheeks. When the dust settled, Amara was gone. Again.

'Thiya!'

Thiya followed the sound of Lochan's voice to the other side of the road where Kayan was trapped. Lochan tugged on the branches that circled Kayan's arms and legs. The leaves rustled, but the branches didn't move. Thiya tried to help, but like Amara's vine bangle, the branches had pressed themselves against Kayan's flesh, bending around every dip and curve, and Thiya couldn't slip her fingers underneath. Even the slightest twig, thinner than her little finger, wouldn't move.

Muffled words caught in Kayan's throat. Thiya pulled the leaves from his mouth. At least they came away with ease.

'Amara?' Kayan asked.

Thiya shook her head. 'Isaac took her, again.' Thiya tugged on a leaf. The leaf snapped off, but the branch remained snug against Kayan's skin. 'Amara said he wants me to free Aunt Yesha.'

Kayan stilled. 'Yesha's alive?'

Lochan scoffed. 'No, she's not.' He tugged on another branch and huffed when it would not move.

Thiya repeated everything Amara had told her.

'You can't free Yesha,' Kayan said.

'We don't even know she's alive,' Lochan said, at the same time Thiya said, 'I wasn't planning on it.'

Kayan raised an eyebrow. 'Even if freeing Yesha means saving Amara?' He shook his head before Thiya could answer. 'We need a new plan.'

Thiya grabbed her dagger and sliced into the vines. The blade didn't even leave a scratch. 'I'm saving Amara. That's always been the plan.'

'Of course,' Kayan said. 'But if Yesha really is alive, we

need to keep you out of her hands. I dread to think what she would do if she got to you.'

'Revenge,' Lochan said. 'If I was trapped for so long, it's what I would want.'

'But the mages who trapped her died in that confrontation,' Kayan said.

'Whatever she's planning, she hasn't gone to the trouble of creating daayan and terrorising the country for years so she can retire to a cottage by the sea,' Thiya huffed.

'We need to get you out of here. Can't you burn the vines?' Lochan asked. The gash on his forehead had started to clot now, but a thin red line ran all the way down to his chin.

Kayan shook his head. 'The fight with Isaac drained me. I would burn myself. You two should go ahead. You need to find out if Yesha is alive. Destroying her daayan might weaken her and bring her out into the open.'

'What about Amara?' Thiya growled.

'I will get her to safety. I can free myself when I recover my energy and then I'll follow.'

'We're not leaving without you,' Lochan said.

'You're wasting time,' Kayan said, his voice soft. 'If Yesha's alive, we need to stop her. Stopping her might stop the daayan. It might stop Isaac. You can ask the mages in Tumassi for help.'

'They might not help,' Lochan said.

'They will.'

Thiya glanced down the road. Isaac was getting further

away with Amara, and Thiya was desperate to chase after them. But Thiya wasn't going to stop Isaac by chasing him, that much was clear now. There had to be another way.

'What about the bangle?' she asked. 'Can that block Isaac's magic so you can free yourself?'

'Isaac's magic is working on the branches, not on me. The bangle won't work . I couldn't get close enough to get it on his wrist before this happened.' Kayan grimaced. 'I might have also lost your bangle. I'm sorry.'

Thiya waved away his apology.

Lochan tapped Thiya's arm. 'Your magic!'

'I'm not a terrai,' Thiya reminded him.

'Aethanis are healers,' Lochan reminded her. 'You can heal him or restore his energy or whatever.'

Was that possible?

Kayan shook his head. 'You would be giving me your energy. It would tire you out.'

'We can't leave him,' Lochan pleaded.

Could she do it?

'Tell me what to do.'

Kayan sighed. 'If you must do it, then trust your magic,' he said.

She pulled at a strand of her magic, allowing the darkness and light to flow through her. She wrapped the thread around Kayan and let it sink into him. She reached for more magic and repeated the process until Kayan had sufficiently recovered. She collapsed against Lochan.

'Stand back,' Kayan told them. The strength had

returned to his voice. Lochan half-dragged her to the other side of the road. The moment they were far enough away, Kayan set himself on fire. The branches went up in smoke.

It was the single most amazing thing she had ever seen a mage do, and she had so many questions. How did Kayan not burn himself? There were no marks on him, not even a single singed hair. Even his clothes had survived the flames.

'Err, Thiya…' Lochan pointed down the road.

Thiya followed his finger and saw people approaching. They wore black kurta and trousers, and there was a flash of silver on their left shoulders that she knew to be the royal insignia.

The shara had found them.

16

Thiya could not let the shara catch her. If they caught her, she would be dragged back to the palace and Amara would have no one.

Lochan pulled her towards the trees.

'Leave the horses,' Kayan said, running into the tree line behind them.

Thiya wobbled with fatigue as she turned to face him. 'We need the horses to get to Tumassi.' They had two days to get there by the new moon. Two days to figure out Isaac and Yesha's plans and how to stop them.

'We can't outrun the shara,' Kayan said. 'We have two horses now Isaac has taken Lochan's, so you'll have to share a horse again, which will slow us down.'

The shara were getting closer. Thiya could feel the ground vibrating beneath their feet.

'Then what are we going to do?' she asked.

Kayan smiled. 'We lose them.' He pointed to the thickest part of the jungle where the trees were so close together, horses wouldn't be able to travel. They would have to go on foot, but it would force the shara to dismount as well.

The shara were close enough that Thiya could see their faces. They were as much a part of her life as her brothers, perhaps more so since she spent more time with some of them than she did with her own family. But she couldn't let them take her back to the palace without Amara.

She'd run out of time. Thiya could only stare as they descended.

Fire flared along the path between them and the shara. Horses brayed. Shara shouted.

'Run,' Kayan said.

Lochan half-pulled, half-dragged her into the jungle, Kayan hot on their heels. Leaves rustled as her shara, Chirag, crashed through the trees to her right.

'Please, Princess, you need to come home.' He grabbed Thiya's arm and tugged her towards him. Lochan's arm tightened around her shoulder.

Flames spluttered close to Thiya's ear. Chirag let go of her arm and dived out of the way to avoid being burned. His yelp pierced her heart. Chirag had known about Amara and kept her secret. He'd kept her safe through the years and look how she was repaying him.

Kayan led Thiya and Lochan further into the jungle, and Thiya squashed down the guilt that slithered in her stomach. Kayan veered left, heading off the path and into a denser part of the jungle. Thiya heard more shara shouting at each other as she followed.

Pain pulsed between her eyes, but Thiya didn't let it slow her down. Kayan weaved through the trees, but the shara matched their steps. Always one step behind, always calling to each other, always trying to trap them, to block their path. But Kayan seemed to know the jungle, seemed to know which way to turn to avoid capture.

Thiya's breaths sounded loud and ragged in her ears. She wondered how the shara didn't hear it. She pulled a thread of magic ready to use should she need it, but her world spun and the magic dissipated.

Lochan's heartbeat sounded, much like she had heard the heartbeat of the woman at the guesthouse. His heart was a little faster than her own, while Kayan's was slower and steadier. There were more heartbeats further ahead, and Kayan was leading them directly into their path.

'Turn right,' Thiya said. Kayan continued on his path. 'There's a shara ahead. Two.'

Kayan veered to the right. He'd taken two steps when Thiya said, 'Left.' Another step. 'Right. Now left.' The shara were all around them.

Thiya's headache grew worse. If she kept this up, she was going to be sick.

'Stop.' They were moving too fast and she needed to get her bearings, to figure out where the shara were. She leaned heavily against Lochan, her legs shaking.

'Are you alright?' Lochan asked.

Thiya nodded her head, or she thought she did.

'What's wrong with her?' Lochan asked, in panic.

'She's used too much energy.'

'I'm fine,' Thiya said.

'I'd believe that if you weren't slurring your words,' Kayan said. He looked around. 'Where are the shara?'

All around them and closing in.

'We need to move,' Lochan said.

'Your sister can't go anywhere like this,' Kayan said, his voice soft.

'I'm fine,' but it took all her effort just to push those two words out of her mouth. They had a few seconds at best before the shara caught up with them again. She pushed away from Lochan to prove her point and was relieved when she didn't fall.

Her vision blurred. She knew she couldn't run for much longer. They had to find a way to shake the shara off before she passed out.

'Can you create another fire barrier?' Lochan asked.

Kayan shook his head. 'I don't have the energy to contain it, and with this many trees around, I could burn down the whole jungle.'

Thiya could feel heartbeats drawing closer.

'Run!' she cried.

She didn't wait to see if Lochan and Kayan followed. She picked a direction and charged.

A little bit of magic and she could push the shara over like she'd done to Kayan in the tent. She grabbed more threads of magic, toppling any shara in her path. Her legs threatened to give way with every step. She listened for heartbeats, trying to avoid as many shara as possible, but one approached from straight ahead. She tried to run around him but tripped over her own feet.

The shara grabbed her and pulled her up. She lashed out with her magic but she had nothing left to give.

17

Thiya's eyes closed, her eyelids heavy. Someone shook her. Thiya swiped at the hand.

'Thiya, it's me.' It sounded like Lochan, but his voice was distorted, too loud, too deep. Another voice spoke – Kayan? Thiya tried to answer but her tongue felt thick.

Hands pulled her to her feet and Thiya found herself leaning against someone. Lochan said something in her ear, but the words were fuzzy. An arm slipped around her waist and Lochan nudged her forward. Her feet dragged, but she managed to walk.

She heard a bird cawing overhead, elephants stomping through the undergrowth in the distance, Lochan speaking to Kayan. A few words came to her, but nothing she could make sense of.

Pain pressed against her temples. She just wanted to sit down and rest.

'Where are we going?' Thiya asked, when she finally found her voice.

'Somewhere safe,' Kayan said, his shoulders tense.

'He wouldn't tell me either,' Lochan said.

Kayan looked behind him and frowned.

'Are the shara still following us?'

'No, we managed to get you away from them.'

'Are we heading towards Tumassi?' Thiya asked. She

glanced around, her world distorting for a second before it righted itself, but she couldn't see the road. She had no idea if they were heading in the right direction or not.

'The shara are between us and our horses,' Kayan said. 'We need supplies, and this is the one place I know that will have what we need. Isaac's revelations complicate things.'

'Which revelations are complicated?' Thiya asked. She swallowed back bile. 'That Aunt Yesha is alive? That Isaac is torturing Amara with some aether-infused bangle? That Isaac somehow knew I had magic before the ball? Feel free to include anything I may have missed.' Her legs shook, and if Lochan hadn't been supporting most of her weight, she would have fallen.

'I think you got them all,' Lochan said dryly.

'Isaac knowing you had magic is easy enough to explain,' Kayan said. 'Aether magic travels down the female royal line. All aethanis have been princesses, but all princesses have also been aethanis. It made sense you were one too.' He shrugged.

'We were tested,' Lochan grumbled.

'I know, and I believe you genuinely thought your family's magic disappeared. But there are a lot of people who think your family are hiding their magic, and the family bangles kind of prove their point.'

Her father was not a liar, even if he had insisted they wear the bangles.

'You said they were for protection,' Thiya said.

'That's what they were created for. It's possible your

father didn't know the full implications of making you wear them, but that's something only he can answer.'

Thiya had always thought her father a fair and good ruler. He wouldn't hide their magic away from the world, would he?

'Let's assume Isaac knew I was an aethani. How do you explain everything else? Like the fact Isaac's using aether magic on Amara when he's a terrai,' she said.

'Isaac must be working with an aethani, someone who has manipulated aether within Amara to cause her pain,' Kayan said.

Someone like Yesha

They paused by a stream to drink water. Thiya crouched down by the edge and gulped as much as she could, the cool, crisp taste filling her mouth and sliding down her throat. Invigorating. She paused to breathe then shovelled more water into her hands.

'You'll make yourself sick,' Kayan warned.

She didn't care. They'd lost their food and water supplies with the horses. Thiya had to drink her fill when she could.

Kayan pulled her away and they continued west. She kept thinking about the possibility of another aethani, but her mind kept coming back to one conclusion: the answer Isaac had already given her.

'Could Isaac really be working with Aunt Yesha?'

'She's dead,' Lochan insisted, but Thiya could hear his fear. That same fear churned Thiya's stomach, or maybe it was the water.

She looked at Kayan. 'You're the only one of us who's been to Tumassi. What do you think? Could she still be alive? Could she still be there?'

When the soldiers and mages intercepted Yesha in Sanathri Jungle all those years ago, several escaped with Thiya's father while the others fought her. And then the darkness had exploded and no one emerged. They'd assumed everyone in the jungle had died that day.

'If she's alive, she never left the jungle.'

'Could Isaac have gone into the jungle to meet with her?' Thiya asked.

'He claims he's been into Sanathri Jungle,' Kayan said. 'But he's alive, so I'm not so sure. Everyone else who has gone into the jungle has never come back, unless they are possessed by daayan. But it is the one place aether magic has survived, other than inside you.

'What I don't understand is why he risked going into the jungle in the first place, or why he would agree to work with Yesha, if she really is alive,' Kayan said. 'Isaac's entire family were killed by daayan. There is no way he would help Yesha.'

Lochan slipped an arm around Thiya's waist when she started to lag behind.

'Yesha wouldn't have been able to survive in the jungle

all these years without being seen. She would need food, clothes and shelter,' Thiya said.

'Does it matter?' Lochan asked. 'We still have to go to Tumassi to rescue Amara. Whether Isaac is working with Yesha or not doesn't change anything.'

'It matters because we don't know what we're up against and who we can trust,' Kayan said.

'Is that why we're going to this super-secret place to get supplies?' Thiya asked.

Kayan didn't answer.

They continued to walk, Thiya leaning more on Lochan than she would like.

If Yesha was alive and had something to do with Amara being taken, then she would have to deal with her when the time came – an aethani who had been practising magic for a few days versus an aethani who had the power to destroy the country. What could go wrong with that?

Thiya's rumbling stomach echoed amongst the trees.

'Where are you taking us?' Thiya asked.

Kayan grunted.

'Are we at least going to get there today?' The sun was still in the sky, but it wouldn't be long before it started to set.

'Of course,' Kayan said.

The sun had started its descent by the time the trees thinned and they emerged on the other side of the jungle. Kayan paused, which gave Thiya time to scan her surroundings. She saw the outline of buildings and a lake stretching out behind the town. Kayan led them around the outskirts.

'I bet they have food and horses in the town.' Even as Thiya said it, she remembered the villages they'd passed that barely had enough food to feed themselves, let alone strangers.

'Most of the town is abandoned.'

Thiya and Lochan exchanged a quick glance before Thiya said, 'How do you know that?'

Kayan didn't respond.

'Where are we going?'

Not even a blink of an eye.

Kayan led them to what looked like a fortress built on top of a hill, farmland stretching out behind it. It was big like the palace, but the walls were thicker, taller, more imposing, and it was made from pink stone. It looked pretty, especially with the waning sunlight shining on it, making it glow.

The black gates they stopped in front of, however, were designed to intimidate, with the spiked ends extending above their heads. Thiya almost jumped when she heard shouts echo around the outer wall and Kayan's name whispered amongst the guards.

The gates opened with a creak and Kayan headed through.

Guards inside the gate were armed and tense. There was a mage with them, a terrai judging by the green band around the sleeve of his jacket. He nodded at Kayan who nodded back, but neither of them spoke.

Kayan led the way down a path that curved around a large fountain depicting the God of the Sea, Barun, rising up on a wave and brandishing a spear. Thiya was surprised they chose Barun and not Urvi, since this was farmland. Mother Earth would have been a more appropriate god to honour.

'My ancestors let prejudice rule over reason,' Kayan said, when Thiya asked about the gods. 'They chose strength over compassion.'

'Your ancestors?'

But Kayan kept walking. Several buildings rose up behind the fountain, and Kayan led them to the largest one in the centre. He inhaled a deep breath then rang the bell.

A young man answered the door. He was a few years older than Kayan and had similar facial features, though his skin was darker and his eyes were brown, not grey. His lip curled in distaste.

'We don't need anything burned down today, brother,' he said, then slammed the door in Kayan's face.

18

'Wow, he's more delightful than Ravi,' Thiya joked. At least Ravi had never shut the door in her face, but judging by Kayan's expression, this was the greeting he had expected.

'I don't think Ravi's that bad,' Lochan said.

Thiya snorted. Maybe Ravi wasn't as bad to Lochan, but Ravi once left a snake in her bed. Of course, this had been in retaliation for her locking him in his room and causing him to miss an important meeting, but still.

'What do we do now?' she asked.

'We wait.' Kayan leaned against the wall of the porch, his arms crossed and his expression guarded.

The door opened a short time later and a woman with chin-length black hair peeked out. She squealed when she saw Kayan and pulled him into a hug.

'Why didn't you tell me you were coming?' the woman asked, her voice muffled against Kayan's chest. 'I would have made idli sambar.'

She fussed around Kayan in the way only a mother could, checking how he was, looking for signs of physical injury and commenting on some recent weight loss; he wasn't being fed properly in Tumassi and someone could expect a stern letter heading their way sometime soon.

Thiya's mother fussed over her sometimes, too, but

her fussing was different: the jewellery Thiya wore wasn't the right shade of blue to go with her outfit; she needed to stand up straight and not slouch, no matter how much the bruise on her hip from an earlier training exercise was irritating her; she needed to do something about her hair because her natural curls always looked messy. Kayan's mother fussed because she cared about him, not because of what others thought of him.

'It was an unexpected detour,' Kayan said, when he finally managed to get a word in.

'Yes, we wouldn't want anyone to think you actually *wanted* to see us,' Kayan's brother said, reappearing in the doorway.

Kayan stiffened.

'Nikul!' Kayan's mother scolded her other son. 'Are you in trouble?' she asked Kayan. 'What do you need?' She beamed at Kayan, the wrinkles around her dark brown eyes deepening. She looked like Nikul, but there was something of Kayan in the shape of her mouth and the expression she wore.

'We cannot afford to help him,' Nikul growled.

Kayan's mother raised her eyebrows at her other son. 'We're family. It's what we do.'

'What about Hiral. How do you think it'll affect her if we're fined or executed for helping a mage who should be at his post?'

Kayan flinched.

Thiya had always felt the threat of fines and

executions for a mage's family were necessary to keep the mage in line, but seeing Kayan with his family, she wondered if it was fair. Kayan would have been taken from his family at age ten to begin training, and while he saw his family from time to time their relationship was clearly strained. Punishing a mage's family would only add to that strain.

Maybe this was something else she needed to discuss with her father. It was the mages that kept them safe in the capital, that allowed the larger towns to flourish. Without them, Agraal would have been destroyed a long time ago. They deserved better.

'I'm not a traitor and I'm not in trouble,' Kayan said, 'but we do need some help.'

Kayan was speaking entirely to his mother, ignoring Nikul completely, and Thiya couldn't blame him. Nikul seemed to be going out of his way to make Kayan feel unwelcome. Kayan's mother ushered them all into the house and shut the door.

'Mother, may I introduce my friends?' Kayan stepped away from his mother. 'Prince Lochan and Princess Thiya of Agraal. This is my mother, Dipti.'

After they exchanged greetings, Kayan added, 'I am escorting Lochan and Thiya to Tumassi, but we have misplaced our supplies. I left a tent last time I was here, but we also need horses.'

Nikul snorted. 'How do you misplace a horse?'

The same way you misplace manners, Thiya thought.

'I'll have everything ready for you by the morning,' Dipti said.

Kayan thanked his mother, but Thiya's brain stuck on the word 'morning'. They couldn't wait that long. Amara needed her.

'Is there any way you can get the horses ready sooner?' Thiya asked.

Dipti's smile slipped and she looked at Kayan. 'Sooner?'

'Yes. Like now.' They were leaving as soon as possible.

'I thought you would stay the night.' Dipti's shoulders drooped.

'Kayan can't be a hero at home,' Nikul said. 'Why do you think he hardly ever comes back?'

'I can't just leave Tumassi whenever I want,' Kayan said, his voice calm and emotionless.

'Unless it's for a ball,' Nikul said. 'What's more important than a ball?'

'The letter said he was being honoured,' Dipti said, smiling at Kayan. 'We should be proud.'

'There is no pride in abandoning your family.' Nikul stormed off before Kayan could respond.

Khal! Thiya wanted to drag Nikul back by his hair and force him to apologise for hurting Kayan.

'Be patient with him,' Dipti said to Kayan. 'He's had a lot to deal with since your father…' She sighed. 'Anyway, I'm glad you're here.' She offered Kayan a watery smile.

'What's been going on?'

'The usual – daayan attacks here are on the rise, we

don't have enough people to work the farm and everything is failing.'

'Why didn't you tell me?' Kayan said.

'I didn't want to worry you.'

'I could have sent more money.'

Dipti shook her head. 'It's not about the money. No one *wants* to stay here anymore. It's too dangerous. Nikul's tried petitioning the king for more mages, but his request is always denied. And he wants you home because he thinks you'll be able to protect us.'

'What about the terrai I saw out front?'

'Hunar? He's a good mage and a nice person, and he does what he can to help out with the farm, but he's not you.'

Kayan and his mother discussed supplies, as they walked through the house. They needed clothes, food and water as well as three horses. Kayan promised to send the horses back the moment they reached Tumassi, because they would be needed on the farm. Thiya realised then just how much Kayan's family were sacrificing to help them and she was grateful.

'I will have everything ready by morning. Now I will see to dinner while you rest.' Dipti kissed Kayan's cheek and headed further into the house.

'No, wait—' Thiya cried, but Dipti had disappeared around the corner. 'We need to leave now,' she told Kayan.

'The sun is setting. By the time we get all our supplies ready, we won't be able to leave anyway.'

Thiya glanced out the window at the golden sunlight streaming through. The sun was lower in the sky, but there was still enough light for them to cover some distance before they had to stop. And while Thiya didn't like sleeping in a tent, it would be worth it to be that little bit closer to Tumassi.

'We can stay one night. There's time before the new moon.' Lochan squeezed her hand. 'We will save Amara.'

Unless Amara died first.

19

Thiya reluctantly let a servant lead her and Lochan up some stairs and into what looked to be a newer wing of the house, while Kayan retreated to his own room.

'You can't save Amara if you're too tired to stand, let alone fight,' Lochan said.

She was stuck here for the night while Amara was in the hands of that monster. She wanted to do something. Anything.

The servant stopped outside two adjacent rooms. She directed Lochan into one then followed Thiya into the other. 'My mistress has instructed us to draw you a bath, if you desire, and we'll bring you fresh clothes.'

A bath! Thiya could finally wash all the dirt and sweat off her skin. It had been far too long since she'd last had a bath. The only thing that could make the prospect of a bath better was Amara being there to rub a washcloth down her back.

The servant left to get warm water and Thiya sank onto the bed that filled most of the room, the cream sheets soft and luxurious. Inviting. And yet she couldn't relax.

The servant had the bath filled in no time. The moment she left, Thiya stripped off her clothes and sank into the tub. The heat soaked into aching muscles but still they wouldn't loosen. She laid her head back against the rim and let the worry flow through her.

Where was Amara now? How much had her health deteriorated since the morning? Would she even last till the new moon?

Two days. They had two days to get to her.

The water was cold by the time Thiya grabbed the bar of soap and washed herself and her hair. She got out, wrapped her body in the fluffy white towel and shuffled over to the bed.

The servant had left her a pale pink and gold kurta that hit the middle of her thighs and matching dark brown trousers with a gold cuff around the ankle. Gold mojari completed the outfit. The mojari were a little wide and slipped off the back of her heel when she walked, but they were fine for now. There was even a pot of arnica cream to rub onto her bruises.

She brushed through her curls and left them to dry, before flopping onto the bed and face-planting the pillow, sinking into the soft mattress. It hugged and supported her in equal measure. This might have been the most comfortable bed she'd ever slept in.

Where was Amara sleeping now?

Someone knocked on her door.

'Go away.' The pillow muffled her words, but either Kayan didn't hear, or he didn't care.

'Meet me in your brother's room.'

She needed to get up, but her legs wouldn't move. She needed a nap. A few minutes would do.

Her eyelids grew heavy. Kayan and Lochan's muffled

voices drifted through the wall. They were already talking about Amara and she needed to be there.

Khal. She pushed herself upright, which took more strength than she expected. She waited a moment for the dizzy spell to pass then swung her legs onto the floor and padded to the door.

Lochan didn't respond to her knock, so she let herself in. 'Let's get this over with so I can—'

Kayan was kissing her brother.

Her brother was kissing Kayan!

Lochan sprang to his feet, his face redder than garlic chutney. He made a point of looking anywhere but at Thiya and Kayan, who still sat on the edge of the bed wearing a self-satisfied grin.

Thiya chuckled.

'How are you feeling?' Kayan asked.

'Fine.'

Kayan raised an eyebrow. 'How are you really feeling?'

Kayan knew she wasn't fine, so what was the point in lying? It wasn't like she was fighting with Ravi, who had taken it upon himself in those early years of her training to prove to their father that he'd made a mistake. This was different. Kayan was trying to help her.

'Tired, like I could sleep for a week. My elbow hurts and my back has so many bruises, I think the entire area is now black and blue.'

'Any dizziness?'

She nodded.

'What about fainting?'

'No.'

'That's good,' Kayan said. 'It means you're getting stronger.'

Kayan looked put together in his dark blue kurta with yellow accents, despite the few nicks on his chin where he'd cut himself shaving. His eyes were bright and clear and he looked … not quite relaxed, but not tired either.

Lochan had on a cream kurta with green accents and he had somehow managed to drip water onto his shoulder. Except the stain was mottled and growing bigger.

'Is that blood?' she asked.

Lochan looked at his shoulder. 'Maybe?'

Kayan unhooked the kurta at Lochan's neck and pulled the material aside to reveal a blood-soaked bandage underneath. He sucked in a sharp breath. 'Why didn't you tell me it had started bleeding again?'

Lochan shrugged then winced. 'It's been a busy day.'

Lochan had been too busy supporting her as they ran through the jungle. She hadn't even thought about his injuries. She was a horrible sister.

'How do I heal it?' she asked.

'It'll be fine,' Lochan said.

Kayan frowned as he poked at the injury with fresh gauze. Lochan hissed.

'I think you might need stitches,' said Kayan.

'Will it still leave a hero-worthy scar?'

'Yes.'

'I can heal it,' Thiya said, louder this time.

Kayan shook his head. 'You need to rest. I'll go get the sewing kit.'

'I'm not letting my brother bleed out.'

'I'm not going to bleed out,' Lochan said.

'Tell that to the kurta,' Thiya said, pointing to the blood stain. 'I feel stronger than I did earlier. I can even stand on my own two feet and everything. Please.'

Kayan paused in the doorway. 'Alright, we'll try it, but if you feel it's too much, we stop.'

'Fine.'

'I mean it. The fate of this country depends on you.'

So did Amara's fate. 'I promise I will stop if it becomes too much.'

Kayan waited until Thiya and Lochan were sitting cross-legged on the centre of the bed, facing each other, before he taught Thiya what to do, which basically amounted to one instruction: 'Trust your instincts.'

Thiya pulled a thread of magic and wrapped it around Lochan's injured shoulder. In her mind, she saw the broken blood vessels and torn flesh. She saw the way the muscles strained when Lochan moved his shoulder and knew his pain. And yet he had not let it stop him.

She could fix this.

She pulled more threads of magic and started knitting everything back together. She wasn't sure how much time passed before she was finally done. She blinked as reality settled around her. Lochan's wound had stopped bleeding.

She yawned.

'How do you feel?' Kayan asked.

'Tired.' Another yawn forced its way out of her mouth and Kayan frowned. 'But I was already tired before.' This bed was as comfortable as the bed next door. She lay back and closed her eyes.

'You got rid of my scar,' Lochan whined. Thiya prised her eyes open to see him wipe away the dried blood with a damp cloth. The skin underneath was smooth and brown.

'Don't worry, you don't need the scar,' Kayan said, his voice rough.

Lochan cleared his throat. 'What's our plan?' he asked. 'How do we find out if Yesha is alive or if this is some elaborate scheme Isaac has concocted?'

Thiya had been wondering the same thing. 'We go into Sanathri Jungle.'

Lochan laughed. 'No really, what's the plan?'

'Actually, I agree with your sister. It's where the daayan are, and it's the one place no one's been able to search. It's the perfect place for Yesha to hide,' Kayan said.

'But, other than Isaac, no one who's gone inside has made it out alive.'

'No one else had Thiya on their side. She can keep the daayan from infecting us while we search for Yesha.'

They continued to make plans until a servant announced dinner, and if Thiya drifted in and out of sleep, neither Kayan nor Lochan said anything. Kayan tensed, his movements brittle as they made their way down the stairs for dinner. He greeted his mother, brother and sister, Hiral.

'I thought you were leaving. Did you forget the way?' Nikul asked.

Dipti glared at him. 'Nikul, be nice. We have other guests.' She nodded to someone seated on the opposite side of the room and Thiya gasped.

Ravi stood when he saw Thiya looking and smiled. 'Hello, little sister.' Three shara stood with their backs pressed against the adjacent wall, their eyes alert.

'What in Khal's left testicle are you doing here?' she asked Ravi. And how was he here? They'd left the shara behind. Lochan and Kayan had said so. And yet Chirag was there, standing with the other shara.

They would not drag her back to the palace before she could rescue Amara.

Ravi feigned a hurt expression. 'Aren't you glad to see me?'

No, she wasn't, and judging by his smirk he knew it.

'Why don't we sit down?' Dipti said and guided everyone to their seats.

Thiya ended up sitting opposite Kayan's brother, which gave Nikul ample opportunity to glare at her, though he did send most of his filthy looks Kayan's way. What was his problem? Lochan squeezed her hand under the table – a reminder to be good.

Thiya looked at the twelve-year-old girl next to

Nikul, Hiral. She kept glancing at Kayan from under her lashes. She had the same grey eyes as him, though she'd inherited her mother's darker skin, which created a striking contrast.

Striking. That's what Amara always said about Thiya's long nose and sharp jaw, although in Hiral's case striking looked good.

For a while, no one spoke. Lochan shifted beside her, and even Thiya wanted to break the silence, but she couldn't force any words out, so she focused on the plate of vegetable samosa in front of her.

It was Nikul who spoke first. 'Is something the matter?' he asked Kayan, his voice much too sweet for comfort.

Thiya would have preferred the silence.

'No.'

'So, you're not running from the shara?'

'Stop causing trouble,' Dipti said.

'No.' Nikul banged his fist on the table, sending the cutlery rattling. 'Kayan turns up unannounced with a prince and princess in tow, and then another prince and several shara turn up a moment later. We deserve to know what's going on.'

'I didn't realise I had to wait for an invitation to visit my own home,' Kayan said, coolly.

Nikul leaned forward; his hands braced on the table. 'It's not your home anymore.'

Kayan's expression remained neutral, but his throat bobbed as he swallowed. Again. And again.

Thiya and Ravi had their problems, but neither of them had ever made the other feel unwelcome in their own home. She had always known where she belonged.

Nikul had let his jealousy consume him.

Her eyes met Ravi's and for a moment she wondered if they were thinking the same thing, that at least Nikul wasn't their sibling. And then she remembered he was here to drag her back to the palace, and she scowled.

Dipti cleared her throat. 'This is my home and I say *all* my children are welcome here.' She reached out and gave Kayan's hand a squeeze. 'Whenever they want.'

Nikul's expression twisted.

Thiya didn't care for Nikul, but Kayan did. It was clear that Nikul thinking the worst of him hurt. She could do something to soften Nikul's sharp edge.

'You do deserve to know what's happening,' she said. 'Kayan is helping me, and the shara are after me and my brother because we sneaked out of the palace.'

'I knew you were up to no good,' Nikul exclaimed.

'Kayan's helping me so I can get to Tumassi and destroy daayan, hopefully for good.' She paused for a moment to let that sink in. She didn't tell him about Yesha because she didn't think that was a good idea. And she didn't tell him about Amara because she didn't think Nikul would care.

She also knew it was a selfish reason for going to Tumassi. Amara was one person versus an entire world, but that one person *was* her world.

'How can you possibly destroy daayan?' Nikul's eyes flicked to Kayan, and this time there was no hatred within their depths, only longing.

He wants you home because he thinks you'll be able to protect them.

Maybe Dipti had it wrong, because to Thiya it seemed like Nikul wanted Kayan home because he missed his little brother. It was easier to convince Kayan to stay away than to see him constantly leave.

'She's not a mage,' Ravi said.

But Thiya spoke over him. 'I can destroy them, and I can prove it.'

Nikul didn't bother to hide his hope as he looked at her. Everyone was looking at her, but she would do this for Nikul and Kayan, for the relationship that had been strained because of her aunt and the daayan she'd unleashed.

Thiya reached for her magic. Her rest had helped restore some of her energy.

But Ravi pulled her to her feet and dragged her to the door, before it had a chance to fully register. And then she was out the room, the door slamming shut on Nikul's expectant face.

20

Ravi's grip on Thiya's arm tightened, as he dragged her to a nearby room that turned out to be a study. He released her the moment they were inside.

Thiya stumbled backwards, putting as much distance between her and Ravi as possible. 'What in Khal's left testicle do you think you're doing?'

Ravi closed the door and stood blocking her escape. 'You seem to have an unhealthy obsession with Khalil's testicles, little sister.' He crossed his arms and smirked.

Thiya clenched her teeth. 'Please step aside so I can leave.'

Ravi's smile slipped. 'We need to talk.'

'No.' Thiya spun around, taking in the shuttered windows, the floor to ceiling bookshelves along the left wall and the large wooden desk in front of the windows. There had to be another way out, but short of smashing through the shutters, she couldn't find anything, and she wasn't that desperate. Yet.

'What you tried to do in that dining room was completely irresponsible.'

Thiya's head snapped to Ravi's where she met his disappointed gaze. She heard what he didn't say. *You're just like Aunt Yesha.*

'How do you know what I was about to do?'

'You got that boy's hopes up.'

'That was the point.'

'You are not a mage,' Ravi said.

Hadn't they had this conversation already? 'Then why do I have magic?'

She walked around the desk and sat down.

'You don't.' The catch in his voice made Thiya look up. She saw it before he managed to hide it – the fear and the jealousy. It buoyed her.

She smiled. 'And yet you dragged me out of the dining room when I tried to show you. Why drag me away if I don't have magic?'

Ravi scowled and Thiya's smile widened. She'd won. There was no way Ravi could talk his way out of this now.

'Father was afraid of this.' Ravi sighed.

Thiya's skin prickled. 'Of what?'

'We think this feiraani wants to hurt our family. There is a faction of rebel mages that think we are to blame for the daayan attacks, and they don't believe we are doing enough to stop them. If they can convince the rest of the country that you're a mage and Father hid it, they will lose faith in us and it will destabilise our country. But to convince them, they have to convince you first.

'Kayan tricked you, made you believe you killed the daayan in the ballroom, but you didn't.' Ravi pushed away from the door and approached the desk. 'Father spoke to the mages in the palace. Kayan is able to manipulate your body temperature, make you feel as if you're using magic.'

Ravi patted her arm in what she thought was supposed to be a comforting gesture, but it was *Ravi*. It was weird. She pulled her arm back.

'You couldn't have known,' Ravi continued. 'There's no reason to feel shame.'

What preposterous drivel!

Thiya slammed her hand on the desk. 'I'm not ashamed. And Kayan didn't trick me. I have magic, and I can prove it.'

She pulled at a thread of magic, looped it around Ravi's shoulders and pushed. Nothing happened.

A smug smile spread across his face. 'See—'

'You need to remove your bangle,' Thiya said, catching sight of the flash of silver under his sleeve. 'It's blocking my magic.'

'Or you don't have magic.'

'Remove your bangle and I'll prove it.'

Ravi gritted his teeth and threw his bangle on the desk. Thiya pulled at another thread of magic and pushed Ravi so his back hit the wall.

For a moment Ravi was lost for words, then, 'The feiraani—'

'Isn't here.'

'But—'

'Would you like another demonstration?' She pushed him again.

Ravi straightened, his movements jerky. 'How?'

'My bangle has been blocking my magic. Lochan

doesn't have magic, but it does make me wonder who else in the family does.'

'That's ridiculous.' But there was hope in Ravi's eyes.

'Is it?' She held out her hand. 'There is one way to find out.'

Ravi hesitated for a second then slipped his hand into hers. Thiya bit her lip, unsure how to proceed, but she let her instincts guide her. She pulled threads of magic and looped them around Ravi, but instead of letting them gently sink into him like she had with Kayan, she pushed them inside, overwhelming his senses until she felt his magic pull water droplets from the air between them. They coalesced into larger, visible spheres that splashed Thiya's face.

She turned her head and released Ravi, the water droplets disappearing. She pushed wet strands of hair off her face and smiled. 'You're an aquira.'

Ravi took a step back. 'I'm a mage?' He squeezed his eyes shut. 'I'm a mage.' He let out a shaky laugh. 'Wait, did Father deliberately try to hide our magic from the world?'

Thiya shook her head. 'I don't know. Kayan said the bangles were meant to be a form of protection. Maybe Father thought it stopped daayan.'

'Then why not tell us? And why not share it with everyone else?'

Thiya frowned. 'I don't know.'

'We can ask Father when we get home,' Ravi said.

How was she meant to ask her father if he had

deliberately hidden her magic? She loved her father dearly. She couldn't bear the thought of him being a coward.

'I'm going to Tumassi first.'

'No, you're not.'

She stood so she was level with her brother when she looked him in the eye. 'It's the right thing to do, and you know it.'

Still, Ravi shook his head. 'We need to be careful about this. I told you about the rebel faction. You can't just run off to Tumassi. We cannot afford for anyone in the family to mess up.'

We can't afford for you *to mess up.*

'Surely going to Tumassi and defeating the daayan once and for all would convince the mages we're on their side?'

Ravi's eyes narrowed. 'Not without an announcement from the palace. Come home. We can plan this properly.'

'And how many people will die in that time?'

'We can't save everyone,' Ravi said, 'but a civil war will kill far more people.'

Thiya shook her head. 'Amara is there and I can't leave her. She's been kidnapped by a terrai named Isaac and I am going to get her back.'

Ravi raised a brow. 'The terrai she agreed to marry?'

Why did Ravi always find a way to make her sound like a silly child? Isaac was dangerous.

'Yes.'

'That's not kidnapping.'

'It is when he's dragging her to Tumassi. She's not a mage. She will die.'

'If you're right, we can tell General Sethu and his soldiers can get her back,' Ravi said.

'By the time he gets the message, it'll be too late.' Two days. They had two days to get to Tumassi, and they were wasting one of them here.

'You don't have to be the one to rescue Amara.'

She hated that softness, that sympathy. Especially coming from Ravi.

'You don't understand…' The room was too small. She moved away from the desk, standing close to the shuttered windows, but it was still hard to breathe.

'That you're in love with her? I know.'

Her breath stilled. 'How?'

'I've seen the two of you together.'

She was too scared to look at his face so she stared at the papers on the desk instead.

Thiya didn't hear any disgust in her brother's voice. In fact, he sounded almost understanding. It had to be a trick.

'No one else noticed—'

'Everyone else is an idiot.'

Her lips twitched. 'Why didn't you say anything?'

'You and I don't exactly get along.'

This time she did look up. Ravi leaned against the bookshelf, his arms crossed.

'I know. This is weird.' She waved her hand between

216

them. 'But I mean…' She trailed off, unsure how to complete that sentence without sounding like an arse or accusing Ravi of being one.

'Why didn't I use it against you?'

She nodded.

'Because it's the one thing I've always admired about you. You're never afraid to be yourself.'

'I'm afraid all the time.' Of not finding Amara or finding her too late. Of not being with her. Of Amara being stuck in a life she didn't want. Of failing to meet others' expectations.

Of being consumed by darkness.

Of being like Aunt Yesha.

'You never show it, and you never let it stop you.' Silence fell between them until Ravi broke it. 'If you tell anyone about this conversation, I will deny it.'

Thiya laughed. 'Who would believe me? I'm not sure I even believe it.' Her smile faded. 'You have to let me go.'

'Father—'

'Amara is dying.' She told him about the aether magic inside Amara, slowly sucking her life away. Ravi stared at her for such a long time, she started to worry he was trying to find another way to convince her to go home. But eventually, he nodded.

Someone knocked on the door, soft and tentative.

'Are you still alive?' Lochan asked.

Ravi marched to the door and ripped it open. 'Which one?'

Lochan answered by looking over Ravi's shoulder. He visibly relaxed when he saw Thiya.

'Nice to know you care about my health.' Ravi stood aside to let Lochan enter, then shut the door behind him.

Lochan gripped Ravi's shoulder and feigned an expression that implied he was so happy he was overwhelmed. 'I'm glad Thiya didn't kill you. That would be a hard one to explain to Father... Mother probably wouldn't mind.'

Ravi threw him off.

'She would mind,' Thiya said. She would probably find a way to tie it back to Thiya's short hair and her disinclination to wear skirts. She could almost hear the lectures.

Lochan nodded. 'But she would expect it.'

Ravi scowled. 'What are you doing here?'

'I told you; I came to see which of you was still alive.'

'Now you've seen, you can leave,' Ravi said.

Lochan looked to Thiya for approval and frowned. 'Why are you wet?'

'Ravi is an aquira.'

Lochan snapped his head in Ravi's direction. Ravi grinned.

'He's also agreed to stop pursuing us,' she told Lochan.

'He did?' Lochan's eyes widened.

'Don't act so surprised.' Ravi scowled.

'But it's ... surprising.'

Thiya had to agree with Lochan, and yet Ravi had

surprised her several times tonight. 'Well, tomorrow, we are going to Tumassi and Ravi is heading home.'

'No.'

Thiya froze. 'You promised—'

'I did no such thing.'

'Told you it was surprising,' Lochan said.

'I'm coming with you,' Ravi announced.

Thiya pushed away from the desk. 'Absolutely not.' They might have reached an understanding, but Ravi would eventually say or do something to annoy her. She did not want him in Tumassi when that happened.

And yet Ravi had different ideas, because of course he did. 'I go with you to Tumassi or you come back to the palace with me.'

'It's too dangerous.'

'All the more reason to have me along.' His hand rested on the hilt of his sword, his eyes glinting. Thiya wasn't surprised he hadn't taken it off here. Ravi never removed his sword if he could help it because he always hoped for an opportunity to use it. 'Having another mage could come in handy.'

'You don't know how to use your magic.'

Ravi shrugged. 'I'll learn.'

'What if you're possessed by a daayan?'

'Why little sister, I didn't know you cared,' Ravi teased.

Thiya scowled. Of course she cared. He was her brother. But she wasn't going to admit it to him. He would be insufferably smug for the rest of her life.

'I don't,' she lied.

Ravi strode over to the desk and picked up his bangle. The enchanted bangle that had been infused with magic that never faded, unlike the enchanted swords. Until she'd given hers to Amara, Thiya had never taken her bangle off, it had never been replaced. There was something different between the bangles and the swords.

But Ravi waved the bangle in her face before she could pursue the thought further. 'I'll wear this. It'll protect me. Don't worry, little sister, I'll be just fine.'

'You don't know that it'll protect from a daayan attack. I was speculating. Plus, it will block your magic.'

'I either use my magic to help you, or I protect myself against daayan. Which will it be?'

'I'd rather you return to the palace.'

'That's not an option.' He held up the bangle. 'How about another compromise, since you care so much? I will use my magic to help you, but I will keep the bangle right here should I need it.' He slipped the bangle into his pocket and patted it.

Thiya crossed her arms. 'I don't care.'

'You do.'

'I don't!'

Thiya's eyes narrowed. 'Well, you care about me as well.'

Lochan pushed between them. 'Please remember that we're guests in someone else's household. I would hate for them to think we're animals.'

'Sorry.'

Ravi grumbled something that could have been an apology or an insult.

'Good. Now please try and behave during the rest of dinner.' Lochan headed for the door. Just as he reached it, someone rang the doorbell.

21

The doorbell rang again. It was louder here in the hallway, the high-pitched vibration echoing through the walls. Thiya reached for her dagger.

Ravi, Lochan and Thiya's sharas were already in the hallway, waiting. They tried to usher the siblings back inside, but Ravi waved them off. Lochan moved in front of Thiya, while Ravi stayed by her side. They drew their swords and pointed them at the door.

But the front door was shut and locked, the window beside it shuttered. No one should have been outside so long after curfew.

Everything was quiet. Still. A part of Thiya wondered if they had imagined the sound, but then Kayan emerged from the dining room.

Nikul stepped out behind him.

'Go back inside,' Kayan urged his brother.

'No.' His jaw clenched. 'This is my home.'

'Mother and Hiral—'

'Are safe. I'm staying with you,' Nikul said.

'If there is a daayan on the other side of the door, you cannot help.'

'Neither can they.' Nikul jerked his chin towards Thiya's brothers and the three shara.

'You should head into the dining room as well,' Kayan told them.

'Actually, I'm a mage.' Ravi puffed out his chest.

'We stay with our charges,' Chirag said. He moved closer to Thiya.

'I'm not leaving now,' Lochan said.

Kayan swore.

Someone knocked on the door again and Thiya froze.

'Nikul?' The muffled voice trembled.

'That's Hunar.' Nikul started for the door, but Kayan pulled him back.

'Are you trying to get us all killed?' Ravi hissed.

'Leave him alone,' Kayan said.

Ravi opened his mouth to argue, but Thiya cut him off. 'Enough.'

Ravi scowled, but to her surprise he closed his mouth and returned his attention to the door.

'It's Hunar,' Nikul repeated. 'The terrai that protects this town.'

Kayan frowned. 'He still shouldn't be outside.'

'Something must have happened,' Nikul said.

'Obviously,' Ravi said.

'Nikul?' Hunar's voice wavered. 'I lost track of time when visiting Charan and I forgot my keys.' He paused. 'P-please can you let me in? It's so d-dark out here.'

Nikul started for the door again, but Ravi flung an arm out.

'We can't let him stay out there all night,' Nikul cried.

'We can't let him inside, either. We don't know what else is out there,' Ravi said. 'Don't you have stables he can stay in?'

'This is my house,' Nikul growled. 'I am not leaving him outside like an animal.'

'He could be possessed by a daayan,' Thiya said.

Nikul shook his head. 'If he were possessed, he would have forced his way inside by now.'

'That's not true,' Kayan told his brother, his voice soft. 'There are some mages, when possessed, who keep ahold of their faculties initially. Or the daayan uses their memories to their own advantage.' He shook his head, his voice hollow. 'They appear normal, and in the dark it's hard to tell if their eyes are black.'

'I get what you're saying, Kayan, but this isn't the front line.' Nikul broke out of Kayan's hold and headed for the front door before Kayan could stop him. He had almost reached it when the town's warning bell sounded.

'I guess that answers the question about whether the terrai is possessed or not,' Ravi said.

'That bell could be for someone else. What if Hunar is in trouble? We can't leave him outside if there are daayan.' He rounded on Kayan. 'What if it were you? Wouldn't you want someone to help you?'

It had been them not that long ago, and Prisha had opened the door.

Kayan sighed. 'There's only one person who would be able to help me.' He looked at Thiya in silent question. She'd used a lot of energy today, but could she still kill a daayan?

She pulled at a thread of her magic and nodded.

'Everyone stand back,' Kayan said. But before any of them could move, the door shattered open.

Thiya screamed. Sharp pain laced her forearms everywhere the flying wooden debris struck. She'd raised her arms to protect her face, but she lowered them now.

Stood in the doorway, framed by the night sky, was the mage she had seen earlier. Hunar. Even half-hidden in the shadows, there was no mistaking those black eyes and grey veins.

He was possessed.

Several daayan flanked him in their shadow form. They swirled around each other, changing shape so fast they were hard to distinguish.

Kayan's flames shot towards them and they spun apart. She didn't know which daayan to attack first, couldn't tell which was the biggest threat. Hunar had his magic which the daayan could use, but the shadow daayan could possess them. Before she could decide, Hunar shot a huge splinter of wood from the broken door at Ravi's shara, Prem, piercing his heart. Ravi roared in outrage as Prem sagged to the ground.

Kayan threw more flames at Hunar, who dived out of the way then directed the stem of a potted plant to wind its way around Kayan's arms, pulling them behind his back. Smoke curled up around Kayan's arms as the plant burst into flames. What remained of the burnt leaves and charred stem slithered back into the pot.

Thiya reached for the threads of her magic when

Chirag pulled her to the ground. His sword glowed white as he swung it towards a daayan. The darkness of the daayan faded a little but the nick of the sword wasn't enough to kill it. The daayan veered to the side before diving for them again.

As Kayan and Hunar continued their fight, Thiya pushed herself to her feet.

'Stay back, Princess.' Chirag used his body to shield her. His sword sliced through the air as more daayan attacked.

Thiya looped her magic around the nearest daayan and pulled the threads. The daayan exploded in a shower of darkness.

Chirag yelped. 'That was you?'

'Yes.' Thiya stepped out from behind him. She looped her magic around another daayan and squeezed until it too exploded.

A sword skittered across the floor and struck the wall behind Thiya. The green glow along the blade faded. Another daayan flew at her and she destroyed it. But there were more coming. Too many.

Daayan swarmed Lochan. He shouted as his shara, Yug, ran to him. One daayan darted forward. Thiya's magic was in her hands, but Lochan's sword got to the daayan first. The sword glowed a cool blue colour and the daayan flinched out of the way.

Thiya's vision swam. She blinked. Yug was in front of her. He reached for her hand, his grey-veined fingers beckoning. Lochan's shara had become possessed.

Chirag slashed at Yug's exposed wrist with a sword, but Yug didn't even flinch. He grabbed Thiya's hand and tugged, his fingers slick with blood.

Thiya reached for her magic. Pain pounded behind her eyes and she almost dropped the threads. Before she could destroy the daayan, Chirag drove his enchanted sword into Yug's chest.

Yug hissed. His grip slackened. Chirag kicked Yug off his sword and he fell on his back. Still.

'I could have saved him.' Her voice sounded hollow.

'Your life was not worth the risk.' Chirag swung his sword around to swipe at another daayan.

Thiya squashed her unease as another daayan lunged for her. She looped her magic around it and squeezed until it exploded. But more swirled around her in a menacing cloud of darkness. She destroyed them one by one, Chirag's sword flashing at her side. A wave of dizziness overcame her once more and she leaned into the wall for support.

More daayan came in through the open door and darted for Lochan. He caught one with his sword but another one attacked. Lochan was already swinging his sword towards it, then another and another. A deadly dance. But there were too many. He didn't notice the one approaching from behind.

Thiya aimed her magic towards it. The thread of dark and light contracted, squeezing and pressing against the daayan before it exploded.

Thiya reached for more magic, but she blacked out for a second. Two.

Fire danced before her. Hunar had picked up more debris from the shattered door with his magic and was shooting pieces at Kayan. Kayan set each one aflame before they hit him or Nikul. Ash and smoke floated around them.

Chirag's sword slashed the air in front of Thiya. The light burnt bright against the onslaught of darkness. One daayan managed to slip under Chirag's sword and headed straight for Thiya. It brushed against her skin, trying to find a way inside, but her magic rose up to destroy it. Her body ached with tiredness.

Lochan shouted. His enchanted sword had stopped glowing, the magic used up. Thiya destroyed more daayan surrounding Lochan, but the daayan seemed to have realised Lochan had no defence. More dived at him, and Thiya could not destroy them fast enough.

Water splashed Lochan: small droplets rather than the stream Thiya had seen the aquira at the palace use, but it was enough to send the daayan scattering.

Lochan swiped a hand over his damp face. 'Thanks.'

Ravi smiled brightly. 'You're welcome.' More droplets of water splashed out around him. Some hit Thiya's arms. 'Oops.'

There were fewer daayan surrounding Ravi. He was drenched, as was the floor around him. Water splashed at random intervals and directions, making it harder for the daayan to find a way to attack him. One daayan swerved out of the way of more water droplets and over Ravi's head.

Ravi shouted. Thiya turned in time to see a daayan dive towards Lochan.

Her breath stilled.

She reached for her magic. Her knees buckled and her back slid down the wall. Ravi looked like he was trying to make his magic work but wasn't having much luck either.

Lochan was still on his feet. Thiya waited for his eyes to turn black, but nothing happened. Lochan spun around as another daayan dived for him.

That's when Thiya noticed it. Lochan's bangle glowed with a rainbow shimmer every time the daayan came into contact with him. They couldn't hurt him.

Thiya laughed, relief and tiredness making her delirious. Lochan grinned, then his expression froze.

He lunged forward and dragged Thiya away from the wall.

'What—'

Lochan pulled her into his chest.

Chirag's sword clattered to the floor. His eyes had turned black.

Chirag headed for Thiya; his limbs now controlled by the daayan within. His fingers wrapped around her wrist. 'Come with me,' he said, forcing her towards the door.

She tried to break away, but Chirag's hold tightened.

'What are you doing?' Chirag growled.

'Let go of my sister.' Lochan pulled Thiya back. Chirag's nails sliced through her flesh and she hissed.

Lochan struck Chirag with his sword, but Chirag didn't notice the blood pouring down his arm. He shoved Lochan out of the way, the sword spinning across the floor.

If Chirag hadn't held her, Thiya would have collapsed. Still, she twisted her wrist to break his hold, but he lashed out with his other hand.

'Stop fighting.'

'No,' she said. She reached for her dagger, but her blade slipped through her trembling fingers.

Chirag had almost dragged Thiya to the door when he burst into flames.

Thiya stared at his remains. Chirag had always protected her, even after she'd run from him and jeopardised his career, but she couldn't save him. He deserved so much better.

Thiya spun around to see Kayan with more fire in his hand. Hunar was patting out flames from the bottom of his kurta with the palm of his hand. His possessed eyes met Thiya's and those black, bottomless depths sent a shiver rippling down her spine.

'Thiya. Help,' Kayan said.

She glanced to the side to see grey veins spreading up Nikul's neck and down his hands from under his kurta. Kayan crouched down by his side.

'Protect them,' Nikul said. His fingers twitched and then the darkness spread down to his fingertips. 'Keep them safe.'

Kayan nodded. Of course he would protect his mother and sister.

Thiya could save him and Hunar. Two daayan. That was all Thiya had to kill. She could do that. No one else had to die tonight. She reached for her magic.

Her stomach heaved.

'Enough,' a deep, familiar voice said. 'I only came to talk and this is the reception I get? Standards have declined in the last few years.' Ravi clicked his tongue.

His eyes had turned black.

22

Ravi paused near the open doorway, his head cocked to the side as if waiting to see what she would do. The shadow daayan had disappeared; Thiya couldn't sense them. She didn't trust the stillness.

The daayan controlled Ravi's movements, his words. But who was controlling the daayan?

'Who are you?' Thiya asked.

'What do you want?' Lochan asked at the same time.

'I'm disappointed in you, Thiya.' Ravi clicked his tongue. 'Really disappointed.'

Those black eyes looked at Thiya like they could see right through her. She fought the urge to shift under that stare.

'Who are you?' she asked again, but she knew. Deep down, she knew.

'I'm your Aunt Yesha.'

So, she was alive.

Thiya's world flashed red. 'What did you do to my brother? Leave him alone. Leave them all alone,' she cried, even as she leant against the wall to stay upright.

'Unfortunately, I can't do that.'

'What do you want?' Thiya eyed Hunar and Nikul who were just standing there. Waiting. It made the hairs lift on the back of her neck.

'I want you to come to Tumassi,' Yesha said. 'I thought you would have come here for your girlfriend, but Isaac clearly underestimated your affection for her.'

How dare she! 'I love Amara!'

'Then why are you hiding?' Yesha looked around and wrinkled Ravi's nose. 'Why are you not on your way to Tumassi?'

'I am.'

'You moved off the path. I tracked you down to Mengaru, but I don't know why you're here.' She waved Ravi's hand in a circle to encompass the house.

'How do you know where I've been?'

'I have my ways.'

'The daayan?'

'I created the daayan. I can control them if I wish.'

'You created them to destroy.'

'Oh no, I created them to survive, something your father could have easily helped me with. They destroy because that's how they survive. Really, Thiya, I thought you would understand that.' There was that disappointment again. It reminded Thiya of her mother.

'My father thought you were dead.'

'He would have known I wasn't when he saw the daayan,' Yesha said.

'How?'

'Because he knew what I could do, knew what he'd turned me into. He'd seen the daayan before. I'd used them on his command, to torture those who opposed him.

It was easy. A little bit of aether and I could manipulate his enemies into scratching themselves till they bled to death or get them to poke out their own eyeballs.'

'You're lying.' Her father was a kind, sweet man. There was no way he would advocate that kind of torture let alone command it.

'Why?' Yesha asked, keeping Ravi's voice calm. 'Because you don't want to believe your father could be so cruel? He let me create daayan. He let me terrorise this country. He's turned a blind eye to it as long as he could keep his family safe.'

'Then you're no better than him. Your daayan possessed people and then forced those people to kill others.'

Yesha moved Ravi's body closer to Thiya. 'I told you; I am not responsible for what the daayan do.' Yesha waved a dismissive hand and Thiya's gaze followed that hand down to Ravi's pocket. His light green kurta was slitted up to his thighs, and Thiya only needed to lift it a little to get to his bangle.

'Once I release them into the world, they are free to do as they wish, unless I choose to take back control.' Yesha smiled, viciously. 'It would take far too much of my energy to control them all. But I had to make an exception tonight because I wanted to see you myself.'

Thiya lunged for Ravi's pocket and pulled out the bangle before Yesha even had a chance to react.

Thiya punched Yesha with a swift uppercut to Ravi's jaw.

Ravi staggered back. Thiya took his arm and slipped the bangle over his wrist.

The darkness vanished and Ravi's brown eyes stared back at her.

'What in Khal's left testicle was that?' he asked, rubbing his jaw.

Kayan grunted and Thiya spun around to see him struggling to restrain Nikul. Hunar glanced from Thiya to the bangle on Ravi's wrist. He cocked his head.

'So that's how he hid you,' Yesha said from Hunar's mouth.

Thiya stared at Ravi's bangle, identical to her own. Her father had hidden her from the world – had hidden all of them.

'Why do you need me to come to Tumassi?' she asked instead. 'What do you want from me?'

'I told you,' Yesha huffed. 'I need your help.'

'With what?'

'I need you to help free me.'

'Why should I? You kidnapped my girlfriend.'

'Ah yes, Parag's descendant. I understand your anger, but you're mistaken. I did not take her just because she's your girlfriend. I have other uses for her.'

'Like what?'

'Her uncle was one of the mages who tried to kill me and the reason I am trapped. I promised myself revenge – that their families would pay.' Yesha reached out Hunar's hand towards Thiya's face but then thought better of it.

235

'I'm sorry you will be hurt, but this is the way it has to be. If it makes you feel any better, Parag is the last mage who needs to be punished.'

'Amara has done nothing wrong. Let her go.'

'You think I want to do this? My whole life, I have sacrificed myself for this country. My father knew I would be an aethani from the moment I was born. I trained with the best mages. Father wanted me to be the best, and I was. The people were in awe of me, and they loved me. I did everything my father asked. I banished our enemies; I healed this land and our country prospered. I even broke the laws of magic and healed my brother when no one thought it possible, and it was still not enough.' Her chest heaved, and the sound of Hunar's rapid breathing echoed across the quiet room.

'What do you mean, you broke the laws of magic?' Kayan asked, his hands gripping Nikul who struggled beside him.

Yesha spun Hunar around to face him. 'Aethani can heal, but we are not meant to bring back the dead. I could feel my brother slipping away, even as I tried to heal him. He was the only son. My father was adamant he could not die, even if the sky god willed it. He thought I wasn't trying hard enough. He thought I *wanted* my brother to die.'

Thiya almost felt sorry for her. Almost. She understood the pressure to be perfect. She'd dealt with her fair share of a parent's criticism.

'I told my father I wanted my brother to live, but the darkness that kept my magic balanced, that kept *me* balanced, was holding me back. He said, if I didn't want him to die, I would find a way. So, I did. I split my magic. I healed my brother. I brought him back to life.'

'How?' Kayan asked. 'That darkness is a part of you. You shouldn't be able to separate it from yourself.'

'It was hard, but not impossible, and once I figured it out, nothing could hold me back. I did things no aethani has ever been able to do before. My father was proud of me. My brother adored me. My people loved me. But when my father stepped down from the throne, he passed everything to my younger brother. His throne should have been mine. He wouldn't even be alive if it weren't for me. I sacrificed everything to do my father's bidding – I sacrificed having a husband and child for him – and he betrayed me. He'd promised to make me queen and he went back on his word. He decided I couldn't be an aethani and a queen.' Yesha approached Thiya. 'My father punished me for my magic, and your father will do the same to you, mark my words.'

Thiya swallowed.

'I'd had enough. I wasn't going to let my father or my brother use me any longer. I fled the palace, but my brother and his mages caught up with me at Sanathri Jungle. We fought, and I was trapped. I have waited years for you to free me. I've tried several times to get you here, but this time it seems to be working.'

Thiya thought of Yug wanting her to leave with him, and the daayan in the palace grounds who had asked her to follow. And then there had been the person who had killed her shara all those years ago. The person who had tried to take her.

'No.'

'Not even if I promise to release Amara?'

Thiya paused. 'Unharmed?'

'Don't,' Kayan warned.

Yesha stepped closer. 'You have my word.'

Amara wouldn't be in pain anymore. She could go home. Thiya could hold Amara in her arms.

Ravi nudged her arm. 'You cannot be considering this.'

'Of course she's not,' Lochan said. 'Right, Thiya?'

No, she wasn't. Was she? It was a stupid choice. They didn't know what Yesha would do once free, what destruction she could cause.

'What will you do if I free you?'

'She'll go after Father,' Lochan said. 'You can't—'

Thiya held up a hand to silence him.

'Naturally, your father will have to pay for what he did,' Yesha said.

'You'd kill him?'

'He doesn't deserve to rule this country. Our people deserve someone better.' Yesha used Hunar's hand to grab Thiya's.

'And that someone is you?' Thiya asked, incredulously.

'Who better to heal the country than an aethani? We

238

are healers after all. All I need is for you to free me, then we can create a great country, together.'

Thiya looked at their joined hands.

Yesha cared only about herself, but her father had always taught her the royal family served the people. Except her father had lied when he'd hidden her magic from her. And she had no doubt Yesha was lying now.

She extracted her hand from Yesha's. 'What if our people don't agree with you? What if they don't accept you as queen?'

'Why wouldn't they?'

Ravi snorted.

'You sent daayan after them,' Thiya said. 'You ruined their homes, their families, their livelihoods.'

Yesha moved closer, Hunar's nose inches from Thiya's. 'My brother did that!'

Ravi and Lochan moved, but Thiya held out her hands to stop them. Yesha wasn't going to hurt her if she needed her.

'If my father knew you were still alive and let our people suffer when he could have stopped it, he should answer for that. But you created the daayan. You made a choice to terrorise the citizens of this country.'

'I didn't have a choice.'

'You've always had a choice. You could have spoken to people, told them the truth like you're telling me now, but you chose vengeance and violence.'

Yesha slammed Hunar's fist into the wall next to

Thiya's head. 'Your father lied to his people for years. They wouldn't believe me.'

Ravi drew his sword, but Thiya stayed him with her hand again. 'What if they don't believe you now?'

'Sacrifices have to be made,' Yesha said, her voice soft. She backed up a step. 'It'll be for the best. You'll see. If you free me, I won't need to create more daayan.' She made it sound so reasonable – no daayan, Amara would be safe. Fewer people would get hurt.

'You can't free her,' Kayan shouted. Nikul was struggling to break free from his arms.

Yesha spun around to face Kayan.

'She's lying to you,' Kayan said. 'Amara won't be safe if she's freed.'

'I don't recall inviting you to join our conversation,' Yesha said. 'But if you're that desperate, let's see what you would do if the life of someone you love is on the line.'

Nikul threw Kayan off him and marched to the dining room door. He turned the doorknob and pushed. The door rattled on its hinges but didn't open.

Nikul slammed his body against it. From inside, Thiya heard a muffled scream.

Thiya saw Nikul ram into the door again. The door splintered.

Hiral screamed.

Someone shouted Thiya's name.

Lochan tried to grab Nikul's wrist and put his bangle on him, but Nikul pushed him away. Ravi cursed.

Then Hunar was there and he ripped the door off its hinges with his magic. The door crashed onto the ground. Thiya glimpsed Dipti shielding Hiral with her body before Nikul and Hunar both went up in flames.

23

Thiya didn't sleep well that night. Dipti's screams rang in Thiya's ears, her anguish at losing her eldest son sending a sharp pain through Thiya's chest. Hiral's tear-stained face haunted her dreams. And Chirag…

Chirag's death had hit Thiya harder than she'd expected. She knew the shara were there to protect her family and she knew shara dying for them was a possibility, but she'd never really thought much about it beyond an abstract idea. Chirag had a family. He'd had a wife and two sons under five. He had a mother who struggled to walk. They would never see him again. And it was all her fault.

She flipped over in bed, her hands curling under her pillow. The diya on the bedside table flickered then stilled. She hadn't been able to blow out the flame. It was the first time since she was a child that she'd had to sleep with a light – not that she was sleeping.

Thiya glanced at the navy-blue shutters. In her bedroom at the palace, she would have heard the waves crashing against the cliff edge. Here there was silence – silence which gave free rein to her thoughts.

Yug, Chirag, Nikul, Hunar and Prem, all dead: she was endangering everyone who tried to help her.

Thiya pressed her face into her pillow and screamed. There were so many things she could have done differently.

Maybe everyone would have been fine if she had asked Chirag for help. Or if she had accepted her magic sooner, maybe she would have been strong enough to stop Yesha.

Or maybe she would have got others killed instead.

She flipped onto her back and closed her eyes, hoping sleep would catch up with her this time, but Chirag's face danced behind her eyelids. She saw the way his face twisted in pain a moment before the flames consumed him.

Did Kayan blame himself for Chirag's death? Or Nikul or Hunar's?

None of them had been his fault. They'd been hers. And Yesha's.

Thiya had thought Yesha had messed up a spell when she'd been backed into a corner in Sanathri Jungle all those years ago.

But Yesha had wanted to attack Thiya, her friends and family. She'd wanted to kill Chirag and Nikul, even though she pretended otherwise. She'd taken away Kayan's chance to repair his relationship with his brother. And she held Amara's life in her hands.

Thiya was nothing like Aunt Yesha. She would never choose to harm someone.

Even if it would save Amara's life?

She couldn't free Yesha to save Amara. There was far too much at stake. She knew it. And yet the thought of Amara dying made her chest squeeze.

By the time Lochan knocked on her door, Thiya's eyes burned from lack of sleep.

'The sun will be up soon,' Lochan said. 'Get dressed and meet us in the kitchen.' He paused and frowned at her appearance. 'You look terrible, by the way.'

'Thank you.' It wasn't like he looked much better. There were dark circles under his eyes and his curls were matted and tangled.

'You're welcome.' He walked away.

Thiya retreated into the room and closed the door.

Someone had left clothes for her on the dressing table. She shook them out to reveal thick brown leggings and a dark green cotton kurta. After she'd changed, she folded her borrowed pyjamas and left them on the bed. She slipped on her boots, buckled her weapons into place and headed downstairs.

A single torch was lit in the hallway, but it was enough for Thiya to see the signs of the fight from last night. The door from the office was now propped up against the main entrance, the hinges melted along the edge to keep the door in place. Shattered pieces of the plant pot and mud were scattered across the floor, and there were scorch marks along the walls. She spotted her dagger amongst the mess and she bent down to pick it up from a pool of dried blood.

She stared at the blood for a moment, numb, before she slid it into its sheath on her thigh.

She followed the smell of cardamom, cinnamon and ginger to a small room at the back of the house, not far from the dining room.

The kitchen was made from the same pink stone as the rest of the house and the light from the torches along the wall made it look bright and airy, despite the shutters being pulled closed over the windows. Lochan and Ravi were already seated on a small wooden table directly in front of the doorway, and Kayan and his mother were behind the counter. Dipti looked up with red-rimmed eyes when Thiya entered.

'Would you like some chai?' she asked, gesturing to the steaming saucepan on the stove. Next to the saucepan was a tava where it looked like Kayan was cooking thepla. A pile was stacked onto a plate on the other side of the counter where Kayan rolled out more dough for the spiced flatbread.

When Thiya nodded, Dipti poured some into a mug and passed it to Thiya along with a bowl of jaggery. Thiya added a pea-sized amount of the sugar to her chai and took a sip. The liquid warmed her insides as it slid down to her stomach. Thiya sank into the chair next to Lochan and took another sip.

'I told you the bangle would keep me safe,' Ravi said.

'But you weren't able to put it on yourself.'

'Then it's a good thing my sister loves me.' He removed his bangle to take a closer look. 'Remember, it's right—' he choked.

His eyes turned black. Grey veins spread through Ravi's body, and Lochan scrambled back, his chair scraping across the stone floor. The bangle slipped between Ravi's fingers and clattered onto the table.

The daayan had been there lurking since last night, ready to take over Ravi's body. Her energy now recovered, Thiya reached for her magic and looped the threads around the daayan inside Ravi. Darkness exploded out of him like confetti.

Ravi sucked in a sharp breath and then another. He touched his chest and his forehead, the table and his tea. He took a large gulp of the chai then spat it out when it burnt his tongue.

He pressed his hand over his chest. 'What in Khal's left testicle just happened?'

Kayan had come around the counter. He picked up the bangle and examined it, slipping it over his hand then removing it again.

'You put this on after you were possessed.'

'I put it on him,' Thiya said.

Ravi nodded. His throat bobbed like he was trying to hold back tears.

'The bangle suppresses magic. It must have suppressed the daayan inside you as well. Bought you time until Thiya could destroy it.' He handed the bangle back to Ravi. 'Keep this safe.'

'Kayan…' Lochan said.

'Don't. I know you're sorry, but there is nothing you have to be sorry for. You tried to save Nikul with your own bangle. That you risked your life to try means the world.'

Everything had happened too fast for Thiya to keep track of, but she remembered Lochan trying to give Nikul his bangle, the daayan-possessed Nikul fighting him off and Kayan making a split-second decision to protect his mother and sister. There was nothing Lochan could have done.

A sharp clang from the counter caught Thiya's attention. Kayan rushed back to his mother's side. He picked up a cloth to wipe away the spilled tea while Dipti turned her back on them, her shoulders shaking on a sob.

'Why does the magic in the bangle still work?' Ravi asked. He held the bangle between pinched fingers and frowned. 'Lochan's sword ran out of magic during the attack yesterday. Why didn't the bangle? It's been around much longer. The magic should have run out by now.'

'The bangle was made using all five elements,' Kayan said. He wrung out the cloth and hung it to dry over the edge of the sink. 'The magic is balanced. It's able to sustain itself. The swords only contain one element. Sometimes two. Without that balance, the magic eventually burns out.'

'Could we make some more?' Lochan asked.

'It would take more time than we have. Especially since we only have one aethani.' In other words, the only way to protect the citizens of Agraal was to stop Yesha. Now all Thiya needed to figure out was how she was going to do that. Last night hadn't been easy.

Dipti managed to stop her tears and shoo Kayan away from the stove. He glanced at the shuttered windows. 'The sun is almost up.'

'Good.' Dipti sounded determined as she marched towards the door. Kayan followed.

Thiya hadn't noticed the shrouded bodies beside the door until now. Five of them, waiting to receive their last rites.

Lochan and Ravi stood. Thiya followed a second later.

Lochan pressed a backpack into her hands. 'The servants packed them for us,' he said.

Thiya glanced over, wanting to thank Dipti but she had already opened the back door and headed outside. Thiya could make out her silhouette against the grey sky.

Dipti and Kayan moved the bodies onto the lawn, laying them side by side.

Last rites were always performed at dawn, allowing the release of the deceased's soul into Gayan's care, and it seemed Kayan wanted to observe them before they left. Thiya didn't blame him. As much as she wanted to be on her way, she owed it to Ravi's shara, Chirag and Yug to make sure their souls didn't wander the earth for eternity. So, she stood beside Kayan and Dipti and her brothers while Kayan set the bodies alight to release their souls. And she sang the prayers asking Gayan for a peaceful transition to the next life.

The sun hadn't fully crested the horizon by the time the last rights had been completed and they were ready to leave. Ravi and the shara had arrived on their own horses, and Thiya held the reins to Chirag's brown horse.

Kayan laid a hand on his mother's arm. 'I'll come back as soon as I can.'

'Stop the daayan,' Dipti said, jerking her chin in the air. 'Get justice for Nikul.'

Kayan nodded then pulled his mother into a hug and kissed her cheek. When they broke apart, Dipti hugged Thiya.

'I've put some pads in the front of your pack,' she whispered in Thiya's ear. Heat flooded Thiya's cheeks. She'd forgotten about her monthly bleeds, but she'd be due soon.

'I'm sorry—' Thiya wanted to apologise for what happened to Nikul, but she couldn't find the words.

She shook her head. 'You take care of yourself,' she said in that warm, scolding voice only a mother knew. Then she turned and walked back into the house without another word.

Thiya climbed onto the horse.

Ravi's eyes widened. 'You're not afraid of horses?'

'I was never afraid of horses,' Thiya said as her new horse followed Kayan out the gate.

'But Mother said… Ah, is this another one of your power struggles with her?' Ravi asked. 'A way for you to assert your independence?'

Thiya blinked.

Ravi shrugged. 'What? I notice things.'

Clearly. First Amara, now their mother. Thiya wasn't sure she liked Ravi knowing her secrets.

'What's the plan when we get to Tumassi?' Lochan asked. 'Yesha has to know Thiya's not going to help her.' Lochan looked at Thiya. 'You're not going to free her, right?'

'Of course not.'

'Good, because our priority is to stop Yesha,' Kayan said, his voice hard.

Thiya's fingers tightened on the saddle. 'And find Amara? You promised to save her in exchange for my help.'

Kayan twisted so he could look at her. 'I will do everything I can to save Amara,' he said, 'but this is bigger than one person.' The same hardness in his voice was mirrored in his expression and Thiya knew deep down he was right. But this was Amara he was talking about.

'Yesha knows you,' he said. 'She will expect you to save Amara at any cost. It's what you've always done. It's why she offered you that choice to save her. She'll use Amara again to force your hand. You need to ignore it.'

But how was she meant to ignore Amara?

'Can you do this?' Kayan asked. 'There is no point going to Tumassi if you can't. If you release Yesha, this country will be in a far worse situation than it's in now.'

'I can do this,' she said, trying to inject as much confidence into her voice as possible. She would find a way to save Amara while defeating Yesha. She would do both.

'Good.' Kayan nodded. 'The best way to stop Yesha is to contain her magic and stop her from making more daayan. Then we can deal with eliminating the daayan already in existence. Would one of you be willing to part with your bangle?'

'Didn't you try that already?' Thiya asked.

'Yes, but Isaac and I were too evenly matched. It was impossible to get close to him. I think I know another way to make this work, if I can get a bangle.'

'You can use mine,' Lochan said.

'Actually, you should wear yours. We can use Ravi's,' Thiya said.

'Why can't we use yours?' Ravi countered.

'Kayan lost it, and if you're wearing your bangle you won't be able to use your water magic.'

'She has a point,' Lochan said.

'I can barely use my water magic now,' Ravi said.

'You just need to practise,' Kayan said. 'I can teach you while I teach Thiya how to magically restrain Yesha so we can slip the bangle over her wrist. It will be the best way to stop her.'

'I already know how to keep Yesha from fleeing. I'll hold a dagger to her throat.' Thiya patted her thigh to check her dagger was still there. 'Let's see her move after that.'

'And what will you do when she kills Amara before you manage to get the bangle over her wrist? Or she sends daayan after you or Lochan or someone else you love?'

'Well, how do you suggest I stop her?' Thiya asked.

'You need to hold her with your own magic. Control her body, her muscles. Her magic.'

'Act like a daayan?' Thiya wasn't sure she liked this idea.

'No.'

'Are you sure? Because it sounds like I need to act like a daayan.'

Kayan huffed. 'If you want to think of it that way, fine, but you are not going to be keeping control. You won't be destroying Yesha or using her to hurt others. I only need you to hold Yesha long enough for us to slip the bangle over her wrist, so we can restrain her.'

'So, no pressure.' So much of this plan depended on Thiya.

'You just need to practise,' Kayan repeated. 'Let's focus on Ravi.'

'Excuse me? Why am I the practice target?'

'I can't be the target because I have to guide the horse,' Kayan said.

'Then I volunteer Lochan.'

Kayan shook his head, and Thiya was sure he was hiding a smile. 'Lochan has no magic, and we want Thiya to be able to hold Yesha's magic as well as her body. Thiya needs to practise on a mage.'

'Sorry, brother,' Lochan said, not bothering to hide his grin.

'Why don't we start with you,' Kayan said. 'I want you to pull water into your hands.'

252

'I want to shoot icicles,' Ravi said.

'We can get to that, but for now it's easier for mages to channel magic through our hands and you need to learn how to control yours.'

When Ravi started to collect water in his palms, Kayan told Thiya to concentrate on Ravi and his magic. With Kayan's guidance, she saw inside Ravi, saw the way his blood pumped around his body and the way his muscles moved. She saw how his whole body connected and the sheer complexity took her breath away.

She took hold of Ravi's body. Her magic slid into his muscles and forced them to stop. Ravi stiffened for a second before fatigue washed over Thiya and she was forced to release her magic. Kayan encouraged her to try again, but holding a person in place was harder than Thiya had anticipated. She couldn't shake the feeling she was going to let everyone down. Again.

24

No matter how much Thiya practised that night, her magical abilities barely improved. She still couldn't hold Ravi for more than a few seconds. Yesha's magic was stronger than his and she knew how to use it in ways Thiya couldn't even imagine. There had to be another way.

'How do I split my magic like Yesha did?' she asked.

Kayan spluttered, the water he'd been drinking spraying across Ravi who was sat opposite him in the tent. 'You don't.' He swiped the back of his hand over his mouth.

Ravi grumbled and shuffled closer to Lochan, who was supposed to be keeping watch. Thiya was sure this tent was smaller than the other one. That tent had felt small with the three of them. This one was suffocating with four.

'What if that's the only way to stop Yesha?'

Kayan shook his head. 'It can't be done. Yesha is lying.'

'Come on, Thiya, do you really think she brought Father back from the dead?' Ravi asked. 'She's delusional.'

'The daayan are made from the dark part of aether. How did she create them if she didn't split her magic?'

'All the more reason for you to not split your magic. It's a violation of nature,' Kayan said.

'But—'

'I wouldn't even know where to begin teaching you how to split your magic,' Kayan admitted. 'I'd never even heard of such a thing before last night. Light cannot exist without the dark.'

But the daayan were made from dark aether and they could clearly exist without the light.

'We already have a way to stop Yesha,' Lochan said. 'You don't need to destroy yourself to do it.'

Except their plans relied on her being able to master something she was still struggling to do. And she only had another day to learn.

'You don't need to become Aunt Yesha,' Ravi said. 'We can stop her together.'

They set off again early the next morning, and Thiya got to work practising her magic once again. She was determined to succeed.

Ravi coughed and spluttered as Thiya forced him to pull water from the air and drench himself. He had been volunteered again.

'I think we can agree Thiya has the hang of that,' Ravi said, spitting water out of his mouth.

Thiya didn't know why he was grumbling. He was getting on better with his magic than she was with hers. He could still only pull small droplets out of the air, but he could aim them and accelerate them with enough force to cause minor injuries. Thiya had already healed a fracture Ravi's water power had caused on Lochan's cheek.

She shifted in the saddle. The closer they got to Tumassi, the snippier Ravi became. Thiya couldn't blame him. There was a stillness to the air that set her on edge.

'Yes, I think she's getting there.' Kayan smiled. Thiya had managed to force him to conjure fire earlier. She'd also held Kayan's magic as he tried (and failed) to conjure flames. And not just for a second. She had lasted a minute before she thought she would collapse. She could have held on longer if she hadn't been afraid of falling off the horse.

It was like the magic spoke to her, invited her inside. It wanted her to use it.

It was with a renewed sense of vigour that they entered Tumassi that evening as the sun started to make its descent. Unlike the other larger towns and cities, there was no one standing guard along the main road, checking to see if they'd been possessed by daayan. In a town full of mages, there wasn't much point.

Tumassi looked like a town, the peaks of the Dhandra Mountains rising behind it to the west. Thiya knew it had been a town at some point before she was born, before the daayan. But now, buildings rose up in front of her in various states of disrepair. A restaurant had its windows broken and a dress shop still had mannequins in the display, the clothes faded and dusty.

Kayan led the way down the wide streets and into a

residential area. He stopped in front of a house where the front wall had been knocked out and replaced with large wooden doors.

The doors were shut, but Kayan dismounted and pulled them open. Thiya scrambled off her horse and led him inside behind Kayan. Lochan and Ravi followed.

The house had been converted into stables. Thiya could still see the foundations of the interior rooms that had existed before, but now straw lined the floor.

'Who's there?' a man asked from inside.

'It's just me.' Kayan moved further into the room. 'I brought some horses with me. Can you take care of them? They've had a long journey.'

'Sure thing.'

Thiya heard the man get up. He came into view a second later as he started rummaging through some feed. He had on the black uniform of a mage with the white cuffs of an airu. An air mage.

'Where'd they come from?' the airu asked.

'The palace,' Ravi said. 'They need to go back.'

The airu raised an eyebrow, but all he said was, 'I'll make a note.' He headed to the other side of the room. Kayan, Lochan and Ravi removed the saddles and bridles of the horses and put them away.

'Who are your friends?' the airu asked. 'I haven't seen them before.'

Kayan paused, considered his options then said, 'Prince Lochan, Prince Ravi and Princess Thiya.'

257

'Only mages are allowed in Tumassi, you know that.'

'I am a mage.' Ravi puffed out his chest again.

'You try telling them to leave,' Kayan said.

The airu looked between the three of them and swallowed. Clearly, he didn't want to disobey rules but the three of them outranked him. 'I need to check this with Captain Nirvan.'

'You go do that.' Kayan strode from the room before the airu could respond and Thiya rushed to follow him out of the stables. He headed down the road.

'Should we be worried?' Thiya asked.

Kayan shook his head. 'Not till morning. The captain will be on the front line now, and if we manage to stop Yesha tonight, the rules won't matter.' Kayan rounded a corner and headed down another street.

Night had truly fallen. The streetlamps remained dark and the shutters had been pulled tight across windows. The only light came from stars scattered across the sky, the faint light picking out the edges of houses and trees. The night of the new moon. Yesha's plans for Amara were happening tonight and Thiya *had* to stop her.

Kayan's steps never faltered. Light flashed across the sky. An explosion rumbled in the distance.

'What was that?' Thiya asked.

'Daayan,' Kayan said without pause.

'Daayan don't explode like that.'

'No, but our weapons do.'

'Weapons?' Ravi asked, his eyes alight.

258

'You'll see,' was all Kayan said.

Kayan stopped at another house that looked like it had been converted for storage. He emerged quickly with several weapons tucked into his arms and led them to a nondescript house in the middle of an unremarkable street. The house was as dark and quiet as the others, but Kayan set the torches alight before guiding them up the stairs and into a bedroom on the second floor.

The room was stark, with nothing but a bed in one corner, a wardrobe in another and a chest of drawers pushed under shuttered windows. There were no signs anyone lived here, and yet Kayan headed straight to the wardrobe and pulled out two sets of mages' uniforms. He threw one at Thiya and another at Ravi and told them to put them on.

'You'll be safe here for tonight,' he told Lochan.

Lochan shook his head. 'I'm not staying behind.'

'The front is not safe for anyone who's not a mage,' Kayan said, clasping Lochan's hand.

The front line, where the explosion had come from. Where the daayan were. Thiya should have been scared, and yet her magic was humming, as if it had found its sense of purpose.

Lochan jerked his chin high. 'I'm not staying behind,' he repeated.

Lochan had always been by Thiya's side, whenever she'd needed him, even when he didn't agree with her. He'd never let her down, and they wouldn't have got this far without him. He deserved to see this through to the end.

'He's coming with us,' she said, cutting off Kayan's protests. She held up the uniform. 'Where can I change?'

Kayan scowled and, for a moment, Thiya thought he was going to argue some more. Then he sighed. 'There's a bedroom next door you can use.'

Kayan had lit the torch in this room, and Thiya could see it was similar to the first in terms of sparse furnishings and lack of personality, though there was a scorch mark on the ceiling Thiya didn't look at too closely. But at least this room looked lived in. The quilt had been thrown back and was half falling onto the floor and there was a pile of night clothes in the centre of the bed.

Thiya changed into a black silk undershirt, black leather trousers and a black leather jacket with red cuffs. The leather was thinner and softer than she'd expected, and the mage's uniform moulded to her skin. It was a little big around the shoulders but otherwise a decent fit that didn't hinder her movements.

The uniform was warm, but not hot. Maybe because night had brought a drop in temperature that was already leaching the heat from the house. She wondered if it would be as comfortable during the day. Would she survive to find out?

She made her way back to the other room. The door was ajar, so she pushed it open and walked inside.

Everyone had changed into black mages' uniforms, including Lochan. He tugged awkwardly at the red cuffs, his back to Kayan.

'Thank the gods you're back,' Ravi said, jumping up from where he'd been perched on the edge of Kayan's bed. 'I hate lovers' tiffs. Never leave me alone with these two again. Kayan is still trying to convince Lochan to stay here and it's cute and disgusting.' He pulled a face and pretended to shudder.

'We weren't having a lovers' tiff,' Lochan said, his ears turning pink.

Ravi raised a brow. 'Then what would you call it?'

The red deepened. 'Why would you—' Lochan looked from Kayan to the floor. 'What do you—'

Kayan was fighting a smile. Ravi loved teasing Lochan as much as he loved teasing her. Thiya would have loved it too, except they didn't have the time.

She cleared her throat. 'Shall we go?'

Lochan nodded.

'Are you sure you won't stay?' Kayan asked. Lochan glared at him, and Kayan held up his hands. 'I thought I'd ask one more time, but if you're going to be stubborn, at least take this.' Kayan held out a sheathed sword. 'I enchanted it myself. Took me two years of practice before I could get it to work.'

Lochan blinked rapidly a few times. 'Thank you,' he said, his voice thick with emotion. He took the sword and clipped the scabbard onto his belt.

Ravi mimed throwing up. Thiya whacked his arm.

Kayan attached a pair of manacles to his own belt. 'For Yesha.'

'Let's go,' Lochan said, and Thiya wondered if he was scared of being left behind. He trudged down the stairs and the rest of them followed. Kayan held out four pairs of glasses with darkened lenses.

'Put these on,' he said, handing them a pair each.

Thiya stared at them. She'd seen soldiers and shara wearing them during the day, but they weren't common, and especially not at night.

'What are they for?'

'Do you remember the flashes you saw in the sky?' Kayan asked. Thiya nodded. 'These stop them from blinding you.'

Thiya slipped on the glasses.

'Now you're ready for the front line,' Kayan said.

25

The front line separated the town from Sanathri Jungle. It was a literal line made up of mages, mostly feiraani, but with a few airu, aquira and terrai thrown in. Thiya first saw them when they walked past the last building in town, standing in the empty field facing the jungle.

Sanathri Jungle was nothing like Thiya had ever imagined. She'd heard the stories, but it wasn't just made of darkness, it seemed to absorb what little light tried to penetrate, like a void.

For the first time since she escaped the palace, she hesitated. The jungle looked like it would have swallowed Amara whole the moment she entered.

The jungle unsettled the mages as well. They looked tense. Thiya noticed all of them wore dark glasses.

Shadows shifted amongst the trees, twisting and reforming. Mocking. Not as dark as she'd originally thought, but more sinister. A chill rippled down Thiya's spine.

The shadows twisted away from the trees, rising higher into the sky like a cloud of darkness.

'Hold.' Someone yelled down the line. A few mages shifted forward, but no one moved. Even Thiya stopped, the mounting tension keeping her in place.

The cloud broke, the smaller pockets of darkness

drawing closer. They were halfway across the field when Thiya realised what they were.

Daayan.

Thiya had thought the daayan attack at Kayan's home had been scary, but this was more chaotic. The daayan were unfocused and not in sync like they had been in Mengaru, and they bumped into each other as they crossed the field. And there were just more of them.

Her magic hummed louder, demanding to be used. She reached for it, but Kayan stalled her with a hand on her shoulder.

'Wait,' he said.

'Now,' someone shouted and light exploded in front of them. Even with the sunglasses, Thiya had to turn away. She blinked a few times, the remnants of light plastered to the back of her eyelids.

'What in Khal's name was that?'

'A flash,' Kayan said.

'Of course. A flash. That makes complete sense. What a great explanation.'

'It's a combination of chemicals that create an ultra-bright light. We set them up on the field during the day and airus knock the containers together when we need them. The light disorientates the daayan. Look.'

Thiya followed his pointed finger to see daayan disappearing back into the jungle. Only a few continued towards the line of waiting mages – more than Thiya had ever seen together, but fewer than the initial swarm.

'This way,' Kayan said, nudging Thiya to the left. Thiya already had her magic in her hands but Kayan placed his hand over them. 'The daayan will continue to come. If you want to stop them, you need to get to the source. Remember?'

But before they knew it, daayan were upon them. Fire erupted from the line of feiraanis – streams of flames rushing out to meet the daayan. Behind them, more daayan emerged from the jungle. Thiya's magic sang in her veins. The threads rose to the surface without conscious thought, wanting her to destroy the daayan, but they'd discussed this already. They needed to stop Yesha to stop the daayan.

This time when Kayan urged her forward, she went. They walked behind the line of mages. They needed to reach the edge so they could sneak past the front line and into the jungle. But Thiya kept her magic in hand, just in case.

A daayan fled from the feiraanis' fire in front of her, and Thiya thought it had returned to the jungle. Several twisted and darted around the flames, searching for a way through. Thiya didn't see the one slinking along the ground until it reared up before an unsuspecting mage and took possession of their body.

Fire curled in the possessed mage's hand. Her eyes flashed black in the light of the flames. Thiya aimed her magic at the daayan inside, just as the possessed mage spun around and took aim at the person beside her. Thiya's aether destroyed the daayan, black sparks exploding out of her skin just as a terrai opened up the ground and swallowed the once-possessed mage whole.

Thiya stared at the place where the possessed mage had been. She waited for the outrage, but no one noticed one feiraani disappearing into the ground and, if they did, they didn't care. Even Kayan continued walking past, a reminder that she had to get to the source. Helping one mage wouldn't help them all.

Kayan skirted around where the once-possessed mage was now buried and continued down the line. Before they could head into the jungle, fire flashed in front of them. The feiraanis on the front line had joined their magic together to create a web of fire in the hopes of catching a couple of daayan. The web moved and swirled in unison, never breaking its shape. But the daayan were fast. Thiya could barely follow them as they darted through the sky, testing the defences.

Another flash went off further down the line, but Thiya ignored it because more daayan were streaming their way, blocking their path to the jungle.

A web of fire to Thiya's right faltered as the daayan approached, a few fiery strands directly overhead pulling away from the others.

'Sajan! Concentrate!' a mage at the end of the line shouted.

A dark shadow almost made it through the gap, but the mage who had faltered regained his concentration and the net spun, caught the flailing strands and reformed.

Thiya had never used her magic against this many daayan before. She didn't even know if it would work, but she had to try to help. They'd never make it into the jungle otherwise.

Thiya pulled at strands of magic and wrapped it around the nearest daayan. The daayan exploded, the drops of darkness disappearing into the night, but two more took its place. She pulled more magic and destroyed several daayan nearby, but the moment they exploded, more pushed in from behind.

Kayan pressed a hand on her shoulder. 'You'll tire yourself out before we even get to Yesha. The mages are trained to handle the daayan.'

Thiya didn't feel tired. She felt invigorated. But she knew the exhaustion would catch up to her later. She let the magic drop and sent out a silent prayer to any gods listening to protect the mages.

But Kayan was right, the mages did know what they were doing. As daayan escaped the fiery nets, airus blew them back inside. The daayan faded under the relentless magical attack.

Kayan moved toward the jungle – until a feiraani blocked their path.

Kayan stopped instead of going around the mage, and Thiya dug her heels in to avoid crashing into his back.

'Kayan!' the feiraani barked. Kayan stood up straighter. 'Where have you been? I expected you back several days ago.'

Kayan inclined his head. 'Captain Nirvan.'

So, this was the man who ran Tumassi. Thiya had never met him. She'd been expecting a beast of a man, but he looked like a swift gust of wind would knock him over. Though he had to be an impressive mage to earn the position of captain – and to have survived so long in Tumassi.

'I'm sorry I'm late, sir,' Kayan said, his tone full of respect. 'I was unavoidably delayed.'

'Unavoidable, huh?' His eyes flicked from Kayan to Thiya and her brothers. 'Where's Isaac?'

'He came on ahead. We're trying to locate him.'

And then Thiya planned to teach him a very painful lesson about what happened to people who hurt Amara.

The captain nodded, before his eyes swung to Thiya. 'Who are you?'

'Thiya.'

'Well, Thiya, I know all the mages in this town. So, what are you doing here?'

At that moment, a flash exploded behind him, lighting up the night sky and another swarm of daayan emerged from the jungle. It was smaller than the first attack, but still more than the mages were used to judging by their exclamations.

The feiraani had their fiery nets up across the line before the light from the flash had faded. The captain shouted orders.

A daayan broke through the mage's defences and

headed for them. Thiya destroyed it, the darkness showering out around them as the daayan exploded.

'What was that?' the captain snapped.

'She's an aethani,' Kayan said.

The captain's eyebrows shot up. 'This was the reason for your delay?'

'Yes, sir.'

The captain turned his shrewd gaze on Thiya. 'Well done,' he told Kayan.

Kayan's head snapped up. 'Sir?'

'Thiya, we can station you at the centre of the line, so you can see everything that's happening. I'll have the runners constantly bring you updates in case you miss anything. Maybe we can get the airus to fly you from one end of the field to the other, just in case…'

Blood pounded in her ears, as he rambled on.

'No,' she said.

The captain cut off and stared at her.

'I'm not here to stop the daayan,' she said. 'I mean, I am, but…'

'She's going to stop the source, in the jungle,' Ravi said.

The excitement slipped off Captain Nirvan's face. 'I cannot let you go into the jungle.'

'With all due respect, sir, you don't have the authority to stop me.'

The captain puffed out his chest. 'I am in charge of all mages in Tumassi.'

'Except me.'

'And me.' Ravi stepped closer to Thiya.

The captain's lips curled before recognition dawned. 'Prince Ravi, Prince Lochan and you must be Princess Thiya?' He paused. 'You're right, I cannot stop you, but most people who go into Sanathri Jungle never come out again.'

'So I've heard,' Thiya said.

'You have a gift. You can do so much good here.'

'I can,' Thiya agreed, 'but it's a temporary solution. To stop the daayan, I need to stop the source – my Aunt Yesha.' It was also the only way to save Amara, but he didn't need to know that.

'Yesha is dead.'

'No, she's not. This is her doing.' Thiya pointed to the new swarm of daayan that emerged from the jungle to join the others.

Captain Nirvan's eyes widened. 'That's impossible.'

'It's not,' Kayan said. 'And we're pretty sure she's getting ready to take over the country.'

'Is that why your family is finally getting involved?' The captain looked between Thiya and her brothers, his eyebrows furrowing.

'We didn't know—' She shook her head. 'It doesn't matter. We both want the same thing – to stop the daayan. But to do that, I need to stop Yesha.'

'I want to keep my mages alive to see another day. Let your brothers sort out your family's mess. You stay here and help them.' He jerked his finger towards the mages.

Thiya shook her head.

A mage shouted in the distance. The captain glanced over his shoulder to see daayan swooping in for another attack.

'Are you going to abandon them like your father?' Captain Nirvan asked.

'That's not fair,' Ravi said.

'No, that's not fair.' The captain pointed at a mage who had just been possessed by a daayan. Grey veins started to spread up his neck. Thiya reached for her magic but a feiraani set the mage on fire, a terrai buried the body and another mage took his place. The process was almost as efficient as the daayan, but that one second where the fiery net faltered allowed another daayan to slip through the defences. Thiya wrapped her magic around the daayan and it exploded.

Dizziness took hold. She shook her head and the feeling dissipated, but there were more daayan. She didn't have the endurance of these mages. She wouldn't last an hour out here, let alone an entire night.

And Amara still needed her.

Thiya pushed past the captain and ran towards the jungle before he could stop her.

26

Captain Nirvan's shouts followed Thiya, but she didn't dare look back. Amara was in the jungle. She just knew it. She wasn't sure if it was intuition or magic. Khal, it could have been wishful thinking, but she had to follow it through.

She ran along the road leading into the jungle, careful to watch her step. At one point, this road had linked Agraal to Kakodha, their neighbour to the north, but now the road warped and bubbled where weeds and grass had pushed through the surface.

Before long, she heard footsteps behind her.

'It's us,' Kayan said.

A weight lifted off Thiya's shoulders. At least she didn't have to face Yesha alone.

'The captain was so angry,' Ravi chuckled. 'You should have seen his face.'

'Not the right time,' Lochan said. To Thiya's surprise, Ravi stopped speaking.

A daayan dived for Kayan. Kayan shot fire at the daayan and it rolled like a ball, changing direction in mid-air before shooting itself like an arrow at Thiya. Thiya wrapped magical threads around the daayan and squeezed. By the time the daayan exploded, they were almost to the trees.

Another flash went off in the distance. Captain Nirvan shouted instructions, but Thiya didn't look back. The jungle was right in front of her, the shadows shifting and undulating between the trees.

She crashed through the first row of trees and skidded to a stop. She removed her glasses, but the darkness surrounding her was so thick, she still couldn't see her hand in front of her face. She spun around, but the town had disappeared. No wonder mages who entered the jungle never returned. Even tigers would get lost in here.

'What is this darkness?' Lochan asked, breathless.

Thiya knew what it was. She could feel that darkness clawing for her, snatching at her hair and clothes, trying to find a way inside. This was aether, the threads fragmented and frayed where someone had separated the darkness from the light. Her own magic reacted, wanting her to heal the damage.

'Aether,' Thiya said. It seemed to whisper Amara's name.

Kayan conjured flames and tossed them into the air, but the aether surrounding them was so thick, the flames cast little light on their path. Thiya's feet were swallowed by the darkness.

How had Isaac navigated this?

Thiya started down the path again.

'Am I the only one who thinks this is creepy?' Ravi asked.

The frayed threads of darkness made Thiya's stomach

churn, but she had no time to dwell on it. Amara needed her.

When she came to a fork in the path, she went right. She didn't know why, but it was knowledge that sprang to mind the same way she knew Amara was in the jungle or that the sky was blue.

'How do you know where you're going?' Lochan asked.

'I don't know, this way just feels right,' she said.

The same feeling told her to veer off the path. The trees were closer together here, and the ground uneven where the roots had pushed their way to the surface.

She continued forward, climbing over roots and squeezing between tree trunks to find her way.

Light flared overhead, lightening the darkness to a deep grey for a split second. A loud crash echoed through the trees.

Thiya turned right at another fork in the path.

'What if this is a trap?' Lochan asked.

Ravi snorted. 'Of course it's a trap.'

'Maybe we should slow down and think about this?' Lochan asked.

'If we want to find Yesha, we have to go this way,' Thiya said. Yesha would keep Amara close if she wanted to force Thiya's hand.

'Slow down and stay alert,' Kayan said. 'We have to find Yesha, but that doesn't mean we have to walk into this trap with our eyes closed.'

But Thiya couldn't slow her pace. Amara was so close. She felt it in every fibre of her being. Her hands scraped across bark as she pushed her way through the densely packed trees, but she ignored the burning pain.

She rounded another tree before running into a clearing. Lochan, Ravi and Kayan behind.

The aether was thinner here, and light from Kayan's flames penetrated further. At first, Thiya thought the clearing was empty, until she saw a denser mass lying on the ground in the centre.

Thiya gasped. The light from Kayan's flames picked out the silhouette of a woman Thiya would recognise anywhere, even if her clothes were wrinkled and her always immaculate hair hung in greasy clumps around her head.

Amara.

But she wasn't moving.

Amara could not die.

Thiya ran towards her, threads of magic already flowing into her hands, but Kayan pulled her back. She struggled to break free.

'Wait,' Kayan said. 'Where are Yesha and Isaac?'

Who cared? It was Amara. She was right there and she needed Thiya's help. Thiya wrapped a thread of magic around her. Amara's heartbeat sounded in her ear, faint but there.

Thiya's knees shook. She tried to move around Kayan, only for Lochan to block her path. 'Yesha wants you to save her. She's counting on it.'

'I *am* saving her.' She moved to the other side, but Ravi was there, stubborn and immovable.

'Khal's bloody behind! Move!'

Amara's breath rattled in her lungs and Thiya wanted to cry.

'I'm sorry,' Ravi said.

Thiya screamed in sheer frustration.

Light flashed above the clearing, three times in quick succession. The distant sound of the explosions reverberated through the air and drowned out her scream.

'You need to stop the daayan,' Kayan said. 'You're the only one who can. Remember our plan. Stop Yesha, then save Amara.'

Except that had been Kayan's plan, not Thiya's. *She* was going to save Amara. Amara's fingers twitched, almost like she was reaching out for Thiya. Thiya couldn't ignore her.

She grabbed threads of magic and searched for the darkness within Amara.

'I wouldn't do that if I were you,' Isaac said.

Kayan, Lochan and Ravi spun around. Thiya saw Isaac detach himself from a tree and walk into the clearing, stopping just behind Amara.

'Yesha doesn't take kindly to people who go back on their word. She'll kill your girlfriend before you can save her.' The darkness within Amara stirred in response to Isaac's threat and she whimpered.

Thiya dropped her magic. 'I never agreed to Yesha's deal.'

'Even if it's the only way to save your girlfriend?' Isaac taunted.

'Who are you?' Ravi said with his trademark sneer.

'Isaac.' Kayan's voice was rough with emotion.

'We met at the ball,' Isaac said.

'Did we?'

'That's the problem with you royals—'

Thiya stopped listening. Amara was trying to lift her head. Thiya pushed through the gap between Ravi and Kayan and ran for her.

Amara's lips moved, forming words Thiya couldn't hear. It wasn't until she was close that she heard the word. 'Run.'

But Thiya was not abandoning Amara now.

She reached for her hand.

The aether within Amara dug into her flesh, causing pain and she hissed.

Thiya clenched her fists. She reached for her magic, wrapped a thread around Isaac and pushed. His back hit the ground.

'Release her.' She grabbed Amara's arm and pulled at the vine bangle, but it held her too tight. Thiya's fingers couldn't find purchase on the vine to rip it off.

'No.' Isaac jumped to his feet.

'Where's Yesha?' They were all here because of her. She should at least have the decency to appear.

'Yesha will show herself when she's ready.'

'This is ridiculous.' Ravi gathered a ball of water in

front of him and threw it at Isaac. Isaac bent a leafy tree to intercept the water.

Lochan drew his sword.

'Stop,' Isaac said. 'Or she dies.'

A branch from a nearby tree wrapped around Amara's neck and jerked her upwards. Her feet kicked out into thin air.

27

Amara's fingers clutched at the branch around her neck, trying to pull it away.

'Stop!' Thiya cried. 'Stop using her to get to me.' She should have listened to her brothers and Kayan. She should have known she would make everything worse, and now Amara was being strangled in front of her and there was nothing she could do.

A flash lit the sky. The sound rumbled through the earth.

'How many years ago could you have stopped this?' Isaac asked. 'How many people would be alive today if it weren't for you? My family would be alive. I would have been there to protect them rather than in a training camp.' His voice hitched.

'Yesha made those daayan,' Ravi said, 'and you're choosing to work for her. Your family would be alive today if it weren't for her.'

Isaac's jaw clenched. Amara jerked higher into the air. Her feet kicked out.

Kayan shook his head as he looked from Isaac to a struggling Amara. 'Why are you working for her?'

'You don't understand,' Isaac said. 'Yesha is not the monster everyone led you to believe.'

The ground rumbled underfoot, as another possessed mage was buried on the front line.

'Yesha is doing that, you know. She's creating the daayan and sending them out to attack the mages,' Thiya cried.

Isaac shook his head. 'She has no choice. The mages that attacked her broke her magic. She needs help, but your family is ignoring her.'

Thiya wanted to scream. The person who held Amara's life in his hands was an idiot.

Ravi snorted. 'I refuse to believe anyone is that gullible.'

Isaac rounded on Ravi. 'It's the truth!' He inhaled a deep breath and said in a calmer voice. 'She cannot stop the daayan, but you can.'

'Yesha's lying to you,' Thiya said.

Isaac looked at her, his lip curling. 'Your father knows the truth and he hid you because he didn't want to risk his *precious princess*. But he was fine to let the rest of us die.'

Ravi snorted. 'That's what she told you?'

'That's what happened!' Isaac shouted. 'Some rebel mages asked me to go into Sanathri Jungle. They knew your family were behind the daayan attacks, they just needed proof. I found their proof. Yesha told me the truth.' He pointed a finger at Thiya. 'You paid off the rebels so they wouldn't reveal your secret. You knew you could stop the daayan, and you let my family die.'

Thiya shook her head. 'I didn't know. My father hid it from me, too. But I'm here now, and I want to help you.'

Another flash lit the sky and Isaac jumped at the deep rumble. The increased light showed the skin around Amara's lips and nails turning blue.

'You need to help Yesha,' Isaac said.

'I can't help her if she's not here. Where is she?' Could she heal Amara before Yesha found out?

'She is here,' Isaac said.

Thiya spun around, expecting Yesha to be standing behind her, but there was no one else in the clearing. There were no other heartbeats lurking nearby.

Amara's heart beat faster in a final attempt to keep her alive even as her body shut down.

'Let her go,' Thiya cried. 'Let Amara go and we can talk about it. You have me. Whatever my father may have done, Amara has no part in it. She doesn't deserve to die.'

'Yesha told you she would let Amara go if you free her,' Isaac said, his voice calm as if he didn't hold a life in his hands.

Amara's heartbeat stuttered. She stopped clawing at the branch pressed into her neck, her hands falling slack at her sides. Thiya needed that branch gone now.

She pulled threads of her magic and wrapped it around Isaac. She felt the steady rumble of strength and satisfaction as well as the shifting of worry within him before she aimed Isaac's magic at Amara and the branch that held her aloft.

Light danced across Thiya's vision, but Thiya held onto Isaac's magic. The branch loosened and Amara crashed to the ground.

Thiya's knees wobbled. She waited for Amara to suck in air. Nothing. The aether from the vine bangle around her wrist was still inside her, sucking out what little energy remained.

Thiya ran for her, but a root pushed up from the ground and wrapped around her ankle. She went flying, crashing to her hands and knees. Her chin hit something hard, sending pain stabbing across her jaw. She tried to get to her feet but the root held firm. Lochan and Ravi ran for her, but a tree branch swept out and knocked them down. Lochan's head cracked against a tree and he slumped to the ground. Kayan rushed to him.

Ravi stood back up and threw water at Isaac.

'Did you just give me a bath?' Isaac laughed.

'That was meant to be an icicle.'

Isaac shifted the ground beneath Ravi throwing him onto his back.

Amara was far too still, her lungs not pulling in air.

Tears prickled the backs of Thiya's eyes. She reached for her magic, wrapping threads round Amara's lungs and forcing them to expand. Air rushed inside then deflated as she breathed out – and fell still.

Thiya reached for more magic, but it felt heavy in her hands. It was harder to wrap the threads around Amara's lungs. Sweat beaded Thiya's brow, but she pushed past the fatigue.

Nothing happened. Amara's chest was still.

No, no, no! This couldn't happen. A tear slid down Thiya's cheek but she brushed it away. She reached for her magic once more when Amara sucked in a breath.

Yes! That was it.

Isaac shouted out before the ground opened up at Amara's feet and swallowed her whole.

28

Thiya stared at the spot where Amara had disappeared. The earth lay flat and undisturbed, as if she had never been there in the first place.

Thiya searched for a sign of Amara with her magic. By some miracle, Amara's heart was still beating. It was slow, but it was there. But for how long?

Thiya wrapped a thick strand of magic around Isaac – he had buried her; he could unearth her as well.

A daayan detached itself from the darkness and infected Isaac before Thiya could take control of his magic. She took another thread and wrapped it around the daayan inside him. She squeezed and the daayan exploded, but just as quickly another one took its place. Thiya tried to wrest control of Isaac's magic, but the new daayan fought back.

'If you want me to free Amara from her earthly confines, stop fighting.' The words came out of Isaac's mouth, but they didn't belong to him.

'Yesha?' She panted.

'Free me and I'll release Amara,' Yesha said.

'She's dying,' Thiya pleaded.

'Not yet.'

Amara's heart spluttered.

Thiya was done with Yesha's games. She scrambled

forward, ripping her ankle away from the root. She reached for Amara, fingers digging into the soil until Yesha made the dirt itself smash into her face and knock her away.

Tears streamed from her eyes. Kayan and her brothers shouted something, and she thought she heard the crackle of flames. Then Lochan was by her side, helping her up.

'Are you alright?'

Thiya nodded. Ravi was already there, where Thiya had been moments before. He stared down at the ground. 'Err … Thiya…'

Thiya stumbled forward, but Isaac blocked her path. Over his shoulder, Thiya saw Amara's head sticking out of the earth. Yesha had lifted the earth to expose her face. Amara spat dirt from her mouth and coughed.

'You're welcome,' Yesha said, sarcastically.

Thiya reached out, but Isaac pushed her back.

'Not yet. We had a deal.'

Free Yesha to free Amara.

Thiya glanced at Amara. She was breathing, but it was erratic.

Several flashes lit up the sky in quick succession.

Yesha was in the jungle with them and she was still creating more daayan to attack the front line. She wouldn't stop until Thiya stopped her.

Kayan's gaze burned into the back of her head. But Amara didn't have time. Thiya would stop the daayan after she saved Amara.

'Let Amara go and we can talk.'

Isaac rolled his eyes. 'That's a shame,' Yesha said. 'I was starting to like your girlfriend.'

The darkness inside Amara shifted.

Amara's heart spluttered and stilled.

29

NO! It felt like an airu had sucked all the breath out of Thiya's body. Thiya ran, collapsing onto her knees next to Amara. She waited for Amara's heart to beat again. Her fingers found no pulse.

This couldn't be happening. After everything she had been through to get here, Amara couldn't die. Thiya reached for her magic and wound it around Amara's still heart. Nothing.

There had to be some kind of mistake. Amara couldn't be dead.

'What did you do?' Thiya screamed. She hugged Amara's head.

She couldn't be gone.

'I told you, if you want Amara back, you must free me,' Yesha said from Isaac's mouth.

Thiya shook her head. 'I will never help you now.'

Yesha clicked Isaac's tongue. 'That's a shame.'

'Thiya?' Amara's voice was distorted, like it was coming from a distance, but Thiya would recognise it anywhere. Yet the Amara in her arms hadn't moved. 'Thiya, what's happening?'

She rounded on Yesha. 'What was that? Where is she?'

'Here, with me. To free her, you have to free me.'

'Stop Yesha and the daayan will follow,' Kayan whispered in her ear. Thiya hadn't heard him come up behind her. Lochan brushed against her other side.

'Ah yes, the person who sacrificed his own brother,' Yesha said.

Kayan flinched.

'Will you sacrifice your heart, Thiya?' Yesha asked.

The ground rumbled. Thiya heard shouts in the distance. She didn't know what was happening on the front line, but she knew Yesha was responsible.

'You can stop that,' Kayan said. 'You can save everyone.'

Everyone except Amara. She glanced down at Amara's unnaturally still form; her eyes closed like she was sleeping.

Yesha stepped closer. 'My fate is Amara's fate.'

'Do it now,' Kayan said, his voice urgent.

Another flash lit up the sky. Yesha was never going to leave them alone. She would keep hurting people Thiya loved until she got what she wanted.

Thiya's magic was already at the surface. All she had to do was push it out.

'Don't,' Yesha warned. 'If you kill me, you kill Amara. Tell me, how will you feel if you murder your girlfriend?'

Thiya let go of her magic. 'She's still alive?'

Even as she stared at Amara's lifeless body, hope sprung in Thiya's chest. She could get Amara back.

'She's lying,' Ravi said. He threw water at Isaac. It cascaded off his head and down his back, but it did absolutely nothing to stop Yesha.

'Why does that keep happening?' Ravi grumbled under his breath.

Yesha blotted the water off Isaac's forehead with the back of his hand.

'Because you are arrogant, just like your father,' Yesha said, coldly. 'I told you; my fate and Amara's are entwined. Isaac's face turned to Thiya. 'Free me and you free her. I don't want to hurt you, beti.' Thiya's body clenched at Yesha's familiarity. 'I never wanted to hurt anyone. All I wanted was to be free to live my own life, but the men of our family are far too stubborn for their own good. Don't make the same mistakes they did. Don't make me hurt more people.'

'Don't listen to her,' Kayan said. 'She made a choice to hurt people. None of that is your fault.'

Thiya shook her head. It wasn't her fault, but her family had pushed Yesha to her choices. Thiya needed to stop her. They needed to get the bangle on Yesha's physical form, not Isaac.

'What would Amara tell you to do?' Lochan asked.

'Why don't you ask her?' Yesha said.

But Thiya didn't need to ask. Amara would tell her to save the world. Except the world would not be the same without Amara.

An idea started to form. She kissed Amara's forehead then stood on shaky legs.

'Where are you? How do I free you if you're not here?' Thiya said.

'You can't,' Kayan said.

'I'm right here,' Yesha said from Isaac's mouth.

'Inside Isaac?'

'No. Here.' The last word came from somewhere behind Thiya.

She spun around, but there was no one there.

'I can't see you.'

'Then you're not looking hard enough.'

This time the words came from Thiya's right. She spun around again, but there was no one there.

'Look harder,' Yesha said.

Thiya listened for heartbeats. Kayan's was slow and steady as always. Ravi's heartbeat was a little faster, as was Lochan's. And there, underneath that, Thiya heard the echo of another heartbeat, distinct but faded. There but not there.

A woman flickered into existence in front of Thiya, her edges blurred like a painting that had caught the rain. Ravi swore. Lochan stepped closer to Kayan.

What in Khal's left butt cheek was this? Was she one of the gods, sent to test Thiya's patience? Or was she a demon sent by Khalil, the God of Mischief?

'What are you?'

Thiya glanced at Isaac who now stood to attention, his eyes black and his body completely still.

Yesha's voice came out of the darkness. 'Are you scared?' She flickered out of existence as fast as she'd appeared, but her voice still remained.

290

'N–no.'

The ghost of a hand brushed Thiya's chest. She saw brown skin, a shade darker than hers, before it disappeared into thin air. Thiya's skin crawled. There was no way she could take hold of Yesha, let alone get a bangle on her wrist.

'Your heartbeat says you are.' Yesha flickered from one end of the clearing to a step in front of Thiya. 'Don't worry, Thiya. I'm not going to hurt you.'

Except she was hurting Thiya by hurting Amara. And it was time Thiya put her new plan into action. She probed the area, trying to find Yesha's prison, but all she found was the darkness.

'How do I free you?' she asked.

'Thiya, don't,' Kayan warned.

Yesha materialised in front of Kayan. 'You really need to learn when to keep your mouth shut.' Her ghost-like hand slid into Kayan's chest and wrapped around his heart. Her fingers clenched.

Kayan gasped and clutched at his chest.

Lochan stepped between them. 'Leave him alone.'

Yesha hissed and rubbed her arm where Lochan's bangle had made contact. She retreated to the other side of the clearing. Maybe Kayan's plan would work after all.

'You cannot free her,' Kayan croaked, his hand rubbing his chest.

In one move, Yesha used Isaac to suspend Kayan above them, tree branches wrapped around his torso and leaves shoved in his mouth.

'I told you to stop talking,' Yesha said.

In response, Kayan conjured fire and attempted to throw it but another branch wound around Kayan's wrist, snapping his hands together so they touched palm to palm.

Thiya felt the burn of Kayan's gaze. *Don't do it. Don't free Yesha. You can't trust her.*

She didn't. She met his eyes, trying to silently reassure him. *Trust me.*

'Now, where were we?' Yesha asked. 'Ah yes, you want to know how to free me. You have to use your magic to heal me, to make me whole.'

Yesha didn't have a body. Thiya could heal a wound on Lochan's arm, but she couldn't even begin to comprehend this. She reached out with her magic, probing the surrounding area. The air was thick with dark aether, but there was something else as well – threads of light aether, suppressed by the darkness but fighting to remain. Parts of the light were familiar, a heartbeat echoing amongst them… Amara.

How was she meant to heal that? 'What happened?'

Yesha glowered. 'There were ten of your father's mages attacking me. All because I refused to serve my brother. I was forced to defend myself, but killing someone using aether magic takes a lot of energy, and killing ten was too much.'

Kayan grunted.

'Judge me all you want, feiraani, but they came to kill me, not the other way round.'

When Yesha spoke again, her voice came from the other side of the clearing, so forlorn that Thiya would have thought it belonged to a child.

'So, they kept attacking and I grew weak. I was too far gone to heal myself, so I did the only thing I could do. I split my magic. I'd done it before to save my brother, I could do it again. But something went wrong. In anchoring myself to this world, I also created my own prison. I was wrenched from my earthly body. I was pulled apart and now I'm trapped here within my own aether. Flickering in and out of existence. Here, but not here. Dead, but not dead. But you can free me,' Yesha said.

Ravi snorted. 'You can create daayan, but you can't free yourself?'

Yesha hissed somewhere beside Ravi, and he moved closer to Thiya.

'Gayan wants me. Every day I feel him trying to pull me away from this world, but I will not let my brother win. I have to keep using my magic to anchor myself. The daayan are a side effect of that.' She was in front of Thiya again, her eyes wide and pleading. 'You've seen the duality of magic. The light and the dark. I can use the light to keep me from Gayan's clutches. If I don't manipulate the dark and create daayan, I strengthen my own prison. I have no choice. If you free me, I won't need to create daayan anymore.'

Thiya could still hear the deep, rumbling sound of explosions from the front line.

'You can make that stop,' Yesha said, her head tilted to the side like she was listening. 'You can heal my magic. Every time I try, I get too close to Gayan, but you can destroy the prison and bring me back into this world.' She flickered and disappeared. 'Don't you think I deserve a chance to live?' she asked from somewhere to Thiya's right.

Thiya nodded because she'd finally figured it out.

She reached across and tapped Ravi's bangle. *Get ready.*

She reached for her magic and looped it around the dark aether that was Yesha's prison. All she had to do was heal Yesha's magic, bring the light and dark back together and make Amara and Yesha whole. But as she started doing just that, Thiya realised she could also wrench the threads apart further and send Yesha into Gayan's arms where she belonged and lose Amara forever.

She heard Lochan and Kayan shouting, heard Yesha's voice cut through them all, but she didn't pay them any attention.

She knitted the threads back together the same way she'd knitted Lochan's flesh. Her limbs grew heavy, and still Thiya continued, pulling Amara and Yesha from the aether and returning them to their bodies.

30

Thiya crashed to the ground.

Something pressed against her shoulder. She tried to wriggle away but the pressure became insistent. She heard the rustle of leaves in the trees and the frantic voices of her brothers.

Her body ached. It was like she'd run several thousand laps of the palace grounds and then been ripped apart and put back together.

'Thiya, are you alright?' Lochan asked.

She wasn't sure. She tried to move her arm, but it was too heavy.

Shapes formed in the darkness: the outline of trees, Lochan's head, the stars. The darkness that had surrounded the jungle had disappeared.

Kayan's voice drifted across the clearing. Flames danced around his head, and Thiya saw he'd managed to disentangle himself from the trees. His words were soft but urgent. Insistent. He was crouched in front of someone, trying to wake them up.

Amara.

Thiya pushed herself upright. Lochan put his arm around her, supporting her weight.

Kayan was pulling Amara out of the hole where she had been buried. He laid her on the ground and pressed two fingers to the pulse on her neck.

Thiya pushed herself to her feet. Her head swam. With Lochan's help, she stumbled over to Amara. Kayan shifted aside to make room for her.

Amara's eyes flickered but remained closed. Thiya brushed a finger over a bruise on Amara's cheek, and Amara whimpered. She wanted to laugh. Amara was alive.

'Where's Yesha?' Ravi asked.

Kayan glanced at the bangle in Ravi's hand. 'What—'

'There!' Ravi took off through the trees. Thiya saw a flash of white. A moment later, Ravi flew backwards through the clearing and landed flat on his back, his bangle clutched in his fist. He groaned. Lochan ran over to him.

A woman appeared between the trees. She was tall and slim like Thiya, her wavy hair hanging half-way down her back. There was nothing striking about her, but she was pretty in her own way, with her dark eyes, delicate features and a wild energy. There was not even a scratch on her.

'That wasn't very nice,' the woman said, straightening the pallu of her white and silver sari.

'Yesha?'

The woman paused and stared at Thiya. That stare made Thiya want to crawl into the ground.

'You wanted to imprison me again,' she said. She ran her fingers down the pleats to crease them into place, then draped it over her shoulder. She took a silver chain Isaac held out to her and snapped it around her waist. 'It's amazing how dishevelled one can get when one is stuck in a magical prison for years.' She smoothed her hands down her sari and straightened. 'How do I look?'

'Like a queen,' Isaac said. Thiya noticed his eyes and skin had returned to normal.

'Perfect.'

'You're not a queen.' Ravi spat.

Yesha snarled. 'The throne should have been mine.'

'We can get you a throne for your jail cell.'

Yesha walked past Ravi with a dismissive glance and crouched in front of Thiya. 'You broke our deal when you sent your idiot of a brother to contain my magic with his bangle. It's a shame, because I thought we would have made a great team. But now you need to pay for your deception.'

Light glowed between Yesha's hands. Not light: magic. Thiya recognised the swirling threads of dark and light. But as she watched, the threads split apart, separating into two masses – one dark, one light.

Yesha created a daayan out of the dark threads, sending the corresponding light threads into the ground to be absorbed by the earth. Before Thiya could even react, the daayan jumped onto Amara.

The breath left Thiya's lungs on a silent scream. Grey veins spread across Amara's body. Thiya braced herself, but Amara didn't move.

'Consider this a warning. She'll be fine as long as you don't follow.' Yesha stood. 'Now, I need to get going.' She blew Thiya a kiss and then the woman who had been waiting for revenge for thirty years walked away, the light and dark threads of her magic hovering in the air in front of her.

Thiya had messed up. She'd thought she could have it all, and now Yesha really was her problem to fix.

'We have to go. We have to stop her,' Kayan pleaded.

Thiya looked from him to Amara, where her heart beat too slowly. Thiya didn't know how much longer Amara would last, especially with the daayan lying in wait inside her.

'None of this will end unless you stop Yesha once and for all,' Kayan said.

A flash lit up the sky. An explosion rumbled the ground under her feet.

Kayan took hold of Thiya's shoulders and twisted her to face him. 'Would you destroy an entire country to save one person?'

Thiya could save Amara, or she could stop Yesha. She'd made the wrong choice before, but not this time. Lochan had asked her earlier what Amara would want her to do. She had known the answer then and she'd ignored it. This time she would listen.

She was going to save her people from Yesha's tyranny.

She paused long enough to kiss Amara's forehead.

It might have been her imagination, but she thought Amara's heart gave a little thump. 'I love you.'

Yesha manipulated the daayan inside Amara. She was too weak to scream, but Thiya knew that was how she was going to die – in pain and screaming on the inside.

Bile rose up her throat.

'Stay with her,' she told Lochan as she got to her feet. She didn't want Amara to die alone.

Thiya followed the flashes to the edge of the jungle.

'Thiya!' Ravi ran up behind her. 'Where are you going?'

'To stop Yesha.'

As much as she wanted to be there for Amara, to hold her one last time, there were people who needed her more.

This was where Amara would want her to be.

Yesha stood on the edge of the tree line, watching the destruction her daayan wrought, Isaac beside her.

Yesha created a stream of daayan to attack the front line.

A flash went off, and Thiya had to squeeze her eyes shut and look away. She blinked back tears. When she could see again, the field between the trees and the town was swarming with daayan, like a sea of darkness.

The captain shouted a command, then small nets of fire combined into a large one that spanned the entire line.

The daayan pounded against the shield and it began to falter. Holes appeared, which were quickly filled by jets of water, gusts of air and balls of earth, but daayan slipped past.

'Are you ready?' Kayan asked.

Thiya nodded. Ravi held up his bangle.

Thiya's ears rang from the sound of another explosion, but the swarm of daayan was so thick, she barely saw the flash of light. Through the ringing, she heard the captain shouting instructions.

Ravi and Kayan were making their way through the tree line so they could position themselves behind Yesha and Isaac. Thiya pulled strands of her magic and waited.

Closing her eyes, Thiya blocked out the sounds of fighting around her and cast her awareness into Yesha. She saw the way Yesha's muscles contracted as she moved, and the way her blood flowed through her body. She felt Yesha's heart beat faster as her daayan destroyed and mages fell.

There was a small thread where Yesha's magic should have been, and Thiya followed it to the two balls of thread between Yesha's hands, fractured and broken. Thiya almost reeled back, but she caught herself just in time and tried to take control.

Yesha pushed her out with her magic. Thiya jerked.

Ravi and Kayan were almost upon her. Thiya opened her mouth to shout a warning when Yesha's magic assaulted her senses and her muscles locked.

Yesha's voice sounded inside Thiya's head. 'You don't have the power to stop me.'

Thiya tried to push her out, but she was much too strong. Yesha held Thiya's magic in place with ease, and Thiya was powerless to do anything but watch as Kayan and Ravi advanced.

Isaac spun to face them at the last moment. The ground exploded under their feet and they both went flying. Ravi's head cracked against a tree branch and he crumpled to the ground. Kayan rolled and was on his feet before he had come to a stop.

Isaac advanced, but Kayan was ready, and the branch that Isaac sent to sweep Kayan's feet out from under him went up in flames.

Ravi staggered to his feet. He bent forward to pick up the bangle and Thiya saw the bleeding gash at the back of his head. But he still stalked towards Yesha, the bangle held in one hand and his sword in the other.

Khal! He was going to get himself killed!

Thiya pushed against Yesha's constraints again. Ravi was getting closer to Yesha.

Her fingers twitched.

Thiya looked inside herself, at the fractured pieces of Yesha's magic flowing through her bloodstream and holding her muscles in place. But where her own magic came in contact with Yesha's, it healed. Fractured pieces joined together, becoming whole. Yesha's hold started to weaken.

Ravi was upon Yesha and Thiya could do nothing but watch as he reached forward with the bangle.

Yesha spun around. Her hand extended towards him. Ravi knocked her hand away with his sword arm and aimed a kick at her midsection. Yesha fell to the ground. Ravi lifted his sword above his head and aimed a blow.

Yesha created another daayan. The daayan flew towards Ravi who had to jump back to avoid being infected. He splashed water at the daayan. The daayan tumbled off into the distance, but another daayan took its place.

Ravi dropped his sword. He drew his arm around in a circle to create a water shield.

'It worked!'

The daayan bounced off the shield, but the shield shattered, water droplets flying everywhere. Yesha sent more daayan after him.

Ravi was moments from death. His bangle lay on the ground a few feet away and Kayan was fighting Isaac. Across the field, Thiya couldn't even see the mages anymore behind the sea of daayan. There was no one to help Ravi but her.

She pushed against Yesha's magic and with Yesha distracted, her hold on Thiya weakened further. Thiya's magic flowed through her veins. Free.

She wrapped a strand of magic around Yesha's heart and stopped it from beating. Yesha doubled over and clutched her chest. She lashed out with her magic, trying to constrain Thiya's. Ravi lunged forward and ran Yesha through with his sword, the bangle glistening on his wrist as the daayan tried to attack.

Ravi twisted the sword and pulled it up, slicing through Yesha's body.

Yesha cried out and released her hold on Thiya. She collapsed to her knees. Threads of light wrapped around Yesha's body, even as she fell forward. But Thiya grabbed hold of those threads, stopping Yesha from anchoring herself to this world again.

With one last beat of her dark heart, Gayan pulled Yesha into his arms for good.

31

Yesha lay on the ground, her eyes open and glazed over. The daayan vanished.

Isaac howled and ran to Yesha's side. 'What have you done?'

Thiya stepped back. She'd done what she had to, to keep everyone safe, but it didn't stop the heavy feeling in her chest. She had to look away, even as Isaac rounded on her.

Ravi stepped between them. 'Leave my sister alone.' He lifted the blood-soaked sword between them.

Isaac whipped branches out and smacked the sword from Ravi's hand, but Kayan managed to slide behind him. He pulled Isaac's hand back and slipped a bangle over his wrist. The branches slid back into the trees.

'This isn't over,' Isaac said. He struggled against Kayan's hold, but Kayan held firm.

'I think it is.' Kayan pushed the manacles over Isaac's wrist and melted it so it stuck to the bangle.

Ahead of them, they saw Captain Nirvan approaching with several mages. 'Who's there?' he called.

Flames lit up the space between them, the light so intense, Thiya had to turn her head. She blinked back tears.

'It's Kayan of Mengaru.'

The captain took in their dishevelled forms, Isaac with his hands bound and Yesha lying in a crumpled heap on the floor, blood staining her white sari. He kicked Yesha with the toe of his boot until she flopped onto her back.

'So, this was Yesha,' he said. 'I was expecting someone more … intimidating. She looks a lot like you.' He nodded at Thiya.

'They're nothing alike,' Kayan and Ravi both said at the same time.

'And Isaac?'

'He was helping her,' Kayan said.

'Are you sure?' Captain Nirvan asked.

Kayan nodded, his expression solemn. 'We need mages to guard him. The bangle blocks his magic, but I want to be prepared, just in case.'

'Are you sure he wasn't possessed?'

'She did what you could never do,' Isaac said, his expression twisting, 'and that usurper killed her for it.' He spat at Thiya's feet.

Ravi yelled at him.

Kayan looked at the captain. 'I'm sure.'

The captain squeezed his eyes shut. He called out a couple of names and the mages rushed forward. 'Do you want them to create a second restraint?'

Kayan shook his head. 'No, I don't think that'll be necessary.'

'The magic won't fade?'

'No.'

304

'Take them both to the mess hall,' Captain Nirvan said. 'I'll create a rota for the mages to keep watch and escort them back to the palace where your father can order Isaac's execution.'

Mages collected Yesha's body and headed off towards the town. Ravi dragged Isaac behind them.

'I guess I owe you thanks.' Captain Nirvan held his hand out for Thiya to shake. Then he followed his mages.

Thiya wanted to get back to Amara. But another mage approached before she could leave.

'Is it really over?' he asked. Daayan were a reality the country had faced since before most of these mages were born. They didn't know a life without daayan and fighting. But now their futures had just opened up.

Laughter and shouts of joy were drifting from the front line, but also pain. Because they had lost friends that night.

And so had Thiya.

'It's really over,' she said, before heading back into the jungle.

Amara lay on the ground in the centre of the clearing, her clothes covered in dirt and the hole she had been buried in gaping open next to her. Lochan sat beside her.

Thiya ran towards them. She knew what she was going to see, but she still wasn't prepared.

A chill seeped into her bones. She prayed to every god

she thought would listen, though she didn't know what she wanted them to do. Amara's suffering had ended, and there was nothing that would ease the sharp pain in the centre of her chest where her heart had once been.

Lochan shifted to make room for her. His dirt-stained fingers held Amara's hand.

Amara lay on her back, her eyes closed, but her chest still moved.

A strangled sound caught in Thiya's throat as her knees hit the ground. 'How?'

'She held on,' Lochan said.

'But—'

'She held on.' Lochan transferred Amara's hand to Thiya's and stood. He made his way to the other side of the clearing to give them some privacy.

Amara was not alright. There were no signs of the daayan that had possessed her, but there were dark shadows under her eyes, and her cheekbones were far too sharp. Thiya cradled her head in her lap and ran her fingers down her cheeks.

'Amara? Can you hear me?'

Amara's light even breaths stuttered.

'Please open your eyes.'

Her lashes fluttered. Thiya's world stilled. She held everything that was important in her arms and she was never going to let go.

'That's it. Just like that. You can do it.'

Amara opened her eyes and smiled when she saw

306

Thiya. 'Where…' She cleared her throat and tried again, but her voice was still a breathless whisper. 'Where's Isaac?'

'Somewhere he can't hurt you.'

Amara nodded. 'Thank you.' She squeezed Thiya's hand, a slight flutter of fingers with little strength, but it was something.

Kayan walked into the clearing. 'Ravi has everything in hand,' Thiya heard him tell Lochan. 'Your brother is a surprisingly good leader.'

'Don't tell him that,' Thiya said. He would be insufferable, especially now that he had helped stop Yesha.

'I promise to keep it to myself.' Kayan crouched down beside Thiya and she saw there was a welt on his cheek and dried blood on his lower lip. He smiled at Amara. 'I'm glad to see you alive.'

'What's the plan now?' Lochan asked.

'Ravi is going to escort Isaac back to the palace tomorrow, where he will likely be executed,' Kayan said, his head bowed. 'I'll follow them after I've checked on my mother and sister. Isaac has no other family and I—' He inhaled. 'I should have seen what was happening sooner. Maybe if I had paid more attention, I might have been able to stop him.'

Lochan squeezed Kayan's shoulder. 'This wasn't your fault.'

'Our father could have stopped things much sooner,' Thiya spat. 'I'm going to have a few words with him about bangles when I get back.'

307

'It's not going to change anything,' Lochan said.

'No, but I might be able to leverage his guilt to help the towns and villages he failed.' She glanced at Kayan. 'Like your farm.'

Kayan smiled. 'It will be nice to go back there and just stay, spend some time with my mother, be there for my sister. Who knows, maybe I'll make an excellent farmer.' He laughed.

'Do you think I'd make a good farmer?' Lochan teased.

'I think you can do anything you put your mind to.' Kayan tugged Lochan to his feet and the two of them drifted away to talk about the future.

Thiya already knew her future was by Amara's side for as long as Amara wanted her. She was never letting go of Amara again. She squeezed her hand.

Amara's dark eyes sparkled and Thiya was overwhelmed by the love she saw shining out of them. Love for her.

EPILOGUE

Thiya woke up in the most comfortable bed she'd ever slept in. Afternoon sunlight spilled through the parted curtains of the room in the inn. Beyond the window, Thiya saw the snow-capped peaks of the Dhandra Mountains.

They had left Tumassi yesterday, Ravi heading for the palace with Isaac, and Kayan and Lochan heading to Kayan's home. Thiya and Amara would eventually go back to the palace, but for now they needed time to recover.

Amara stirred beside her.

Thiya brushed her finger over Amara's cheek. The bruise had darkened to purple, and stood out in stark contrast against her hollow cheeks. She'd lost a lot of weight over the last two weeks.

Amara's hand slid around Thiya's waist. Her eyes fluttered.

'Look who finally woke up.' Thiya kissed the top of Amara's head.

'Hmm…' Amara buried her face deeper in Thiya's chest. 'Good morning.' Her rough voice made Thiya's body heat.

'It's afternoon. You slept an entire day.'

Her eyes sprang open. 'Oh. I'm sorry.'

Thiya shook her head. 'You needed the rest.' She traced the welts across Amara's neck, deep and red. 'How does it feel?'

Amara's eyes darkened. 'A little sore, but I don't want to talk about it. Distract me.'

'I know something that might help.' She hitched her leg over Amara's hip and rolled so Amara was under her.

Amara's breath caught in her throat. She bit her lower lip and looked at Thiya from under long lashes.

Thiya leaned forward, her breath fanning across Amara's lips. Amara gulped. Her eyes fluttered closed.

Thiya scrambled off the bed. She was almost to the door of the adjoining bathroom when Amara cried, 'Tease! Come back.'

She glanced back to see Amara lying in the crumpled sheets, scowling at her. Thiya laughed and pushed open the door.

The bathroom was made of cream tiles. It reminded her of the bathhouse in the palace, except there was no bath. The floor was tilted towards a drain in the far corner, and there were two knobs along the wall.

Thiya turned the knobs the way the innkeeper had shown her last night, and water started to flow from the ceiling in a steady stream.

The door opened behind her.

'That wasn't fair,' Amara said, faking outrage. She paused, her eyes widening at the site in front of her. 'What is that?'

'It's a shower.'

Amara had had a bath before they'd left Tumassi, but Thiya thought hot water hitting her back would help her relax more.

Amara closed the door and stepped into the steam that had started to form. 'This is amazing.'

Thiya grinned. 'Wait till you get underneath.'

Thiya helped Amara undress. She hissed when she saw the deep welts along her arm from the vine bangle and the scratches across her skin. She'd healed the worst of Amara's wounds, but she didn't have the energy to heal them all. She ran her finger over the raised red skin. It was a good thing Yesha was already dead.

It took all of Thiya's efforts to turn away. She managed to keep her voice neutral as she told Amara how to work the controls.

'I'll be just outside.'

'Stay.'

Thiya hesitated in the doorway.

'Please.'

Thiya's body heated in a way that had nothing to do with the temperature in the room. She crossed her legs and leaned against the door.

'It's not fair that you're fully dressed and I'm not.'

Thiya's insides knotted at the invitation. This girl was going to be her undoing.

She smirked. 'What are you going to do about it?'

Amara grabbed the front of her pyjamas and pulled

her under the stream. Her pyjamas soaked through within seconds, the material clinging to her skin. Amara's eyes darkened and Thiya looked down to see the material had turned see-through.

Amara tugged at the hem of Thiya's top and pulled it up over her head. She dipped her hands under the waistband of her trousers and slid them down, her fingers lingering on her bottom.

Thiya's heart beat faster. She kicked off the trousers the rest of the way. No sooner was she free than Amara pushed her back into the wall. She pressed her body against hers, stood on tiptoes, her head tilted up.

Thiya met her halfway.

Amara pulled back before their lips could touch and Thiya groaned.

'Not so nice, is it?' Amara nipped her ear.

'Tease.'

'I learnt from the best.'

Thiya laughed. She reached into the alcove behind her and pulled out a bar of soap. She lathered it between her hands before she started rubbing it into Amara's skin. The smell of cinnamon and roses filled the room.

Amara's eyes brightened.

'I'm glad you like it,' said Thiya. She leaned forward and planted a quick kiss on Amara's lips.

'We got our cottage in the mountains,' Amara said and Thiya smiled. She thought she was going to be doing a lot of that in the near future.

'We can sit by the fire and watch the sun set tonight, if you want?'

'Do I get spiced wine?' Amara asked, her eyes sparkling.

'As long as I get chai.'

She took the soap from Thiya and started lathering her up, her fingers light and teasing, the pressure never quite enough. Thiya's entire body hummed.

Amara's fingers stilled.

'What's wrong?' Thiya asked.

'I know it's meant to be a fantasy, but I don't want this to end.' Amara shifted back, and despite the heat of the water, a chill filled Thiya's chest. 'I want the sunsets and the fire. I want to wake up in your arms every morning.'

She took Amara's hand. 'I'm yours, for as long as you'll have me.'

'Forever.' Amara pressed those joined hands to her lips. 'I want you forever.'

'Good, because I have no intention of ever letting you go.'

Amara laughed, and it was the sweetest sound in the world.

'I've been thinking about something,' she said.

'Oh no!'

'Stop.' Amara pressed a finger on Thiya's lips. Thiya nipped it. 'I've been thinking, the gods wouldn't have brought us together only to force us apart. We belong together and my parents will just have to get used to that.'

Thiya grinned so wide she thought her cheeks would split. 'I like this feisty Amara.'

'I'm serious,' Amara said. And she proceeded to show Thiya just how serious she was.

The sun was about to set behind the mountains as Thiya slid into the armchair alongside Amara, her long limbs loose and relaxed. Thiya brushed her finger over Amara's cheeks and her eyes flickered open.

'You're going to miss it,' Thiya whispered, because there was something about this view that demanded silence.

A chill wind blew over from the ice-capped mountains and onto the veranda where they sat. The fire in the pit next to them crackled. Thiya pulled the blanket tighter around Amara. Amara smiled.

'I got you some spiced wine,' Thiya said.

Amara's smile grew wider and she took the mug.

Thiya brought her own mug to her lips and drank deeply. The rich taste of the chocolate sweetened with jaggery was something she would never have imagined.

'That doesn't look like chai,' Amara said, peaking over at Thiya's mug.

'It's hot chocolate.'

Amara's eyes brightened. 'I can't remember the last time I had that.'

Five years ago, when they'd sneaked down to the kitchens and helped themselves. They'd just had a shipment from Kakodha, and Thiya hadn't been able to wait to drink some.

'Would you like some?' She handed Amara her mug.

A little boy shouted from inside the building. 'Mama, you're going to miss it.' Thiya heard his excited footsteps pattering down the hallway outside before they were cut short.

'I don't think you should disturb our guests, beta,' his mother said.

'But I want to see the stars,' he whined.

'We can't, beta. There's curfew.'

'But the daayan are gone. Thiya said—'

'It's *Princess* Thiya. Show her some respect.'

'But she said I could call her Thiya,' the boy said.

'The palace hasn't said it's alright to go out at night.'

It would take a while for the palace to make an official announcement, but there was no need for curfew anymore. Despite Thiya's insistence, the innkeeper had shuttered all her windows and doors last night. It was a hard habit to break.

'But Thiya is from the palace.'

The boy broke loose from his mother's arms and ran onto the veranda. He flopped down into the sofa.

'Ishann!' The innkeeper followed, but she hesitated in the doorway.

'Please join us,' Thiya said. 'It's safe and I've heard it's supposed to be spectacular.'

Thiya had wanted to stay up and watch the sunset last night, but she and Amara had both been exhausted. Tonight, however, she wasn't going to miss it. They'd all missed too many sunsets.

The innkeeper hovered in the doorway. Thiya felt nothing but awe as she saw the last of the sun's rays disappear behind the mountain. What should have been the start of curfew was now a glorious sunset.

The sky was awash with colours of orange and purple. The sight made her breath catch in her throat.

The innkeeper stepped out onto the veranda, her eyes transfixed by the sky.

The oranges darkened to red. The purple deepened before the sky darkened to shades of blue and black. Pinpricks of light revealed themselves. Some grew larger, while others were content to stay small.

'My grandfather used to tell me stories of the stars,' the innkeeper said.

Thiya wrapped her arms around Amara's waist and snuggled closer. She watched a sky she'd never really seen before, and listened to those stories that had almost been lost.

Amara twisted around to look at her, to capture her lips in a kiss. Soft and sweet and absolutely perfect.

ACKNOWLEDGEMENTS

Writing a book is a solitary activity, but it doesn't come into the world in isolation. There are a lot of people who had a hand in getting this book into the world, and they have my utmost gratitude.

To Holly for convincing me to enter a competition that set me on my journey. This book would not have been written without you. Thank you for cheering me on in my best moments and consoling me in my worst. You're the best.

To my agents, Gemma Cooper and Zoë Plant, for seeing the potential in a rough second draft and wanting to work with me.

To Divya for your invaluable feedback and support.

To everyone on the Firefly team who had a hand in making this book shine, but especially to my wonderful editor, Hayley Fairhead, who helped me break this book down and build it back up into something truly amazing, in a way that made sense and felt achievable.

To Cynthia Paul for capturing Thiya and Amara so perfectly for the cover.

To everyone in my writing groups: Wattpad, SCBWI, Southbank Writers and Write Magic, who have encouraged me and cheered me on.

To my parents for allowing me to live at home rent-free so I can write.

To Julie D'Aubigny for being so awesome and for inspiring the character of Thiya.

Thank you!